I0581172

Books by S.C. Giedzinski

Nine Million Marshmallows and More
Island Rain

ISLAND RAIN

S.C. GIEDZINSKI

This book is a work of fiction.

To be more precise, the story that follows is fictional. This page is not, nor are the next four pages. Names, characters, places, and events in this story are the product of the author's imagination. Any resemblance to actual events, small watercraft, other literary works, construction firms, television programs, persons known to the author, coastal islands, or anything else in the real world, is purely coincidental. Drink responsibly. Results may vary.

 Brantwood Press

ABOUT THIS BOOK

The first draft of *Island Rain* began on July 1st, 2017. The previous day, I locked myself in a room and refused to leave until I produced a complete outline for a new novel. That July would be my first attempt at National Novel Writing Month.

I was 18 years old, fresh out of high school, and itching to write a book that I could finally publish. While locked in that room, I happened to be on vacation with my family in Surf City, North Carolina. We always stayed at my great uncle Peter and great aunt Gail's house—a house called Innisfree. It was the perfect summer escape for a new high school graduate like me. My story began there, and with a title: *Island Rain*. I picked this book's title before writing a word of it.

I worked on the NaNoWriMo draft for ten days before giving up. In under 12,000 words, I burned through two thirds of my outline. That outline, however, held up far better. For the first time, I paid attention to what I believed a young adult audience would want: Murder, romance, beaches, nerds, parties, betrayal, mischief, queer teenagers, closeted teenagers, mean, weird, or sensitive teenagers, and teenagers who just want to be left alone. I created a chimera of these components that I hoped to blend, under the assumption that my fellow young readers shared my interests. I engineered a story, then I kept it in my pocket until I felt strong enough to write it.

A year and a half later, I rebooted the project in earnest. While studying creative writing at the University of Maryland, *Island Rain* chapters became my primary workshop material. By mid-2019, I had a full-length draft of something that felt real—not good, but real. Celia, Abby, and all the other members of the JPWH Novelist Support Group contributed immense feedback and edits that took *Island Rain* to new heights. My family, friends, and enemies all read and reviewed bits and pieces of this story.

As I revised and expanded it, that draft became the centerpiece of my Arts Scholars capstone project: *The Murderous Art of the Mystery Novel*. To my surprise, someone decided to feature my presentation in a special session with the University of Maryland deans. A few students presented massive charitable programs, others made groundbreaking medical discoveries, and I wrote a teen mystery novel. This star-treatment worked wonders for my ego.

I commissioned my incredibly talented friend Bethel Afful to make the book's cover, and I crafted two unique bound copies of my latest *Island Rain* draft. I gifted one to my great aunt Gail, as I dedicated the book to her and Peter, who passed away in 2018. Shortly before Innisfree went up for sale, I stashed the second copy on a bookshelf there for a future owner to find. To my knowledge, it's still on that bookshelf.

In the summer of 2019, I began querying literary agents with my final manuscript of *Island Rain*. I wrote almost a hundred letters and received three responses, all of which amounted to nothing. The querying process robbed me of a lot of time and motivation. Despite the calculated marketability of my book, I found it impossible to secure representation for a debut novel as a student author. Perhaps I never emailed the right person, or perhaps my letters weren't up to par. I gave up my mission to publish this book by the end of 2019.

By then, a new project needed my full-time attention: *Nine Million Marshmallows and More*, a short story collection that I prepared as another capstone project for a different academic program. Abandoning old unfinished projects in favor of new unfinished projects is an unshakeable habit of mine—my files are a graveyard of over a hundred unfinished stories, some as long as this one.

I finished my short story collection in the early days of the 2020 pandemic shutdowns. Self-publishing *Nine Million Marshmallows and More* taught me the tricks and procedures I needed to navigate the user-unfriendly hellscapes of certain websites essential to the process. Out of resentment for the bland, unaesthetic, and low-budget stigma of self-published books, I registered "Brantwood Press," a fictitious publishing house, in my name. The imprint is legally real, but only exists to lend a trade-published appearance to my books' covers and copyright pages. I suppose I could have kept that a secret, but it's too interesting not to mention here.

After two years of a pandemic—and two years selling a tiny book that primarily functions as a coffee table decoration—an old friend asked me whatever happened to *Island Rain*. I said I finished it. Why not publish it, then? After all, I designed the story to be viciously marketable. Maybe I felt phony publishing something that echoes a million similar mystery stories. Maybe I lost my own voice trying to find one that young readers wanted.

Gail and Peter named their house for Yeats' poem *The Lake Isle of Innisfree*. Innisfree was a place to be free of the loudness and seriousness that clouds the adult world. In a house named for freedom, I began a story about breaking free. Then, I locked my story in a room and let it fade away. I've loved, hated, and battled these pages for half a decade. I waited too long to tell my story, or maybe just long enough.

I bottled the fears and desires of my young adulthood, and I tossed them into the surf. I let them sink and spin in the waves of the two then-strangest years of my life. I never expected anyone—not even myself—to read them again, but here you stand on the shore of Innisfree, a glass bottle rolling at your bare feet.

Pull the cork.
Bottoms up.
Turn the page.

CONTENTS

1: The Island.. 1

2: The Party 17

3: The Tower 33

4: The Puzzle 47

5: The Job 63

6: The Mansion.............................79

7: The Evidence............................93

8: The Water 107

9: The Emergency 121

10: The Delivery.........................135

11: The Suspect 149

12: The Beach.............................163

13: The Hunt...............................179

14: The Storm.............................193

15: The Night 207

16: The Team 221

17: The Murder...........................237

18: The Future 251

For Gail and Peter

1: THE ISLAND

After burning all eight of my college rejection letters, I sat down for dinner with my mom. Silence lingered over us for a few minutes. Outside the window, an evening breeze scattered the last smoldering papers over our patio, whipping them into the sky like joyless confetti.

My mom ignored the ashes. "It's your first dinner as a graduate. Feel any different?"

I felt the same. Dinner looked the same, too: Pasta from a bagged mix, steamed broccoli, and weeks-old potato chips. I poked at the noodles with my fork, and their warm smell drifted through the empty house.

"I feel good," I told her, not feeling good at all.

My mom straightened in her chair, which meant she had something important to say.

"Well, you don't have to worry. There's always community college."

"I don't want to think about that."

"It's good to think about your future."

"I don't want *community college* to be my future."

"That's not how community college works. It's just one step."

I stabbed my fork into a broccoli stem, hoping for a satisfying *crunch*, but the fork tines fell straight through and clinked against the plate. I stuffed the broccoli into my mouth before I could say anything regrettable in response. Mom slumped down over her plate again but didn't eat anything. She reminded me of a psychic staring into a crystal ball.

"What do you want your future to be?"

"I don't know, but not just soft broccoli. I don't want to stay in Ohio."

"Well, after community college, if you really put in the effort, you can go anywhere."

"Why can't I just go somewhere this summer?"

Mom sat upright again; she caught on quickly. After asking once, I took a risk by asking again. Facing a summer spent trapped in my house—listening to my mom either complaining or crying—I could wait for divine intervention, or I could act. But she held her ground.

"You mean with Carson? I already said no."

"But I have nothing to do here all summer."

"If you wanted to have a vacation, you should have kept up your grades. When you fail math, English, and history… If I just gave you a reward, I'd be a bad parent."

"Like Dad?" The words slipped out too easily.

"Rain, please…"

Silence. She wouldn't defend him. She wouldn't let another argument spiral into yelling, tears, and stomping feet. Somehow, I *wanted* that to happen. I wanted to scream about everything: Graduation, life, Dad. I wanted to see him again—just to tell him how badly he messed everything up for both of us—but I couldn't do that. I couldn't do anything but wish, ruminate, and eat soggy food. As a last resort, I offered all my bargaining chips.

"If you let me go with Carson, I'll get a job on the island. They have a bunch of restaurants and shops where I could work. And I'll make new friends! I'll find the good people and spend time with them. I'll eat healthy. I'll text you every day! And you can always ask me to come home. It's just one summer…"

My mom glued her eyes to the crystal ball of pasta. She processed my words like a computer making a thousand calculations. She sat up straight once more to deliver her verdict.

"You'll *call* me," she ordered. "You'll call every day. You'll be safe. And you'll drink plenty of water."

I couldn't believe my ears. I stood up, glowing with excitement.

"Yes! I will! Thank you!" I tried to hug her from across the small kitchen table, but it didn't really work. I dashed away and up the stairs to start packing. She watched me and smiled—for the first time in weeks.

"And you'll bring the notebook!"

The notebook. I should have guessed she'd toss in that final condition. My dad gave me that notebook, inscribed with his mantra: *"Tell Your Story."* I couldn't bring myself to write in that horrible book. I couldn't accept that notebook no matter how many times my mom reminded me of it. Even so, I couldn't throw it away. Not yet.

"Okay. I'll bring the notebook."

I hardly slept—mostly because I couldn't wait to leave, but also because Carson arrived just a few hours after dinner. He wanted to leave early and arrive at the island in time for dinner. At around three in the morning, I locked my front door and met my best friend out in the driveway.

"Hey, Carson."

"Hey, Rain! Wait, hold on, man. Is that everything?" Carson whisper-shouted, his upper body leaning out the window of his idling pickup. I flung my one duffel bag into its red-painted bed next to Carson's three larger bags. It landed with a *thunk* that echoed off a neighbor's garage.

"Yeah, that's it. Why are you whispering?"

"It's three in the morning!" he hissed even louder.

"That was your idea! And it's not my fault your truck is always so loud."

I leapt into the passenger seat and patted the dashboard of the old truck, then Carson rolled it slowly out of my driveway and down our street. Once we hit the next road, my heart picked up its pace, and so did the truck. I'd succeeded, after all. After so much arguing and back-and-forth with my mom, I finally escaped my hometown.

We reached the highway before sunrise and had to battle the orange glare when the sun rose in front of us. On top of that, Carson kept whining that he had to piss, so we stopped for breakfast at the nearest golden arches. I unlocked the bed of the truck and fished through my duffel for my wallet, but I accidentally knocked the notebook out of my bag. It flipped down from the pickup and opened onto the sun-soaked pavement, white pages gleaming. I scooped it up and shoved it back into the bag, but not before Carson saw.

"So… you writing now?" He raised his eyebrows.

"Ha, good one. It's empty. C'mon, you know I never write." I flipped roughly through the creaseless pages. "I never even wanted this notebook. My mom made me bring it."

"Is it the one your dad gave you?"

I nodded. I could trust Carson. Junior year, when a Bunsen burner ignited my already fire-like hair in honors chemistry, Carson Welling put it out with his hat. When three girls rejected Carson's senior promposals on three consecutive days, I talked one of them into dancing with him when prom night finally came. So, when my senior year spun out of control and I needed a clean slate, Carson offered me one: Warley

Island. Who wouldn't die for a chance to spend all summer on a beautiful Carolina beach?

"Are you gonna ditch the notebook before we get there?"

"Probably."

I tried not to think about the notebook after that. We ate a quiet breakfast—it was still too early for real conversation.

Back on the road, we struggled to occupy ourselves. The GPS on Carson's phone estimated a ten-hour drive from Ohio to Warley Island. We must have opened and closed the windows a dozen times, letting the highway breeze rattle our eardrums over and over. I played my Spotify playlist, then he played his. In our deepest boredom, we even played the license plate game. I thought that was a little dumb, but Carson got me hooked after he saw a plate from Alaska.

"Do you want me to drive a bit?" I offered, already knowing his answer. We had to stop for gas anyway, so he pulled into a small station in West Virginia and agreed to a switcheroo.

"Did I tell you what Cody's doing now?" he asked while we stretched our legs. The remarkable life of Carson's older brother was old news to me. "He's still in Nashville. He got a new record deal with some label down there. And he says he plays cool gigs at restaurants and parties, too. He doesn't tell us much, but I bet he gets all the ladies down in Tennessee."

"Do you guys visit him at all?" I climbed into the driver's seat and adjusted the mirrors.

"Nah, he doesn't really want us to visit yet. He says Nashville is just a steppingstone to LA, and that we should wait to visit him when he really makes it big."

I hadn't seen Cody since he graduated, but apparently, he'd turned himself around. The Cody I knew failed music classes, got busted for smoking pot at homecoming, and barely remembered three guitar chords. By some overnight miracle, Cody transformed into his family's golden goose, flying from the nest into a mad world of roadies, groupies, and record deals.

That level of success scared me. I saw it with my father. Fame is like a drug; it eats away people's everyday lives. My dad received his first book deal a few months before I could walk, and then his writing career completely took off. He topped national bestseller lists with every new title. While traveling the world for readings, signings, and panels, he forgot about everything else—specifically, me.

I hoped Cody might escape that unending fame-vortex.

"Alaska!" Carson shouted.

"Shit! What?" I swerved more than enough to worry my only passenger.

"Whoa! You good?"

"Yeah, fine. What did you say?"

He pointed to an *Alaska* license plate on a boat trailer to our left. Only the plates for Hawaii, New Hampshire, and Wyoming remained.

"Good eye."

"You still good to drive?"

"Yeah. Til lunch, at least."

After another tank of gas and driver switch, we stopped at a diner near Raleigh. Carson parked directly in front of the diner's windows, backing into the parking spot with great difficulty. He insisted on this parking arrangement so we could watch our bags while we ate. Subtext: Carson wanted to show off his shiny red truck to everyone in the diner, but I didn't have the nerve to tell him that a 1990 Chevy Sport Pickup wouldn't turn many heads.

"I think she's into me," he grinned after we settled into our green booth seats. I cocked my head in confusion, then understood: He meant the apathetic waitress who took our drink orders. I shook my head, but he nodded back with the certainty of a man pouring his life savings into lottery tickets.

From the start of high school, Carson clung to his mission of becoming the next Hugh Hefner. He wore the nicest pastel shirts and the brightest khaki pants. He tweezed and mangled his eyebrows until they nearly vanished in tenth grade, and he used up hair gel faster than most people go through peanut butter. Over our high school years, he'd put on a few extra pounds, but he still carried himself with the manufactured confidence of a wannabe ladies' man.

"Carson, c'mon. Can't we just order food for once? No flirtation schemes? You've gotta know by now that not *every* waitress has the hots for you."

"There was that one time though…"

"No, no, she gave you the phone number of the *rejection hotline*. That doesn't count. Besides, *she* must be twenty-five."

"Older chicks dig me. What are you ordering?"

"No offense, but they don't. Probably the Rueben."

"Sauerkraut? Nasty. And c'mon, I know you're just jealous."

As Carson suggested, I checked on the truck through the diner's window. The ongoing procession of vacationers rumbled eastward on the nearby highway, many cars hauling boats behind or bicycles above.

"How much do you know about Warley Island?" Carson mumbled through a mouthful of fries once our food arrived.

"Um… It's an island," I answered, expecting more words but finding none. I knew more: Carson's parents always rented out the Welling family's summer home in Warley. They handed Carson the keys for one summer as a graduation gift, thinking he deserved some reward for miraculously passing calculus. "I know you go there for a week every summer with your family. What else is there to know?"

"Okay, I don't even know where to start. Basically, Warley is a long barrier island, which means there's ocean on one side and the intracoastal waterway on the other. The intracoastal is brackish, which means the water—"

"Do I really need to know all this? I just wanna enjoy my sandwich, here." It tasted better than expected.

"Ever heard of Captain Heron's treasure?"

I glanced up, then quickly down. Carson noticed, though, and he seized the opportunity to elaborate. While I failed history, he practically *taught* that class.

"Okay. So, during the War of 1812, there's a British blockade all up the east coast. American ships are shit-outta-luck, just totally trapped. Only the British merchant ships get through. The whole thing sucks for the Americans, so a lot of people want some sort of revenge on the British. That's where Captain Heron comes in. This guy gathers together a group of American sailors who all want to fight back, and they take three ships to attack the blockade. That plan doesn't go so well, and they lose one of the ships. Womp-womp. So instead of taking out the British navy ships, they decide to go after the merchant ships instead. Those are easier targets, and these guys become this merry band of American pirates, all led by Captain Heron."

"Cool," I said. "So, Johnny Depp is doing great. Where's the Flying Dutchman?"

He scoffed. History: Like writing, not my thing.

"Now, their piracy works for a while. They steal gold and shit from the British ships and divide it up fairly. Heron keeps his share in a big maple wood chest on his ship. But everything goes south when someone sells them out to the British. After they re-supply at Warley Island for food and rum, the British Navy surrounds the last two pirate ships twenty miles offshore. Cannonballs fly, then both pirate ships sink, along with Heron and all of his crew."

Mic drop. Or more accurately, fork-and-knife drop. Carson always ended his stories with the good guys dying in a fiery battle. That spoke volumes about history as a whole, I think.

"So, is that it?" I laughed, finishing off the last of my sandwich.

"Almost. Remember Heron's maple wood chest? Well, when people finally dove down to the shipwreck like thirty years ago, it wasn't there! Heron must have brought it ashore somewhere before the sinking, and we don't really know where, but a lot of people think—"

"They think that because Warley Island was his last stop, he buried it there?"

An obvious guess.

"Bingo!" He pointed one finger at me just as our waitress placed the check and a pen on the table. "I got the check this time," he spoke, too loud. "After all, I'm the one with the *steady-paying job*. And the *truck*."

He only had one of those things. I faced the window so that our waitress wouldn't see me cringe, but our equally pained eyes met in the glass reflection. Carson's weak lie hardly impressed her, as I could have predicted. Once she walked out of earshot, he leaned toward me and whispered:

"Actually, I left my wallet in the car. You got cash? I'll pay you back later, I swear."

After I paid for our lunch at the diner, Carson drove again. He droned on about Heron's treasure. Apparently, he and his dad always searched the beaches with metal detectors when they visited Warley. I appreciated Carson taking an interest in something other than finding a date—even in something possibly *more* outrageous and unrealistic. Somewhere along the drive, I agreed to go metal detecting with him. He even suggested seeing the Captain Heron Pirate Museum.

Talk of the treasure carried us most of the way through North Carolina. Finally, we reached a bridge that rose up on rusted stilts over marsh grasses. Carson rolled down the windows, and fresh currents of salty June air filled the car. The intracoastal waterway shimmered for miles on either side. High on the two-lane bridge, I saw the whole narrow island ahead of us: Houses, dunes, piers, and crisp eggshell sands on the ocean side. *Paradise,* I thought to myself, happily pushing Ohio out of my mind.

"Can't you just *taste* the sun?" Carson wafted the sea breeze with one hand. "Enjoy that now. Weather app says a storm's coming later this week."

Two main roads stretched up and down the island's length. The bridge brought us to an intersection with the western road, Warley Avenue. A large plaster shark gobbled up customers entering the trendy Warley Winds beach shop on our left. On our right, the red and white umbrellas of tables at Ritz's Burgers and Fries fluttered in the ocean breeze. Bicycles—some with tandem seats—crossed the intersection as we waited. I hadn't expected the island to be so busy, and I let Carson know.

"Seems crowded."

"It is, man. Beach week! Senior week! People just like us drive in from all over. Hundreds of people! For the next seven days, we *own* this island."

We the graduates? The idea of an island run by drunk teenagers concerned me, to say the least. I never went to parties in high school, but if rumors could be believed, they always devolved into madness. One way or another, alcohol and weed fueled tense emotions; guys fought over girls, and vice versa. If parties in our boring suburb of Cleveland could fly off the rails so easily, what might happen with hundreds of euphoric grads roaming an island for a week? Idling at that intersection in Carson's truck, I felt a pinch of the dread that I thought I left back in Ohio.

Carson laughed at my nervousness. "Relax, Rain. No one's gonna die."

Rolling south down Warley Avenue, I noted the abundance of independent surf shops. Each promoted a different style of Warley hat in its front window, and each took the name of its owner, like Ron's Surf Shop or Surf Supply by Colin. In front of Ron's, a family of five stood around a shirtless, tattooed employee as he demonstrated how to wax a surfboard.

"Does everyone surf here?" I asked, having only seen the sport in movies.

"Only the *coolest* people surf," Carson intoned, briefly lifting both hands from the wheel to aim his index fingers at himself.

Past all the beach shops, surf shops, bars, and small family restaurants, lines of brightly colored for-rent houses emerged. They all had cutesy wood-carved names nailed to posts near their driveways, like *Life's a Beach* and *Turtle Cove*.

Before I could ask about the name of his family's house, Carson turned the truck off Warley Avenue and onto a sandy gravel drive. Gnarled, dry bushes curled up from the ground on either side of the narrow road. My words sunk back down my throat. The shadows of prickly plants above us creeped me out, and the buzzing of insects and frogs in the darkness forced me to wonder if maybe we really *had* taken a wrong turn. Halfway through the sandy tunnel of terror, a snake slithered in front of us. Carson slowed down but moved on after it wriggled out of our path.

"Lots of snakes here," he said. "Not all of them are poisonous, but— Whoa, what the…?"

I followed his alarmed eyes, instantly taking in the catastrophe before us. At the end of the bushes, a circular gravel driveway spread into view. Plastic bags, popped water balloons, crushed beer cans, and even a broken baseball bat littered the area. The cactus growing in the center of the driveway wore a torn pink t-shirt reading "*Warley Island Gal*." Behind that mess stood the Welling' house: Two floors stacked on wood poles above a large garage. I wish I could say the house looked better than the driveway. One garage door didn't quite meet the ground, probably thanks to a dent on its lowest quarter panel. A pair of jeans, two towels, three swimsuits, and two socks hung drying on the wooden railing of the second-floor porch. The sliding door to that porch bore a spider web of cracks patched with rainbow duct tape. On top of it all, a deflated orange raft draped across the peak of the house's roof like a sad rubber hat.

Nailed above the garage, the Welling house's perfectly ironic name: *All's Well.*

"What happened?" I asked. Without answering, Carson stopped the pickup at the edge of the debris field. We both got out, standing frozen in our shock. "I'm guessing this isn't normal?" He held his hands tight around the back of his neck, turning pale and shaking his head.

"Someone must've broken in," he concluded, then he picked up half of the splintered baseball bat on the ground.

"What's that for?"

"See the clothes up there? Whoever they are, they're still inside. But not for long."

I grabbed the other half of the baseball bat and followed him. I doubted I'd be much help against a burglar. My hands shook just holding the half-bat, and I suddenly felt the need to piss.

A set of wooden stairs led up to the house's front door above the garage. Carson whipped out his house key and guided me in that direction. He and I stepped as quietly as we could on the gravel, avoiding aluminum cans along the way.

"No other cars. They've got no escape. Get ready to call the cops." Obeying him, I transferred one nervous hand from the bat to my pocket, ready to make the call.

We crept up the steps one at a time until he stopped. He raised one fist to make me stop too, and we listened. A few feet away, just inside the house, slow footsteps thumped across the floor. That's when it became real for me. My brain finally switched from car-ride-mode to let's-kick-some-ass-mode.

He dropped his fist, and we dashed up the last few steps. He threw the key into the doorknob so hard that it jammed.

"Shit!" He frantically shook the doorknob while light feet rushed around inside. Through the clouded glass on one side of the door, I watched a dark figure approaching the door on the other side.

"Carson! Pick up your bat!"

Too late. The knob turned from the inside and the door swung inward. Carson raised his bat and prepared his mighty battle cry.

"Get ou— Huh?"

He lowered the bat slowly. A blue-haired girl, equally confused, squinted into the sunlight to scowl at us. She looked roughly our age, and she certainly didn't look like a master burglar. If anything, she could have been the vocalist of a 90s rock band. I almost expected her to speak in song lyrics, but she talked much more slowly.

"Whoa, whoa. Bats down, boys. Too early for this shit. What's the matter with you two?" Neither Carson nor I tried to justify our defensive stances on the doorstep, so she continued. "It's not even six o'clock. I still have shit to do. New playlist, new clothes, you know the deal. The party starts at eight. Just come back later, okay? Okay. Buh-bye."

Party? Carson shoved his foot in the door before she could shut it, but that didn't stop her from trying. He gasped.

"Ouch! Who are you?"

She scowled even harder than before. It was really something.

"Bea. Short for Beatrice. Not Tris. This isn't *Divergent.*"

"Okay… I'm Carson. Carson Welling? My family owns this house. And the cops are on the way! Right,

Rain? This is my friend, Rain. Rain, you called the cops, right?"

I shook my head. Did he really think I made a silent phone call right behind him while holding half of a baseball bat?

"Right, right," Bea grimaced, peeling the door off Carson's shoe. "Come on in, *homeowners*." She opened the door further, and a second non-burglar emerged from within. Carson's eyes widened. My jaw dropped.

Cody Welling stood opposite us with a beer bottle in one hand and a packet of Swiss Rolls in the other. Despite all the stories and brags over the past twelve months, Cody was far from Nashville. When he saw us, his beer bottle fell to the floor and shattered, right along with all my hopes for a predictable and peaceful summer getaway.

He didn't drop the Swiss Rolls.

2: THE PARTY

"You asshole!" Carson shouted. He knocked the Swiss Rolls out of Cody's hand.

"Hey! Not cool! I was eating those."

Growing up without any siblings, I never knew just how bad things could get. Sure, I had my own family issues to deal with, but I never had an older brother—not to mention a pathologically lying one. Given my lack of experience, I joined Bea to watch the show from behind the safety of the kitchen island. I kicked off my shoes, and the floor's white ceramic tiles felt cold under my feet. The cabinets, countertops, fridge, and walls matched the sterile white of the floor, all as cold as the ice in Carson's voice.

"Why aren't you in Tennessee? What happened to the house? Who is *Bea*, and what's she doing here? No offense to you, Bea. You seem cool."

Bea tipped her imaginary hat. Cody attempted to regain control.

"Okay, slow down. First of all, I *was* in Tennessee. I just got here, like, a few days ago. Right, Bea? Back me up here. Bea?" He paused. Bea eyed us one by one before shaking her head and cracking open an energy drink to sip in silence. Cody took a step back. "Okay, maybe it's been longer. But it's not my fault. Some damn producer, he scammed me! One minute I was about to make it big, and the next, like—"

Carson slapped a hand on the kitchen island.

"Next minute, you're getting hammered and trashing our family's vacation house? C'mon! Mom and Dad still think you're in Nashville! Let's see what they think of this…"

Carson pulled out his phone and began typing furiously. Cody entered panic mode.

"Hold on," he pleaded. "Talk with me here. Just think for a second."

"And let you drag *me* into this shitstorm? I don't think—"

Cody wrestled the phone from Carson's fingers and leapt over the living room couch to place a barrier between them. Carson tried to cross over the couch too, but Cody pushed him back and held the cell phone up close to the ceiling fan.

"Don't you dare!" Carson shrieked. His voice cracked. Cody's scraggly facial hair twisted upward with his grin.

"Okay, there we go. So, how about this: I give you back the phone, and we all put this mess behind us."

"No way! That's the stupidest thing—"

"*And* if you text them, they're gonna find out about *winter break*."

I could only guess what Cody meant by that. Considering that Carson hadn't told me about *winter break*, I knew the stakes had risen drastically. Cody stood on his toes, and Carson's phone nearly brushed against the spinning white fan blades.

"Fine!" Carson gave in, extending his arms like a mother reaching for her baby. "I won't tell them. But you're going to let us stay here."

"And help us find summer jobs!" I added, remembering my mom's demand.

"Deal." Cody shook Carson's hand, sandwiching the phone between their palms. Despite the couch separating them, Cody pulled his younger brother in for a hug. All was forgiven, just like that, and a much-needed silence fell over the Welling house.

"Boys are weird," Bea murmured, finishing her canned energy drink. She crushed the empty can between her hands and then, to my surprise, placed it in a recycling bin under the kitchen sink. "Does this mean the party tonight is off? Because one of my friends has been subtweeting again and I was thinking I'd key her car if there's nothing else going on."

Carson did a double take.

"Party is on!" Cody hollered, making a two-handed rock and roll gesture. "It's gonna be even more lit now. Gotta give a proper welcome for Carson and… Sorry, it's been forever, my dude. What's your name again?"

Finally, an opportunity to introduce myself.

"Rain," I said. Bea snorted, which caught us all off-guard.

"Sorry, Rain. I just… I thought that was a girl's name."

Shortly after eight, the sun began to set on the grassy shores of the waterway behind the Welling house. The sky glowed in a million shades of pink, yellow, and orange. From the wide window and porch by the living room, I noticed the long wooden dock that stretched out over the grasses behind the house. It terminated with a large gazebo-like structure on the water, about a hundred feet from the last patches of marsh grass.

Carson told me that the Welling house shared the dock with the house next door. Since the neighbors hadn't rented out their house yet, I suggested inviting the partygoers out to the dock. Cody agreed, so we moved two coolers of drinks down the long walkway, plus a Bluetooth speaker and a bag of Doritos. Bea stayed back at the house to greet people, which sounded to me like a recipe for disaster, but I guess someone had to collect Cody's mandatory five-dollar entry fees—it was his only income, apparently.

The covered gazebo area at the end of the dock was the perfect place to watch the sunset. Cody's music choices detracted from that though, and the beat of the Bluetooth speaker echoed far out across the glasslike water.

Before long, our first few guests arrived. In groups of three or four, they strolled down the dock toward us.

"Seven," Carson whispered to me, out of the blue, as he watched a group of girls approaching down the dock.

"Please tell me you're not trying to—"

"Shh! C'mon, Rain. Look at her. The blonde chick leading the pack, walking this way now. Seven, easy. Maybe eight?"

"Nine," Cody interjected. I didn't know he'd been listening. "And I'm not even drunk yet. That's Eliza Murphy. Just wait until you actually meet her."

When Eliza's group arrived at the end of the dock, we did. Although I'm firmly opposed to rating people's looks, I admit that Eliza looked like she stepped off a magazine cover. But that wasn't the whole story, either. There's an unfortunate stereotype of beautiful people who aren't all that bright, but Eliza broke that mold. Remarkably, Carson struck up a conversation with her, and I listened in.

"So, are you here for the whole summer, or just beach week?" Carson asked. I translated his question: "How long do I have to seduce you?" But if Eliza caught that undertone too, she ignored it.

"Actually, I'm here for another year, at least. I graduated last year, and I'm living on the island with my mom because of her company's contract."

"Like a long-term business trip?"

Eliza laughed. "I guess you could say that, but she *owns* the company. GRM Development. She started it after she divorced my dad. It began out of spite, I think—she kept my dad's name and used it for the company—but she's done well with it. Her company builds casinos and hotels usually, but they're working here in Warley to build a new bridge with the mainland."

I recalled the rusted metal bridge that carried us to the island a few hours earlier. Replacing it sounded like a massive undertaking, but a necessary one. Carson, I'm guessing, heard nothing but "Money, money, money." After all, it isn't every day that you meet the heiress of a multi-million-dollar development company.

"What's the timeline for the new bridge?" I asked, giving Carson a moment to compose himself.

"Right now, just acquiring land. Lots of price negotiations with a few holdouts. Then rezoning, which shouldn't take too long, and in a few months, we'll have barges out on the water pouring fresh concrete."

The way Eliza smiled at the idea of fresh concrete, one might've guessed she'd spoken about spring flowers or Ryan Gosling. Before Carson could finally come up with something to say, one of Eliza's friends pulled her away to dance by the end of the dock.

"Nice meeting you!" Carson called, but the thumping of music drowned him out. More people had arrived too, and their voices surrounded us as they drank, danced, and milled about.

"Hey!" Cody called to us from further up the dock. He waved for us to come toward him, so Carson and

I pushed our way slowly through the crowd. The dock only had space for so many people and judging by the lights back at the Welling house, some had opted to stay there.

"Carson, Rain, I want you guys to meet my friend AJ." Cody stood next to a long-haired guy with ocean waves tattooed on his forearms.

"How's it going?" AJ greeted us.

"He works at Ron's Surf Shop. AJ, I guess just tell these guys what you told me."

Even before Cody mentioned the surf shop, I recognized AJ's tattoos. Carson and I saw him waxing a surfboard when we drove down Warley Avenue.

"Yeah, so, I'm AJ. I guess, uh, now that summer's here, we're kinda short-handed at Ron's. My boss keeps saying we gotta hire someone new to help out, and since Cody says you guys are gonna be around for the next few months, I was thinking I could put in a good word if one of you is interested."

Carson and I exchanged a look, but I don't think we communicated anything of significance between us.

"Only one of us?" I asked to clarify.

"Yeah. Sorry, dude. Gotta have good customer service for this season, but I don't know if my boss is up for training *two* new guys. I mean, I can ask, but no promises. Do you guys wanna think it over for now, or—"

"I'm in!" Carson exclaimed before I could even consider the proposition. After enough discussion, Carson and I probably would have agreed to let him take the job anyway, but it bugged me that Carson *assumed* I didn't want it.

"Right on!" AJ affirmed, holding up his hand to make a Shaka sign. "See this? This hand sign? It means *awesome*. Make sure you know that one." Carson nodded.

"I gotta go check on Bea," Cody told us, checking the time on his phone. "She's gonna want me to take her place at the door. Catch ya later." He turned and retreated up the dock.

"Hey," AJ started. "Rain, was it? Sorry I got nothing for you at Ron's, but see if you can find my babe Ryan, around here somewhere. Maybe hanging out back inside. I think Ryan's boss at the Ritz is still looking to hire someone new."

"The Ritz?" I puzzled, imagining myself working at a luxurious hotel.

"Ha! No, not *that* one. Ritz's Burgers and Fries."

Gilded walls and high ceilings vanished from my mind. Instead, I now pictured myself working at the Krusty Krab, predicting that I'd be less of a Spongebob and much more of a Squidward. Flipping burgers wouldn't pay much differently than working in a surf shop, which didn't feel fair. Carson wouldn't have to deal with grease stains, indecisive lines of customers, or copious amounts of fatty foods. Years ago, I swore to myself that I wouldn't start my career working at a restaurant. I planned to do something more interesting, like a paid internship somewhere. But standing there on that dock, hundreds of miles from home with no college plans, no money, and no other direction to turn, I ran out of options. So, I let it be.

"Sounds *awesome*." I told AJ, half-heartedly mimicking his Shaka sign.

"When can I start?"

"Probably Monday. The shop is only open for a few hours tomorrow, and I'm gonna skip out early if I can, so I doubt I'll be there long enough to help you learn the ropes. I'm going out surfing after work tomorrow, then metal detecting later in the week."

"Metal detecting?" Carson perked up. "What are you looking for?"

"Captain Heron's treasure, of course! Or, like, lost jewelry, coins, you know. But mostly the treasure."

Carson could barely contain himself.

"My dad and I do that every summer! Have you found anything big?"

"Just lost earrings, mostly. I did get an old silver dollar last summer, and that was sweet."

"What's your theory on Heron's treasure?"

I half expected Carson to whip out his phone and start taking notes. AJ poured more fuel on the flame.

"Well, everyone says Heron's crew buried their loot on the island somewhere, but people have been searching for so long that I just don't think that's right. Every plot of land has been dug up at least once. My guess is that it's somewhere inland. Not far, but not actually on Warley Island."

"Have you gone detecting over there? I know there are some big dunes over that way."

"That's where I'm driving Thursday! You wanna coming along?"

"Sure! I've got my own detector I can bring."

"What model do you use?"

Around that point, I lost interest. AJ never told me what Ryan—his boyfriend—looked like, and I didn't want to interrupt Carson's treasure discussion. I decided I'd wander around the party and eventually run into Ryan. Granted, I had no way to recognize him if that happened. Wandering wasn't a very thorough plan, but I didn't want it to be. I wanted to wait as long as possible before pursuing my new job as a fry cook.

My wandering led me back up the dock to the house, then up the back steps to the living room porch. A few guests made way for me enter through the sliding glass door, and I nearly jumped at the sight before me. Bea stood inverted on her hands over a keg of beer, assisted by two other girls holding her ankles. Her blue afro floated just over the keg, and the other people in the living room cheered her on amid blasting music. Between cheers, one voice called out exactly the words running through my mind:

"Someone's gonna die."

Generally, in a loud group of people, it's difficult to pick out who said what. But it wasn't difficult to notice a tall girl wearing a white t-shirt with "RBF" printed in bold red lettering. If that shirt didn't broadcast strong enough opposition, she'd also traded her obligatory Solo cup for a heavy paperback book. She held it between her face and the crowd, just below eye level, and she only flicked her eyes up from the pages every thirty seconds or so. I made my way toward her reading nook on the far side of the kitchen, thinking to myself: *What sort of person comes to a party just to read a book?* When I got close enough, I glimpsed the book's cover and nearly spun around on my heels.

"Have you read it?" She asked. I jumped a bit too noticeably. "Whoa, you okay?"

"Yup, sorry. Just didn't think you saw me. And I've read parts of it, I guess."

"So addicting," she groaned, waving the book in the air. "You've only read parts? How is that even possible? I couldn't stop after the first couple pages. I swear, Eldridge is the greatest mystery author of our time. He *was*, I should say. Anyway, what's your name, bud?"

Before I could process the situation, divert to a new topic, run away, or even comprehend that I'd just been called "bud," a sweaty arm draped itself around my shoulder and dozens of blue curls danced into my field of vision.

"Rain!" Bea exclaimed, slurring through my name for three whole seconds. At least she remembered it somehow, after however much alcohol she'd pumped into her body. "How's it going, man? This place is so lit, right? Wow, I'm dizzy! Here, just… Yeah, hold me up, I guess. Thanks. But like, I bet all those bitches from my school are sitting in their rental house, all alone, because everybody's here! We stole the party! You hear that, guys? We stole the party!"

The dancing crowd in the living room echoed her and hollered loudly. I couldn't believe Bea's transformation. She hardly spoke while sober, but after a few drinks, there were *two* open books in the house's unofficial reading nook.

"Beach week slaps. I love you guys so much. Especially Cody: we hooked up last night. Oh! That's a secret. Shh, don't tell anyone! He's a great kisser even though he has that silly beard thing. I bet those girls down the street are j-e-a-u-l-o-s. Jealous. Jello shots? Shit, I forgot to make more."

The RBF girl's eyes whispered: "Rock paper scissors for who calls the ambulance?" I hoped it wouldn't come to that. I first helped Bea lower herself into the seat across from the RBF girl. Bea kept rambling on.

"Some old lady tried to get into the party. So rude. Like, can't you see this isn't about you? This is about us! Live while we're young! At least those girls from my school didn't try showing up. Especially Val. Can you believe she kicked me out for dyeing my hair? And I only did that because she acted weird when I told her I'm bi, so then I'm like, bitch, let me wake up your intolerant ass. *Boom*, hit you with some blue hair. And if that's not enough for Val, she can catch these hands because they swing both ways too."

No one really caught the brilliance of Bea's threat before Cody waltzed into our popular reading nook. He set his cup down on the kitchen island and slid into Bea's seat, which really couldn't fit both of them. Only I remained standing, and the RBF girl stopped attempting to actually read.

"What's up, you guys?" Cody spoke much too loudly.

"Trying to find a job," I answered, mostly to remind myself.

"Receiving an info-dump from your friend," RBF added with a wink in Bea's direction. I thought her words flew over both their boozed-up heads, but Bea understood the gist.

"Shh!" She reminded us. "Don't talk about the secret!"

"Well, Bea, you need to drink some water. C'mon." Cody helped her back to her feet. "Catch you guys later. Pong's in the garage if you want. And Ryan, AJ wanted me to tell you he had to head out. My brother Carson can give you a ride later if you need."

My mind spun as Cody and Bea drifted into the fray. *Was he talking to RBF?*

"Awesome," RBF replied. "See ya, Cody."

"Wait, hold on." I froze, then took the seat that Bea left. "You're Ryan? *You?*"

She smiled awkwardly. I dropped down into the seat left empty by Bea and Cody.

"Last I checked, yeah. Ryan Burnstein."

Oh, shit. My words couldn't build sentences fast enough, but I tried anyway.

"Whoa. Okay, wait… AJ said… He told me to look for his babe, Ryan, and somehow I thought…"

"You thought 'Ryan' was a dude?" She grinned more now. "Well, it's a girl's name, too."

I backpedaled. "I'm so sorry! I mean, I should've known. My name is *Rain!* I get the same crap all the time, and I know exactly how it feels when—"

"Wait, so you thought AJ was gay?"

"Okay, okay, I'm a victim of limited information."

Ryan laughed at my expense, but a laugh is a laugh, so I felt better. "That you are," she agreed, tapping her closed book. "H.M. Eldridge would remind you to separate *assumptions* from *deductions*. People forget to do that. In fact, I bet I can catch you making at least one more assumption. What does my shirt stand for?"

I glanced down again, even though I obviously remembered what the shirt looked like. From the moment I spotted the shirt's red letters, I assumed they stood for "Resting Bitch Face," but after my first lapse of judgement, the truth flowed into place like water into a sponge.

"Okay," I started. "I get it. No more assumptions, just evidence. Now that I know *you're* Ryan, I also know that AJ sent me to see *you* about finding a summer job. You knew that too because I just told Cody, and then you told me to figure out your shirt, which must relate to where you work. The shirt's not just a style; it's a uniform! But how does that help me? Well, I also remember that when Carson and I drove down earlier today, we passed a restaurant with red and white umbrellas, the same colors as your shirt. I would have forgotten the place's name, but luckily, AJ reminded me out on the dock."

"Well?" Ryan beamed. "What's RBF?"

"*Ritz's Burgers and Fries.*"

"Bravo! Bravo!" Ryan applauded, which blended into the sounds of partiers nearby. "Not bad detective work. I guess I can talk to my boss tomorrow, but assuming all goes well, consider yourself hired, Detective… What's your last name?"

"El—" I choked the word *Eldridge* back down into my throat. I nearly spoke my most valuable secret without a second thought. I tried not to imagine what might've happened if I'd really done it. Would she have fainted? Would she have screamed? I could only guess, but I knew she wouldn't have treated me the same if I'd told her the truth so soon. I read my surname silently from the cover of Ryan's book and fibbed: "…Smith."

Her head cocked sideways.

"El-smith? That sounds… unusual."

"It's old. Like, old English. Not many Elsmiths left."

Ryan narrowed her eyes and went in for the kill. "I'm gonna bet that there are *none*, since I'm pretty sure you just made up that name. I've read enough detective novels to catch a quick lie, but it's okay; I'll see your paperwork when you come to RBF, so I'll learn your full name then." She winked again, just like she did to Bea, throwing my mind into a mix of deep concern and frail joy.

A chatter crossed the floor like a wave of water from the front door to the back porch. In seconds, the music stopped. Voices grew louder and everyone moved faster, dropping their drinks and fumbling for their flip-flops. The crowd split and pushed toward the exits. Out of nowhere, Carson dashed into the beer-splattered kitchen.

"Neighbors! They said they're gonna call the cops."

"About time," Ryan smiled, standing and scooping her book off the table. Carson tried not to look too offended; he'd clearly enjoyed his night being the host's brother, especially judging by how he greeted her.

"Hey, I'm Carson. Cody's brother. Just graduated. Do you still need a ride?"

"Hey bud, I'm Ryan, but you probably won't remember my name. Also, I have a boyfriend, and it takes me like two minutes to walk to my place. Plus, I'm just gonna go read on the beach for a while. So, I'd hate to waste your time driving me around while you sweat through that Polo shirt." Ryan shot off another wink, this time at Carson, before waving goodbye to me. "See you soon, El-smith."

Ryan merged into the stream of people escaping downstairs into the garage. Her tight ponytail and familiar book disappeared into the darkness. A bit shaken, Carson took the free seat across from me in the kitchen's abandoned reading nook.

"Geez, Rain. Do you ever meet any normal people?"

"Nope, not really. How many phone numbers did you get?"

"Three."

"Snapchat names?"

"Six. New record."

"Okay, how about *actual* names?"

"Well doesn't Snapchat tell you that?"

Carson and I shared a laugh at his expense.

Despite the pandemonium, the police never arrived. Cody said they busted another party further south, instead. After all, the island police could only handle so much during the chaos of senior week. Without a reason to tidy up, we let the house remain in complete, silent disorder. Half-dried puddles of beer and mixers painted the white tiles of the kitchen. Crushed cans and cups decorated every flat surface and filled every narrow corner.

Carson, Bea, and Cody all migrated toward their bedrooms upstairs. I slunk into my solitary room on the main floor, wondering if Cody and Bea planned to share a room. More importantly, I worried that their room might be directly above mine.

Thankfully, I didn't stay awake to find out.

3: THE TOWER

If there's one thing I learned in the months before my arrival in Warley, it's that no day is as predictable as it seems. As people, we see the order in the world—or at least most of us do. We learn routines. We drive the same streets every day. We use the same words to greet the same people, we go to the same classes, or we work the same hours. Our days feel predictable because we force ourselves to be, but we have no real control over the rest. Routines are violated. Cars spin out. People drift apart. Students are expelled, and employees are fired. Even after months of understanding this, I never imagined what my Sunday in Warley would bring.

Waking up in an unfamiliar room, I jolted upright. I felt like a computer rebooting, forced to restart a dozen programs all at once. Questions flooded my mind, some answered more quickly than others: *Where am I? Did I set up this pullout couch? What day is it? Where's my duffel bag? What time is it? Why am I here?*

When my mind eventually ripped itself from that death spiral, I rolled out of the bed and picked my phone up off the floor. Next to it sat the empty notebook. Late at night, whenever I haphazardly unpacked my duffel bag, it must have slipped out onto the carpet floor. Morning sunlight seeping through the blinds brought it to my attention.

Tell your story, said the message inscribed inside the notebook's front cover. I read that message in my dad's voice. He said it over and over for years, whispering it harshly like a magical spell. That spell, *"Tell your story,"* cast a curse over me. I could hardly look at the notebook without remembering where my father's mantra took him.

I kicked the notebook underneath the pullout couch and threw on some fresh clothes. It wasn't enough. The notebook's persistent aura swirled around my dark bedroom like a swarm of insects. I decided to open the blinds, which covered the duct-tape-patched glass door on one side of my new room. As I reeled them aside with a clatter, the June sun set my room ablaze. I squinted out over the house's front stairs and driveway and stepped barefoot onto the wooden porch outside.

My room's porch extended sideways to the house's front door, where Carson and I nearly attacked Bea. Beneath the wooden porch, fresh piles of party garbage blockaded the garage doors. Ahead of me, the driveway's tunnel of gnarled trees hummed with frogs and insects, already awake in the simmering heat. Like them, I felt the urge to make noise. I felt the urge to escape that awful, taunting notebook. I felt the urge to move.

Throwing on a pair of shoes (one of only two pairs that I packed), I shut the glass door and jogged down to the messy driveway. Through the tangled bushes, across Warley Avenue, and past a dozen colorful beach houses, I ran toward the ocean. My phone told me how early it was, which explained why everywhere looked so desolate. I preferred the empty street to the wild and crowded party, but something felt especially ghostly about Warley Avenue on that morning. Maybe it was the faint ocean spray rising like steam beyond grassy sand dunes.

I followed a sign for *Public Beach Access*, crossed the dunes via a path of wooden planks, and there it was: The Atlantic Ocean. I certainly never saw that in Ohio. We had Lake Erie, but so what? The Great

Lakes end just beyond their horizons. The Lakes are better described as large islands of water in a sea of land, but the Atlantic Ocean doesn't just end like they do. It extends far around, connecting the Southern and Pacific Oceans, the Mediterranean Sea, and five continents. Gazing out over that vast water for the first time, I paused to think of how big it all is. The world, a story that doesn't have an end.

"On your left!" Someone called out. I jumped to the right side of the dune walkway. Ryan rushed by sporting neon athletic clothes and a pair of running shoes—nicer ones than mine. She jumped down the steps to the beach sand and carried on running.

"Cool shoes!" I called to her. She turned around.

"Oh, Rain? Hey! Didn't recognize you from behind." Her breaths followed each other rapidly, like she'd already been running for a while.

"Mind if I join you?"

"Going south? Sure, if you can keep up."

The low tide waves crashed far from us. The earlier tide left us a path of hard, smooth sand between the dunes and the ocean, and that made running easy. Ryan, on the other hand, complicated things. She ran *much* faster than I expected, but I did my best to keep pace.

"What's that tower up there?" I asked her, but she didn't turn around to answer; the waves drowned out my voice. No one ever told me how loud the ocean would be. Each crashing wave roared and echoed continuously through the salty mist. I took a few more breaths and pushed myself to catch up so I could run alongside her. Then I asked my question again.

"Oh, the watchtower?" Ryan nodded toward the narrow, white-painted building that rose up from the beach's grassy dune. "AJ told me about those. I forget if it was the Army or Navy, but they built them during

World War II for photographing missile tests. Once the war ended, the towers stayed, collapsed, or became private property like that one."

One of the waterfront homes sat close to the tower, and its deck connected the two buildings together.

"How… How many? Towers?" I tried to ask but found myself out of breath. Ryan still seemed mostly unphased. She even grinned at my struggle.

"I don't know, five to ten maybe. There's another one you'll see further down, assuming you don't pass out before then."

I held up a Shaka sign to avoid speaking again.

"Ha! I bet AJ taught you that, didn't he?" She knew him well.

The beachfront houses looked so similar that I wondered how we'd find the same walkway from earlier. One after the next, each two-story house held out a sandy wooden deck and bore pastel siding all around. Blue, yellow, gray, and white appeared most often. Further south down the beach, the houses stood farther and farther apart. Dune grasses grew wilder, and beach access paths snaked toward us from the road like splintered tree limbs. Through the morning mist, the silhouette of another lonely tower emerged.

Between us and the tower, a man shuffled up the sand carrying a tackle box, fishing rod, and Styrofoam cooler. The tail of a limp fish poked out from under the cooler's lid, and a small knife slipped out of the tackle box. The man didn't pause to look at us—or down at the knife he dropped. Ryan jogged over to pick it up for him. I stayed close.

"Hey, you dropped this." She pulled the knife out of the sand. Even from a few feet away, I saw the bloodstains on its blade. The fisherman turned. A dirty beard covered most of his face. His gray eyes widened and darted between the two of us.

"Thank you," he spoke, taking the knife from Ryan. Without another word, he proceeded up the sand and vanished over the dunes.

"Creepy," I said. Ryan agreed.

"I would say that guy scared me, but it looked like *we* scared him even more."

I contemplated asking Ryan to turn back. We'd already stopped, and my legs turned to jelly. Besides, if there's ever been a perfect omen of *"Turn back,"* it hobbled through ocean mist with a bloody knife. But after so much running, I never spoke up, so we continued toward the south tower.

This tower wasn't like the first one. Its white paint remained only in sparse patches, and its first floor had no walls, just concrete stilts. The two floors above had glassless windows that invited the sea breeze into the dark hollow within. Empty beer cans and cigarette butts littered the dune at its base, along with something else.

I wish that Ryan saw it first. I wish she warned me to just turn away… But I saw it first. I saw strands of blonde hair poking up between the dune grasses. I saw a face half buried in sand. I saw the body first, and before I could tell Ryan, I puked.

"Rain!" She exclaimed, stopping next to me. "Oh, shit, I'm sorry! I should've slowed down for you. I didn't realize you were having that much trouble keeping up. Do you need water? Because I could go—"

I shook my head and pointed to the tower. I stayed on my knees dry heaving while Ryan stood up. She left me and approached the tower. Her movements were mechanical, careful, and slow like she'd planned it all in advance. Ryan remained unthinkably calm when I couldn't even stand up.

She returned just as I got to my feet again. My legs shook more than before.

"Do you have your phone?" Ryan held out her hand. I reached into my pocket.

"Why?"

"I'm calling 9-1-1."

Oh no. This can't be right.

"So, it really is… A body?"

"Yeah. Now c'mon Rain, the sooner we call, the less likely we are as suspects."

What?

"Suspects?" I gripped the phone tighter, but she yanked it from my hand.

"Yes! There's a body. *Someone* knows why it's here. And since *we* found it, we'll be the first ones questioned."

"No!" I gasped for breath, trying not to panic again. "No, let's just go. Turn back. Forget it. Someone else will call. There's no rush; she's… Dead, right?"

Ryan looked up from my cell phone, raised one hand, and slapped my face.

"Are you insane? Rain, you want us to commit a crime so that the police won't *think* we committed a different crime?"

My cheek stung from the slap, but I focused on stopping her from calling the cops.

"This isn't gonna be like a movie. Real life isn't an Eldridge novel. It's worse; it makes no sense! And if we get involved in whatever *this* is, there's no way of knowing how it will end. What if they *do* think we're suspects? What if they arrest us? Convict us of something we know nothing about? That sort of bullshit happens every day in real life. But if we go back now, we can avoid it all! No one is asking us to be some sort of heroes here."

Ryan dialed the number and made eye contact with me as she raised my phone to her ear.

"Being some sort of hero is usually better than the alternative."

Behind my layers of fear, I knew that she was right.

They told Ryan to stay on the line, and she did. I thought maybe they'd ask her to approach the body again—she said that there was no pulse—but they didn't ask her to do it again. They asked if she was alone. No, she said, I was there too. They insisted we stay put, but once my stomach settled, I forced myself to trudge up the dune and take a closer look. What a horrible decision that was.

To Ryan, the body on the dune belonged to someone nameless. The stranger's head sat wrong on her shoulders; her neck bent itself unnaturally to one side and stretched the skin on the other. Despite her disfigurement, she was no stranger to me. I recognized her face, her dark eyeliner. I remembered her voice, and memories of the party rushed back in a wave.

Carson—in his own way—called her beautiful. She told us about her mother's company, the one contracted to build a new bridge from Warley Island to the mainland. To see her there on the sand, eyes closed, with her head at a sideways angle... It couldn't be right.

Eliza Murphy.

I expected some caravan of vehicles with flashing lights, but at first only one beach patrol arrived. It wasn't even a car, just an all-terrain vehicle with a hefty first aid kit and a flotation device on the back. The officer behind the wheel parked between us and the tower, then he stepped down onto the sand.

"Stay right here," he spoke without introducing himself. He looked young, like he'd recently graduated from college, and his short hair stuck flat to his head like a swim cap. The officer unclipped the first aid kit from the back of his vehicle. He ran up the dune to the base of the tower, moving so haphazardly that I thought he might slide and fall back down the dune toward us. When he reached her, he knelt down and checked again for signs of life.

"Can I see my phone now?" I asked Ryan once the call center told her to hang up. She tossed me the phone, and I sent Carson a text: "*Went for a run. Police here at south tower. Might not be back for a while.*"

I neglected to mention Eliza. In hindsight, I should have neglected to mention *anything* to Carson. But some part of me itched to tell someone about our discovery, like doing so would release the burden suddenly placed on Ryan and me.

The officer returned to us with his first aid kit unopened. He placed it on the seat of his vehicle and pulled out a notebook—smaller than mine.

"My name is Officer Lee. Don't worry, we have more people on the way. I know this is probably very scary, but I need you both to bear with me here. Did you make the call?" He looked toward Ryan.

"I did," she nodded. "I'm Ryan Burnstein. B-u-r—"

"It's fine, the call center got your name down. I have to ask some questions now. You know, paperwork. Shouldn't take too long. Um…" He flipped to a fresh page in his notebook. "Can you tell me what happened? Before you called?"

"We were running," she began. "Rain and I. Running separately, but we ran into each other further north. We decided to pace each other. Then we got to the tower, and Rain looked up and he saw…"

"I saw her hair." I said. Officer Lee's eyes flicked from Ryan to me.

"So, you're… Rain? Rain and Ryan?"

Ryan affirmed. "It's confusing, I know. Rain saw the body and pointed me toward the tower. I walked up to see her, then he did too while I made the call. Those are our footprints next to yours."

I looked over the paths of footprints. Four up, four down—too many. One trail led in the direction the fisherman went, vanishing north toward the nearest beach access path… *He saw Eliza too. And he didn't call the police.* Ryan was right. That made him suspicious, as if the bloody knife wasn't enough.

"Thanks for that. Do either of you recognize her? Anyone you know? Seen her around?"

"Eliza Murphy," my lips spoke without thinking. Two pairs of eyebrows rose. I probably surprised Ryan the most, since she knew I'd only just arrived in Warley. *What were the odds that I'd met Eliza?* Officer Lee, well… If he didn't think me suspicious to begin with, he did after that. The rising sun on the water glared across my vision, and beads of sweat crawled down my face.

"Is Eliza a friend of yours?" Lee asked.

"Not really. I just met her last night at a party…"

My mind snagged: *Underage drinking! Was there weed too? Or worse? Who brought the booze? Would I get in trouble for attending? What about Cody?* I had no time to worry about that. Eliza took precedence.

"…We just talked a little. She told me she'd been on the island a few months because her mom runs a construction company. For the bridge."

Lee's hand scribbled faster in his notebook. My mind flip-flopped between visualizing Eliza's twisted neck and forecasting my immediate future. Of all my predictions—being handcuffed, issuing a false confession, being framed for murder by Ryan, or throwing up again—what happened next topped them all. Officer Lee paused in his writing.

"Wait, Rain? I never got your last name."

Oh no. My stomach rolled. Ryan's ears perked up. Before I could answer him, my phone rang. I checked the caller ID, and my stomach rolled again.

"It's my mom," I told Officer Lee. Then I showed him. He gave a begrudging nod, as if to say: *This is a horrible time, but I have a mom too, so I know you'd better take that call.*

He didn't *actually* say anything. I picked up the call on the fifth ring, stepping toward the water and leaving Ryan with Lee. I knew her well enough to expect her ears to point in my direction, and Officer Lee, well… What else is a cop supposed to do? I remained the center of attention no matter where I walked. Ryan, my mom, and Officer Lee all held their breath waiting for my words, each expecting something completely different.

"Hey." My voice sounded cheerful, but not energetic. Good start.

"Rain? Did you arrive safely? You never called yesterday. That was part of our deal."

Shit, I forgot.

"I'm sorry, I've been busy." I told her, staying as vague as possible. Ryan remained within earshot, but Lee retreated toward the tower again. *Phew.*

"Are you and Carson at the house, then?"

"Yup, we're just settling in."

"Okay, that's good. Are you looking for a job?"

"Yeah, I might have something. I don't know yet." Ryan kept listening to me. My heart pounded harder in my ears, and I prayed that I wouldn't vomit again while my mom quietly droned on.

"Alright, that's good. Have you written in the notebook at all?"

"I have to go," I interrupted. "Text if it's an emergency."

"Okay. Make good choices."

"Okay. Bye."

Beep. Done.

I dropped my phone back into my pocket and tried to pull my brain back to the crisis at hand. I expected Ryan to interrogate me about the phone call, but her attention turned to the tower.

The flashing lights of two emergency vehicles rose up over the crest of the sand, then stopped short. Stepping out from one vehicle, a tall, dark-haired woman wearing orange sunglasses led two other officers to meet Lee at the base of the tower. Her uniform differed slightly from theirs.

"Are they just gonna leave us here?" I asked Ryan rhetorically. "I mean, don't they give us those metal blankets for shock or something?"

"I don't know. Like you said, this isn't an Eldridge novel."

Two more figures emerged over the dune grasses, but not directly behind the tower with the officers. They approached us faster, jogging down the public beach access ramp on the north side of the watchtower. The two familiar figures—one wearing a Polo shirt and the other with a patchy beard—craned their necks to see the officers taking photographs. Like visitors at a zoo peering into an exhibit, they leaned over the railing eagerly.

"Dammit," I muttered. Ryan squinted her eyes at the newcomers. Carson and Cody waved to us and proceeded down the sandy wood-plank steps at the edge of the dune. Ryan was not impressed.

"Oh, c'mon. Did you tell them to come here?"

"No! I just texted Carson to say I'd be gone awhile… I guess I might've mentioned police." In retrospect, I shouldn't have sent the text. After the party, I figured nothing could've awakened Carson. As for Cody, I almost questioned whether he'd wake up at all. Most of all, I wondered about Bea, whose absence concerned me even further.

"Holy shit!" Cody exclaimed. He gazed up at the tower and placed his hands anxiously on the back of his neck. Carson ran toward us and cut to the chase.

"Is that… *That* girl?"

I hated his question; I hated how he forgot her name. Still, someone had to tell him something. I hoped that Ryan would answer him, and she probably hoped that I would. But the fear in Carson's eyes blocked my words from leaving my throat.

"Eliza," Ryan reminded him. "Eliza Murphy."

Cody wandered down to the low-tide waves and started digging in the wet sand. He piled dark brown clumps of mud and shells in the shallow water, then reached into hole he made before the water filled it again. His distractedness upset me in a different way. Cody swept the thought of Eliza under the rug with all his other problems, like debris from a party. *Out of sight, out of mind.*

"Look," Carson pointed to the tower. Two men in dark blue uniforms lifted a stretcher draped in a white sheet. I thought maybe we'd see one last glimpse of her: Maybe a hand, a foot, or a few locks of her long blonde hair. But they covered her up completely, then they took her away to one of the waiting vehicles. *It's like they want us to forget about her as quickly as possible,* I thought to myself.

"C'mon," Carson said. He waved for us to follow him back over the beach access path. Ryan and I did. Cody rinsed the sand from his hands and followed lazily behind us.

"What happened to her?" Carson asked Ryan and me. "Or what do you think?"

"I think her neck was broken," I informed him. "I mean, look at that tower. It's tall. You can do the math."

"You think she was drunk up there?"

"Probably."

Ryan huffed and grabbed Carson and me by our wrists.

"Really? We're diving right into assumptions? Rain! RBF, remember? We don't know how she broke her neck, or even if her neck was broken at all. What if someone set her up to look that way? What if she killed herself? What if she got mugged? What if she got struck by lightning? Abducted by aliens? Don't get me wrong, I want to know what happened to Eliza. Mysteries are my passion! But can we wait until Eliza isn't *a hundred feet away* in the back of a *coroner's van?*"

Not for the first time, Ryan intimidated me. Her height brought her eyes about level with mine and Carson's, and she showed no sign of fatigue, even after running all the way to the tower with me. As she paused, the rear doors of the coroner's van shut together with a loud bang, followed by silence.

"Thank you," Ryan sighed, hurrying us along toward Carson's parked truck.

The drive back to the Welling house should have flown by, but as we rolled north on Warley Avenue, one of the house names caught my eye: *Gone Fishin'*. The whole world slowed down. A chill ran up my spine, bringing back the image of the bearded fisherman on the beach. He creeped me out even *before* we found Eliza, but afterwards, the memory of him really bothered me. We met him very close to the watchtower. Stains of blood covered his knife, but who's to say that blood came from a fish? And his footprints led up to the dune before any of ours.

Ryan sat next to me in the bed of the truck, ready to slap my face again if I offered up my new theory, so I kept the thoughts of the fisherman to myself. Besides, the rushing ocean air made talking difficult.

When we entered Welling house, I finally crossed out one item on my mental list of worries: Bea smiled and waved "*Good morning*" at us, leaning one arm on the kitchen island. Without speaking, she took a sip from an energy drink can, leaned over the sink, and vomited. Bea looked like I felt.

"You okay?" Ryan asked her. She offered up a water bottle and tore a paper towel from the roll near the sink. Bea coughed, wiped her face, then spoke the words on all our minds:

"Another day in paradise."

4: THE PUZZLE

We migrated to the living room, brushed away trash from the couch and chairs, then sat down in a wide semicircle. Naturally, Bea asked what the hell had freaked us out. Our answers to her question differed, but the emotion was the same.

Carson told Bea the short version: Eliza was at the party last night, then we found her body in the morning. Carson hardly remembered what Eliza said to us out on the dock, but he remembered asking for her Snapchat username later on. He even pulled out his phone to show us: *Emurphy98 added.* Carson knew the feeling of never receiving a text back, but that never broke his spirit before. This time wasn't the same. Carson hadn't messaged Eliza yet, and now he never would. Sure, his whole perspective sounded shallow to the rest of us, but I knew he felt the same hopelessness.

To fill in the blanks left by Carson, Ryan described the scene on the dune in detail, from the tower's height to Eliza's winged eyeliner. Ryan kept mentioning the lack of evidence; we couldn't know much from only a couple fleeting glances at her body. In books, Ryan said, a body would always point the way along a trail of evidence, but Eliza's gave us nothing. Ryan tapped her foot anxiously, unable to move on with so few facts. That's what bothered her most, and as a result, she officially lifted her moratorium on speculation.

"Whatever," she said. "Let's hear some theories."

Cody dove right into his concerns. When did Eliza leave the party? Was she alone? Drunk? High? Did she get a ride, or did she drive herself? Walk? None of us recalled seeing her more than once or twice. Cody worried that the police would retrace her steps back to all of us—or specifically back to him. He already found himself in a delicate situation: Hiding from parents, buying cases of beer for teenagers, and trashing an expensive vacation house. Any police involvement could tip the balance out of his favor, maybe even implicating him in Eliza's untimely death.

"I don't know how I feel," I said, when four pairs of ears turned their attention to me. "It just felt wrong to see her like that. At the party, she was happy. She didn't really seem drunk, at least not when Carson and I talked with her. How could she end up dead on a dune, like, what, three miles away? That's not an accident. That's not suicide. Whatever it is… *That's* what has me freaked out."

After a long pause, Bea nodded. "Okay, yeah. Sounds like freaky shit. Glad I wasn't out there with you guys."

Ryan huffed. Bea flipped her off with a yellow-painted nail.

Carson picked up the TV's universal remote and turned the system on. A little distraction couldn't hurt, I supposed, but Ryan objected when Carson selected one of the sports channels.

"C'mon, really?"

"I have to catch up on the World Cup. *Fútbol* is the new *football*, you know?"

Cody stretched from his recliner to steal the remote off the couch arm. Carson scrambled to take it back, but Cody blocked him with one foot outstretched. After Carson slumped back onto the couch, Cody switched the TV over to Netflix. One by one he ran through suggestions, and one by one we shot them down. *Making a Murderer, Riverdale, Evil Genius,* and even *Sherlock* all felt a bit too real under the circumstances. On the other hand, *Moana, The Office, Cheers,* and *New Girl* sounded frivolous. Plus, someone always had an excuse:

Cody already saw *Twin Peaks*, Ryan refused all Marvel movies due to her preference for D.C. Comics, Bea objected to *House of Cards* on account of Kevin Spacey, and Carson vetoed the newest *Star Wars* since he hadn't seen the others yet. All the while, our thoughts kept revolving back to Eliza.

"There has to be something," I insisted, standing up to look for DVDs under the TV stand.

"Do we know that her neck was broken?" Carson asked for the third time.

"Looked broken to me," Ryan confirmed. "But that doesn't mean she fell."

"You think somebody just twisted her head? Like in a movie?"

Cody interjected a sickening crack sound with his tongue, and Bea pretended to gag. Maybe the gag was real, considering her hangover.

"Well probably not. I mean, logically, why do it there by the tower instead of somewhere less conspicuous? Unless they moved the body, which they could have. Almost every killer does that in books. Rain, have you found a movie yet?"

In the cabinet under the TV stand, I found a small cache of Disney movies on DVD. I knew someone would object to those, but I found more than just DVDs down there. The cabinet held three decks of cards, a large jar of pennies, and board games including Monopoly, Life, Risk, and something called Tripoley. Underneath those, I found a white cardboard box that I slid out and carried over to the dining room table. With one arm, I wiped the table's red cups and aluminum cans onto the floor, then I dumped the box's contents in a messy heap.

Two thousand colorful puzzle pieces settled onto the table. A few slid and fell to the floor. Everyone turned.

"If we're in the mood to solve puzzles, we might as well solve one that has all of its pieces." I help up the lid of the jigsaw box to show them. A printed image collage showed off familiar sights: Surf shops, the Captain Heron Museum, beloved local restaurants, people fishing from docks, kites and pelicans flying, fireworks exploding above, and even one photo of the iconic coastal watchtowers. An arc of text broke through the middle of the collage to say *Warley Island.*

Ryan rolled her eyes, but Carson jumped to his feet.

"Challenge accepted!"

"Perfect. If you're doing that, we can watch *Star Wars.*" Cody started up the movie.

"Turn it down though! No spoilers."

Ryan trailed behind Carson toward the newly established puzzle table. Carson shuffled through the tiny pieces with both hands and spread them into a widening puddle of cardboard.

"Well, Rain," Ryan began, waving one hand over the puzzle, "I'd much rather solve a real puzzle. One that matters. But until we know more about the Eliza puzzle, I guess this one will have to be enough."

As the opening crawl of *Star Wars* ran up the TV screen, someone knocked at the front door. Cody called to us without breaking his eyes away from the screen.

"Are we expecting someone?"

"Yup," Ryan answered. She abandoned the puzzle to go open the front door. Under the paranoid watch of the other four of us, AJ entered, and we all breathed a collective sigh of relief.

"Hey guys. Ryan texted me… I heard what happened, and Ron said I could ditch work early. It's Sunday, ya know?" AJ and Ryan greeted each other with a kiss. *Weird*, I thought. Before that instant, I never saw them in the same room. No stranger would have placed AJ with Ryan; as far as I could tell, they came from different worlds. Ryan read giant books, and AJ either surfed or treasure-hunted on weekends. AJ brought the booze to Cody's party, and Ryan never took one sip. Despite all that, their casual kiss in the foyer of *All's Well* didn't look unnatural. Ryan's shoulders relaxed for the first time since we found Eliza. AJ smiled at her when he kicked off his shoes.

"Hey, man. Have you seen the new *Star Wars*?" Cody called back to AJ.

"What? Oh, yeah, I saw it." He glanced over the puzzle. Carson and I sifted through the messy pile to find edge pieces. Back in the living room, Cody and Bea migrated closer to each other on the couch. AJ nodded weakly. "Wow. You guys all seem… Okay. You know, since what happened…"

Bea turned around and smiled up at him. "Don't worry, we're all dying on the inside."

Ryan and AJ joined Carson and me at the puzzle table. AJ reached swiftly into the mess and pulled out a corner piece, which he handed to me. Carson marveled at this with visible jealousy.

"Wow," Ryan grinned. "Looks like you finally found some buried treasure."

"Nah, Rain or Carson would've found it just as easy. It was right on top."

I shrugged. "Now we just need the other three corners, right?"

"Yeah. That's the tough part."

Before we could embark on that next challenge, someone else knocked at the front door.

"Hold up, Ryan." Cody paused the movie. "How many people did you invite to puzzle club?"

She shook her head. "No one else."

"Nose goes," Bea exclaimed, sticking one finger to her nose. Ryan, Cody, Carson, and AJ followed suit. Distracted by the puzzle, I touched my nose last, and the responsibility of answering the door fell to me. The person outside knocked again twice, louder.

"Coming," I called, but I slowed down close to the door. Something caught my eye. Through the clouded glass on either side, I saw that our uninvited guest was plural *guests*. Even closer, I saw that both figures wore dark uniforms from head to toe.

"Cops," I warned, and our manufactured calm exploded into madness.

"Oh shit!" Cody shouted, and his face flushed. Bea flipped backwards over the couch, then lunged toward the kitchen to take over the situation. Her hangover dissipated in an instant, replaced by the cool-headed authority of a drill sergeant.

"Clean up the cans, assholes! Go! Cups, bottles, anything with alcohol! Rain, don't you dare answer that door. I'll grab the trash can. Carson, take those six packs from the fridge, put them all in the kayak that's hung up on the basement ceiling. AJ, if you've got weed on you, flush it. You know the drill. *Why are there pills?* Rain, do me a favor: Grab that keg, take it out on the back balcony, and just *yeet* it into the grass. Cody, get your ass over here. Ryan... Here, take this!"

Bea snatched the trash can from a cabinet under the sink and catapulted it over the kitchen island to Ryan. The half-filled plastic bin bounced once on the puzzle table, scattering puzzle pieces and dropping party garbage all over. Bea hardly noticed. Cody arrived at the kitchen, anxiously awaiting Bea's orders.

"Cody, listen carefully. You are in Tennessee. What sound will *we* hear when you're in Tennessee?"

"Music?"

"Hell no! We'll hear *silence*. So, get under the sink and be silent!"

At Bea's demand, Cody ducked down and climbed into the space where the trash can had been. His head clanged twice against the bottom of the metal sink before she flung the cabinet door shut, and—by anyone's account—Cody returned to Tennessee.

The remaining five of us scrambled to complete our responsibilities. Carson heaved four six packs of beer from the fridge, across the kitchen, and down the basement steps. AJ pushed past me toward the bathroom near the front door, and the toilet gurgled moments later. I carried the keg from the living room to the back porch, then I dropped it fifteen feet down toward the intracoastal grasses. It landed with a swish and a thump in the muck below. Meanwhile, Ryan struggled to gather up trash in time.

"Jesus, you people drink a lot!" Ryan shouted, tearing through the room hopelessly. Bea lent her a hand, squatting down and scooping up four more cups from underneath the coffee table.

"Not so useless now, am I?"

Ryan scoffed. "Barking orders doesn't make you useful."

One of the officers at the door knocked again. Three times. I couldn't wait any longer. Gathering up all my courage, I stepped up to the clouded glass door and pulled it open.

I locked eyes with the man on the right—Officer Lee, who met Ryan and I on the beach. Then my attention shifted to the tall woman on the left, whose distinct orange sunglasses and obsidian-black hair hadn't left my memory since the beach. Up close, I saw the reason for her different uniform: Her badge read *Warley Island Chief of Police*, but even that wasn't the main way she stood out. For comparison, I could imagine Officer Lee partying like Cody or AJ in his former years, but this woman wore the muted expression of a robot. I couldn't imagine how or where a smile might fit on her face. Staring past me and into the house, she extended one hand and introduced herself.

"Chief Fitz."

"Rain." I reach my hand to shake hers, but she simply held out a slip of paper.

"This is a warrant. Read it if you would like. We are coming in now."

I took the paper. Officer Lee pushed the door all the way open for her, and she strolled inside like the single aunt at a family reunion. The rest of us struggled to act natural. Ryan and AJ entered from the back porch, having just thrown the garbage bin down with the keg in the marsh below. Carson, still out of breath from running to the basement, tried to look busy at work on the puzzle while Bea calmly replaced the filter in the coffee maker. Our uninvited guest floated to the center of the house between the kitchen, living room, and dining area. Finally, she removed her sunglasses.

"Good afternoon. My name is Marie Fitz, and I am Warley Island's Chief of Police. For those of you who have not met me before, I hope we do not have to meet again. For those of you who have met me before…" She glanced at AJ. "…Long time, no see. I know we are all here this week to have a good time, right? We are all here to party? I have lived on this island my whole life. News always travels fast around here. How about we skip the first few questions, then? I already know about last night. I already know who was here. I also surmise that you are each aware of Miss Murphy's death.

"I know all of these things because I am good at my job, and I hope that none of you are stupid enough to assume that you can keep secrets from me. You do not want me to be here. I do not want to be here either. If we all have come to an understanding, my friends will have a quick look around, I will ask some of you questions, and we can all go on our way. Clear?"

Nods all around. Fitz commanded it.

"Excellent. What is your name, blue hair?" Bea started up the coffee maker.

"Bea. Short for Beatrice."

"You hosted the party last night?"

"No. Just helped out."

"Who hosted the party then? Cody Welling?" Fitz took a seat at the kitchen island while Lee and two other officers began shuffling around the house. "Yes, I already know who he is." *Did she look up the deed to the house? Did she call Carson and Cody's parents? Or did she see something on social media?* I couldn't say for sure, and that worried me. On top of that, I worried that Cody might sneeze or bump his head under the sink again. His hideaway trapped him on my side of the kitchen island, only a couple feet away from Fitz.

"Yes, Cody hosted."

"And where is he now?"

"Back in Tennessee," answered Carson. "He was only here for a few days. I'm Carson, his younger brother."

I wanted to stop him. *Was that too much information? Would Fitz know?* She didn't seem to care. In fact, her eyes seemed glued to the soiled coffee filter that Bea left on the counter.

"Are you going to throw that away?" Fitz pointed with her laser like eyes. My stomach rolled; Ryan and AJ threw the kitchen trash can down with the keg, to make room for Cody under the sink.

"Sure," Bea shrugged. As casually as possible, she balled up the coffee filter, opened the island's cabinet, and handed it to Cody. Then she closed the cabinet as fast as possible without slamming it. Everyone on the other side of the kitchen island saw none of this. Only Bea and I watched Cody take the coffee filter. Fitz carried on.

"Lee? Check the garage below and the floor upstairs, too. Make sure the elder brother is not here. I am going to have a look down at the dock. Rain and Ryan are going to walk with me."

That was about the kindest invitation I could imagine Fitz offering anyone. AJ squeezed Ryan's hand once. I don't know exactly what he meant by it. Fitz slid open the glass door in the living room that led to the back porch, and we all prayed that she wouldn't lean to look over the railing. I followed her, and so did Ryan, and she led us down the wooden steps to the long dock.

Not for the first time, I wondered if I made a mistake running from Ohio.

Birds circled the covered platform at the end of the dock, chirping happily in the hot sunlight. When Fitz sat down on one of the benches, they stopped chirping. I think Ryan noticed too because she sent me her trademarked raised-eyebrow look. We shared a bench directly across from Fitz.

"Beautiful day," Fitz announced, breaking whatever expectations I had of her. "Not the best day to find a corpse," she added, in a return to her normal form. "It was the two of you who found Miss Murphy, yes?"

"Yes. Me and Ryan. We were running—"

"Thank you, Rain. I like your name. It does not fit you. In fact, your name is exactly the opposite of you, with that hair. Natural ginger, I suppose? Thought so. Your parents must have named you before seeing you, then?"

"My dad. Yeah."

"I apologize for this tangent. But since your name does not suit you, and since it sounds so much like Ryan, I would like to call you by your last name. Would that be okay?"

Oh no.

"Of course." I faked a smile. Ryan nudged my shoulder. Fitz grew impatient.

"Well Rain, what *is* your last name then?"

"Eldridge," I said, and the veil lifted.

One way or another, the word always came out. No matter how far I ran, no matter what I said or did, *Eldridge* always messed everything up. Friends treated me differently, and not in ways that I could clearly explain. People who knew *Eldridge* never looked at me like those who didn't. Ryan—the ultimate fan of my father's work—could be no different, I figured. I thought she might at least gasp or even faint, but she kept it together. Whether for my sake of for Fitz, Ryan never flinched. She stared over the open water of the intracoastal, just thinking.

"Well, Mr. Eldridge, what brings you to Warley Island?"

"Senior week. Like you said, I'm…" The words burned my tongue. "…I'm here to party. Just like everyone else. High school is over. You know?"

"Yes, I do know. I also know that I could ask the same question to anyone from Cody's party, and they would give me the same answer. I don't want their answer, because their answer is not your truth. Do you understand?" Fitz leaned forward. "Your friend Carson has a red truck parked out front. It has a license plate from Ohio. I want to know why you are with him, hundreds of miles from home."

I didn't mind Fitz knowing the truth. It was about Ryan. *What would she think of me?* I think Fitz picked up on my discomfort. She hadn't missed much else, after all.

"If you would prefer, I can have Ryan leave us for a minute."

Ryan stood. I waved her back.

"No, sit. It's okay. I trust Ryan too. Thanks to her, I might have a job soon. Flipping burgers is better than nothing, and nothing is exactly what I have back home. I didn't apply for anything. I applied to college, but eight have rejected me already. Even that… That's not all. My dad died recently, and everyone knows. No one at home will let me stop thinking about him, not even my mom. She's sad all the time now, and everyone else just keeps reminding me how sorry they are for my loss. It doesn't even feel like *my* loss anymore. But out here, away from all that… It's better. I can try to move on a bit, I guess."

I caught Ryan's smile in the corner of my eye. It held something beyond sympathy. Fitz didn't smile, but she clearly relaxed her shoulders.

"Thank you, Rain. I will accept honesty, any day. Next, to you, Ryan: What brings you to Warley Island?"

Just as I gave an honest answer, Ryan offered hers.

"I graduated last year with my boyfriend AJ, in California. I think you know him already. I grew up in the foster care system, then eventually with my aunt until she drank herself nearly to death. AJ helped me deal with a lot of that. He's one of eleven siblings, so even my issues couldn't scare him off. When high school ended, we both wanted to travel, so that's all we've done since. Last summer, this is where we landed. Ms. Roakes hired me when she opened Ritz's Burgers and Fries. When fall came, we drove around the country following the warm air. When summer came back around, we thought about trying somewhere new, but... We like Warley. So, we're back."

Fitz nodded. That's all she did for half a minute. She looked back and forth between us, just nodding and mulling over everything we'd said. Ryan and I waited patiently for another question: Something about Eliza, the party, Cody, or even my father. Instead, Fitz lifted herself from the bench and began walking back up the dock.

"Thank you both. Tell Ms. Roakes I said hello."

Her tapping footsteps faded back toward the house. The swirling flock of small birds picked up their chirping again. Water lapped against the wood posts of the covered platform, but that was all. I felt like I'd dodged a bullet before it could be fired. I felt like a child awaiting a flu shot, only to be told it already happened: *That's it?*

Meanwhile, Ryan's focus returned to the other elephant on the dock.

"Sorry, but... I knew 'Elsmith' was some grade-A bullshit."

"You already knew?"

"Not really. So, please excuse me, but I need ten seconds to freak out a little." Ryan jumped up from the bench, walked to the center of the platform, then took a deep breath. Without warning, she hopped in the air, spun around twice, and pumped her fists in silent glee. If AJ, Bea, Carson, or Cody had seen her from the back porch, they might have questioned her sanity under the greater circumstances.

After a few seconds, Ryan composed herself.

"Woo. Okay. Rain, I get it. What you said makes sense. I won't tell anyone about your dad. And I'll do my best not to treat you any differently."

"Carson knows. So does Cody, I think."

"Beyond them, your secret is safe with me. On one condition."

"No, wait. That's not fair. I know what you're gonna say—"

"Listen! Whether we like it or not, you and I know more about Eliza's death than anyone else right now. There's no way we're out of the woods yet after just two questions! Whatever Fitz says today, we'll be the main suspects tomorrow if this is ruled a murder. But only we know about the fisherman with the knife. If we tell the police, all they have is our word and some footprints, but if we can find out who he is, maybe even get more evidence that he's involved..."

Ryan trailed off, hoping maybe I'd jump in and finish her sentence. I didn't.

"We could prove we're innocent."

"But we already are innocent. Why do you need my help?" I groaned, shaking my head. "My last name doesn't qualify me for this. Yes, my dad was a brilliant mystery writer, but those were just stories! And why does everyone *assume* that his talent was hereditary? You're probably better at puzzles than me. I mean, you've read more of his books than I have."

Ryan sighed.

"Okay, you know how I feel about assumptions. I get what you're saying, and I'm sorry, but have you ever *tried* solving a mystery? It sounds to me like *you've* assumed you're the exact opposite of your father. Maybe that's true. Maybe everyone else's assumptions are wrong, and maybe you're an idiot. So, if you want to spend your life assuming that you're an idiot, be my guest, or you can replace all *those* assumptions with some actual evidence. Go out and *see* what you're capable of. Take on a real mystery. Because he never did."

Ryan held out her hand. I didn't like the idea. Investigating Eliza's death could be dangerous, I knew. Moreover, I hated the feeling of following in my dad's footsteps. Then again, he *wrote* the mysteries; he never lived one. Trying to unravel Eliza's death wouldn't be following in my father's footsteps. It would be something new. It would be my project, not his. For the first time, I could be better than him at something.

Maybe.

I shook Ryan's hand, and she lifted me from the bench to my feet.

"And for the record, I already know that you're not an idiot."

5: THE JOB

The police never found AJ's weed. They never found the beer in the kayak, either. Most importantly, they never found Cody under the sink. Once Fitz asked Ryan and me our questions, she rushed the other officers along to wherever they planned to search next. The six of us returned to our puzzle, movie, and drinks until late in the evening when we had nearly forgotten about Eliza.

Or at least most of us had. I didn't drink anything.

Carson and I agreed to get an early start on Monday, since the surf shop opened at nine. Ryan texted me to say I should arrive early too, but I could only guess whether that pertained to job training or to our new private investigation. I didn't tell Carson about that initially, but I wondered whether Ryan told AJ. After spending over a year travelling the country together, did they tell each other everything? Or had they grown tired of talking? I could only guess based on the two times I'd seen them together, and that limited time left me with nothing more than assumptions.

In the morning, the fridge looked empty to me, but I knew my eyes could only be as big as my nonexistent appetite.

"Oh, I bet Cody stashes the good cereal somewhere." Carson checked the pantry. I tried a bunch of cabinets and drawers, but no luck. Carson moved toward the oven. "Gotta be in here. He never cooks anything."

Sure enough, Carson pulled out two boxes of Captain Crunch and a jumbo bag of Cocoa Pebbles. We also discovered the elusive box of Swiss Rolls, a bowl of peanut butter M&Ms, and a smartphone in a black waterproof case.

"Is that your brother's, too?"

"Must be. He always leaves shit in random places."

I grabbed a bowl and settled for Captain Crunch, since there were two boxes. Carson poured out a heap of Cocoa Pebbles that we both knew would overflow from the bowl when he added milk. That looked like an act of brotherly spite to me. We sat up at the small kitchen table where Bea, Ryan and I hung out during the party. The reading nook.

"So," I began, gathering up as much courage as I could at half past seven. "Maybe we should discuss the elephant in the room?"

"Hm? Oh, yeah. I know! Bea and I are building up some *serious* chemistry. I'm glad you see it too."

What? I would have laughed, but I knew Carson too well. He wasn't joking. In his mind, he developed chemistry with *every* girl. I felt bad for him, but also good for him—I suppose—even if it was all in his head.

"Wait, hold on. I wasn't talking about that. But you know that Bea and Cody are…? You know about them?"

I thought about trying to indicate my meaning with a lewd hand gesture, but I couldn't really pull it off while clutching a spoonful of cereal. "I wasn't really supposed to say anything. Bea gets talkative when she drinks, apparently. She told me and Ryan that she and Cody had… You know?"

"Rain, my room is next to theirs. And yes, they share one. So, I heard some *things* last night. Let's just say… I'm aware of the situation. But just because there's a goalie doesn't mean you can't score. If you ask Cody, he'll always say he's single. Girls want commitment, and Cody won't commit to anyone. As soon as Bea figures that out, she'll ditch him, and I'll be ready. Just you watch."

"Nice, real nice. He's your brother!" I finished up my cereal and drank the oddly flavored milk from the bowl. Carson still had plenty of cereal left. I returned to my original train of thought. "What I was trying to say before all of this: Ryan convinced me to do something stupid."

"Finally! You gonna get drunk, for once? Stoned?"

"No! Not *that* kind of stupid. Basically, Ryan thinks that she and I aren't off the hook yet with the cops. If Eliza wasn't suicide or an accident, then Ryan thinks the police will come back to us. So, she wants to try getting ahead of the police and finding a real suspect, which sounds insane, but we might know where to start. Out on the beach, we saw a fisherman… Oh, hey! Good morning, Bea."

From the stairs, Bea strode into the kitchen and offered a halfhearted wave. The words on her shirt said enough: *Don't talk to me until I've had my coffee.* Carson ignored the shirt, or maybe he didn't bother reading it.

"Hey Bea. How long have you been up? Did you hear us talking before, or…?"

Bea brought her eyes up from the floor just long enough to deliver a perfect poker face, giving no answer to Carson. Then she began tending to the coffee maker. Carson gave up on her for the moment.

"Anyway, Rain, that does sound crazy. I want in."
Shit. Not what I wanted to hear.
"Same." Bea mumbled so we could barely hear.
"You know what we're talking about?"
She shrugged.

The Monday sun left the air hot by the time Carson started up the truck. The bugs and frogs of the mangled trees clicked and buzzed as loud as ever, especially since Carson kept the windows down while we drove. I still liked the heat; it beat the awful chill of Ohio, and the drive to Ron's Surf Shop took only a few minutes.

"AJ and I are going metal detecting Thursday night. You interested?"

I shrugged. "Don't you think Eliza is enough for us to deal with? Captain Heron's treasure will wait."

"Not if someone else finds it first. But about that, what's the deal? Do you and Ryan have some sort of plan?"

"I wish. I mean, we want to find that creepy fisherman guy, but I have no idea where to look."

"Warley isn't a big place. You can bet he'll turn up again sooner or later."

Carson parked his truck in the small gravel driveway next to Ron's. The tiny shells mixed into the gravel turned it nearly white, and they clinked and crackled when I stepped down onto them. AJ burst out from the door of the wood-paneled storefront and onto the porch. Strings of beads, bells, shells, and shark teeth rattled and jingled whenever the door moved.

"Beautiful morning, eh?" AJ unrolled a crisp blue poster and taped it up to the front window. The new poster covered an old one that bore the same sweeping black logo, and I suspected that many more could be found underneath that one. The entire storefront resembled a seashell in that way: Layers and patches covered up the trends and styles of decades past. Carson was enthralled.

"This place looks awesome! What can I do to start out? Is there paperwork? Where's your boss?"

"Oh, Ron?"

Right on cue, a burly man with a wide-brimmed hat leaned outside and whistled at AJ.

"Hey! You seen the blue tackle box?"

"Yeah, no worries, Ron. Sold it the other day. Check the register."

"My man. Right on! Oh, is this Carson? Nice to meet you! I'm Ron. Just come on in, and I'll get you set up behind the register. There's a new shipment of boogie boards coming in today, so that'll be fun."

I tried to get a move on and leave, but AJ shouted out to me: "Oh, hey Rain! You headed over to Ritz's already?" I stopped walking.

"Yeah, it's just down the street. And Ryan told me to arrive early."

"Alright, well say hi to my babe for me."

"Will do."

I crossed Warley Avenue and walked north toward the bridge. Ahead, the open-mouthed grin of Warley Winds beach shop's plaster shark showed me where to find Ritz's Burgers and Fries. Sure enough, I rounded the corner of the main intersection to find Ryan already opening the red and white umbrellas of the tables out front. She wore her familiar white shirt with the red *RBF* on the front.

"AJ says hi," I told her. She jumped.

"Oh, Rain! Hey. Mind helping with the last few umbrellas?"

"Sure, no problem. I guess this means I got the job?"

"Well, not exactly. I haven't talked to Lucianne yet. She's the owner, and my boss. Oh! Don't call her Lucianne. Not yet. She's Ms. Roakes. But hopefully she'll like you. She probably will, and then you can get right to work."

I leaned over the last table and struggled to find the crank to raise the umbrella. I walked all the way around, reaching under the red and white fabric to figure it out, but I had no luck. When I finally looked up at the other five raised umbrellas, none of them had hand cranks. Ryan sat on one of the tables, amused at my realization.

"Oh. Old-school umbrellas. Duh."

I lifted the umbrella's wooden hub up the pole, then I took the metal pin on its chain in my other hand. To my embarrassment, I couldn't reach high enough over the table to lock the umbrella into place. Ryan came to my rescue; she could reach without any trouble. I blushed.

"If that was a test, I think I failed."

"You should be glad Ms. Roakes didn't see that."

"Should we go inside now?"

"Sure. Do you need me to reach the door for you?"

Inside Ritz's Burgers and Fries, the red-and-white color scheme continued across a checkerboard floor of linoleum tiles and up the vertical stripes of the order-taking counter. Light brown wood paneling rose up waist-high along the wall of the cozy eating area, along with a countertop that brimmed the windows for additional seating. Other than those seats, the inside of Ritz's only held three small wooden tables, two of which had already been pushed together. The whole space smelled like French fries and something else that I couldn't quite identify. Not something bad, but something *different*.

"Poutine," Ryan said, which sounded like another language to me.

"Hm?"

"The smell. Poutine. I couldn't figure it out at first either. See the menu though? It's the top-seller."

I skimmed the two columns of lettering hanging over the main counter. Sure enough, poutine showed up three or four times as a side, as an appetizer, or with the *Poutine on the Ritz Burger*. I groaned, and Ryan knew why.

"I know. The pun was Ms. Roakes' idea. Tastes great though."

"But what is it?"

Ryan's jaw dropped as if I'd blasphemed the religion of Warley Island. It was too late; the words had already left my mouth. Ryan rushed back into the kitchen.

"What's poutine? Only Quebec's gift to the human tongue! Cheese curds and brown gravy on a bed of French fries. Don't make that face. Stop making that face. I thought it sounded gross at first, but now I have to stop myself from just eating all of it. So here: Try it. Fresh batch. It's still warm." Ryan held out a red plastic basket lined with wax paper. The messy pile of fries, cheese clumps, and gravy reminded me of Bea's vomit after the party. "If you're going to work here, you should probably like poutine."

Trying not to breathe through my nose, I took the plastic basket from Ryan and gingerly extracted one small fry from the pile.

"Get some cheese, too."

"I thought they were curds?"

"Are you holding your nose?"

I tossed the fry into my mouth but ditched the cheese curd. Meanwhile, the door behind me opened, and a woman entered the restaurant. She could have been anyone for about two seconds, but then she asked a question that could only come from Ms. Roakes.

"Is this the boy?"

Ryan nodded. I swallowed the French fry, doing my best to enjoy it.

"You like that poutine there?"

Ms. Roakes spoke with the slight rasp of a long-time smoker. That could have been her natural voice, I suppose, but I spotted the electronic cigarette in her left hand. She looked anywhere between 30 and 55, if that makes sense. Her overworked amber hair surrounded her face and head like a caramel helmet, and her sleeveless top showed off colorful tattoos on both her arms. She had more than AJ. Most notably, Ms. Roakes stood at least four inches below me, so she had to look up even further to speak to Ryan.

"What's his name?"

"Rain Eldridge," I answered begrudgingly. "And the poutine is great." Ryan flinched again at my last name, but Ms. Roakes didn't seem to care.

"Well Rain, I'm Ms. Roakes. Oh, lord... Rain and Ryan. I don't like that. You see what'll happen? I call out to one of you, and you both come running? No way. Can't have that."

I scrambled to save myself. "I can go by my last name, if that's easier."

"Relax, *Eldridge*. I'm pulling your leg. You want to join the slowest-growing restaurant on the island? Fine. Welcome to my sinking ship. The pay sucks, but I'm sure you need it more than me at your age. I'm off the smokes now, so I guess you'll be making whatever cash I've saved." Ms. Roakes dangled her e-cigarette like a pocket watch on a chain.

"Thank you, Ms. Roakes. I don't really have a résumé, but I'm ready to learn whatever you need me to do. Is there a—"

"Here, let me *point* you in the right direction."

Ms. Roakes vanished into the kitchen. Ryan chuckled. She knew whatever *that* meant, and I didn't have to wait long to understand too. Ms. Roakes returned with a slab of lightweight foam board. It stood taller than her and sported a giant red arrow with one word: *FOOD*.

"Here you go, Eldridge. You can start off outside with the sign, before that storm rolls in later this week. Until then, let's see if you can *spin* this place around."

I'm not sure what hurt me more: The job or the pun.

On the bright side, sign-spinning duty kept me further from the smell of poutine. I dropped the sign enough times to dull the arrow's sharp corners, and if anything brought in new customers at the Ritz, it was my laughable clumsiness with the sign. For the first hour or so, I kept myself occupied with the sign itself, but the growing Carolina heat drove me crazy as noon approached. Worst of all, I had no one to talk to.

I kept an eye out for the fisherman, although that felt like a long shot. No one like him appeared at the busy intersection. There were more young couples on rented tandem bicycles, more families making the short trek down to the beach, and more crowds of half-drunk graduates flaunting their most colorful summer outfits. A few people—mostly fathers herding multiple kids—carried fishing rods down the beach or up to the intracoastal, but none of them matched the distinct look of the bearded fisherman. I wondered how many happy people on the street knew about Eliza. Did any of them care?

By half past noon, I held the *FOOD* sign flat over my head to shade myself. If Ms. Roakes or Ryan saw, I didn't care. All I cared about was sparing myself from third-degree sunburns and locating a suspicious man with a bloody knife. Rather than spotting him, I noticed Bea and Cody returning towel-shaded from the beach. It was hard not to notice them; Bea's hair stood out like a blue raspberry snow cone, and Cody never failed to make his presence known.

"Whaddup, Rain Man?" He shouted as they crossed the street from Warley Winds. I waved. The nickname wasn't new. Bea, on the other hand, seemed a bit more concerned for my safety.

"Damn. How long have you been out here?"

"Couple hours."

"Without that shade, your skin would be the color of your hair by now. Do you get a lunch break?"

"I don't know. Probably."

"Is the food any good here?"

"I'm told it's popular in Canada."

"Well how about you come on inside and eat with us?"

I didn't want to eat any more poutine, but I thought I could use some air conditioning for a while, so I followed Bea and Cody inside. The rush of cool air in the doorway felt heavenly, and I wondered if I'd ever convince myself to go back outside with the *FOOD* arrow. Ryan, at the register, called out to Ms. Roakes back in the kitchen:

"He's alive! And with new customers. Hey Cody. Hi Bea."

I dropped the arrow down next to the fountain drink machine and filled my hand with water to splash on my face. The mixture of sweat and tap water dripped into my eyes and down my shirt, but I smiled anyway because it felt amazing. Bea snorted out a laugh.

"Rain, check this out," Ryan whispered, sliding me a newspaper across the counter before taking their order. "Alright, what can I get for *y'all*?"

As Bea and Cody mulled over the menu options, I picked up the newspaper. *Warley Gazette*, the title read, and I didn't have to look much further to see what Ryan wanted me to. The front page's top story read as follows:

Daughter of GRM Developer Found Dead

WARLEY ISLAND — Late Sunday, a press release from the Warley Island Police Department confirmed the tragic death of Eliza Murphy, young daughter of GRM Development's founder and chief executive, Georgia Ralena Murphy. Although authorities do not suspect foul play, island police are "pursuing all available leads and channels" to fully understand the events that led to Murphy's death, according to WIPD Chief Marie Fitz.

Although few details on the tragedy have been released as of press time, Fitz initially stated that an unnamed female had been found "unresponsive" in the early hours of Sunday morning on a stretch of beach near the south end of Warley Island. The individual was declared dead at the scene, although no official cause of death has been stated. Since that first announcement, a beach access ramp close to 12th Street has been closed, and the adjoining dune area has also been blocked off. The controlled area, monitored by the WIPD, includes one of Warley island's infamous observation towers, which have been afflicted with legal controversy and vandalism for decades.

Eliza Murphy, 19, graduated second in her class from the Gravewood Institute in New York last year. According to her mother, Eliza was an avid and talented photographer. She planned to enter NC State this fall as a political science major, following one gap year spent working with her mother's construction company.

Last summer, GRM Development received a state contract to rebuild the Turner Avenue bridge, which connects Warley Island to the mainland. Concerns over worsening hurricanes and aging girders prompted the expensive project, which is now expected to be completed within three years. The company has previously built casinos and hotels across the Carolina seaboard. There is no apparent relation between the company's highly publicized bridge contract and the death of its heiress.

A public candlelit vigil is being held at the Murphy family residence on Monday evening. For driving directions and timing, please refer to the event's online page at...

"Rain! Food?" Ryan snapped her fingers, and I folded the paper on the counter.

"Oh. Right. Um…" I scanned the menu, but my eyes still saw only newsprint. "I guess I'll try the Ritz Burger. No onion."

"Some poutine on the side?"

"No thanks."

There was an eye roll before Ryan passed my order on to Ms. Roakes, but I could hardly process anything aside from the article. *A vigil? What does that mean?* It felt too soon for something like that. Still, I hastily pulled out my phone and typed the website address into my browser. Sure enough, the page already showed over fifty registered attendees, so I added myself to the *"Maybe"* list. Scrolling down, dozens of posts offered kind words and condolences to Eliza's family, and primarily to her mother. I clicked on a few profiles of the people who posted the messages. Some looked like Eliza's friends: I recognized one or two of them from Cody's party. Others were adults, many of them employees of GRM Development.

"Did you two see this Facebook event?" I held up my phone to Bea and Cody. Bea scowled.

"Damn. So soon?" Bea took a seat at the larger table. Cody joined her, eager to give his horrifying suggestion:

"I'll go, but only if I get wasted before."

"Bad idea," Ryan reminded him. "Bea gave the police a story, and you have to maintain it: You're in Tennessee, remember? You're risking a lot just being out here in public!"

Bea fumed. "Ryan, cool it. Cody won't get busted on my watch. Besides, going to any event drunk has to be easier than going sober. I guess you wouldn't really know, would you?"

Ryan pretended to gasp dramatically.

"Whoa, do I have a belligerent customer? Legally, in this state, I could kick you out if I wanted to. But Bea, listen: It's not personal. I'm only trying to protect your *boyfriend*."

"Boyfriend?" Cody rose at attention.

"Order up," Ms. Roakes interrupted in the nick of time. She handed three plastic baskets of food to Ryan, who sent them down to the table with me. The fried food's warm aroma had a more positive effect on Bea and Cody than on me, but I wasted no time pulling up a chair and biting into my Ritz Burger. Cody shoved a fistful of poutine into his mouth.

"Well, I'm gonna sign up for this thing. What's the website?" Cody pulled out his black-cased phone and I passed him the newspaper. He laughed once then swallowed his fries. "Aw shit. Wrong phone." Then he put his phone down and extracted *another* one from his pocket, this one with a case that looked like an acoustic guitar.

"Why do you have two phones?" I asked, knowing that everyone else wanted to ask the same thing. Unfortunately, Cody had already taken another mouthful of poutine, so Bea answered for him.

"He found the black one on the beach. It's one of those expensive new ones, so we're gonna try to sell it. Could be worth a couple hundred dollars, since it still works."

Of course you are. Ryan could hardly find words. I watched her take a deep breath and try to reply as calmly as possible.

"Okay. Alright. You don't think maybe… It belongs to someone? They probably want it back. Maybe *they'd* pay for it. Can you unlock it?"

Bea tossed the black phone to Ryan, who turned it over in her hands. I stood up to examine it at the counter with her. With a push of the side button, the phone's screen lit up and showed a photo of a cat bathing in a sunlit window.

Locked.

"Good luck," Bea sang. "There's a six-digit code. And face-lock, or whatever. Best if we just sell it. And no, Cody and I will *not* split the money with you."

Ryan met my eyes and whispered mournfully, "Your friends will be the death of me, Rain."

6: THE MANSION

After lunch, Ritz's quieted down. There wasn't much of a dinner rush; the menu options didn't merit one. Ms. Roakes knew that, so I didn't stay at my post any later than what she deemed reasonable.

During the remaining hours at Ritz's, Ryan made her case for avoiding the vigil. Firstly, if Cody would be there, she couldn't let herself be associated with him. I understood that; Cody left a trail of destruction wherever he went, and steering clear meant avoiding the storm that we knew could swallow him at any moment. Plus, none of us knew Eliza well enough to begin with. Even though the article and the Facebook page listed the vigil as a public event, we couldn't guarantee just how welcome we would be. None of us had seen Eliza's house. None of us knew her family. To Eliza, we were nearly strangers. From that alone, Ryan saw more potential risk than reward in attending the vigil—even in terms of our private investigation. When the time came to close up Ritz's, she put her foot down.

"I'm not going. You can go if you want, but it just feels wrong to me."

"Oh. Alright. Well… If I go, or if Carson goes, what should we do?"

"Are you asking me what clues to look for?"

"Basically, yeah. It's not my area of expertise, remember?"

"I don't know. I really don't think you should go to this thing, but if you do, investigating Eliza's death at her own vigil is risky business. If anyone notices you or Carson acting some way that isn't straight-up mournful, they'll know something's off. Just observe. No assumptions. Take it all in, and if something important catches your attention, don't overreact. Like… Do you know that part in *The Eighth Juror*, when Detective Goldberg sees the envelope being hand over?"

"Um… Not really. I seriously haven't read my dad's books."

"Right. Right. Well, keep your cool. And don't let Carson hit on Eliza's cousins, or anything. If something happens, text me. I'll be with AJ at our place."

Carson picked me up in his truck after Ron's Surf Shop closed, which wasn't too much later. We still had an hour before the start of the vigil, which meant plenty of time to get ready. Cody and Bea downed a few beers in the kitchen while Carson and I picked out clothes to wear. That wasn't a problem for Carson; his typical preppy outfits worked fine for the occasion, but I struggled. I hadn't packed any really nice clothes when I left for Warley. None of the five shirts I brought could pass for "mournful," and I hadn't even brought any pants. Reluctantly, I headed upstairs to ask Carson for help.

"Do you have any extra clothes?"

He was in the bathroom checking his hair, already dressed up and ready to go.

"Clothes in your size? Not unless you shrink them in the washer a few hundred times."

"C'mon, you're not *that* much bigger than me. I just need something better than a graphic tee and cargo shorts."

Carson reeled.

"Rain! That's your *best* option? I knew you needed an intervention, but I didn't think it would come today. Let me lay out some shirt options. I'll steal one of Cody's belts. Oh! I have an extra pair of loafers that you can wear, if you have the right socks."

For once, I appreciated Carson's fashion sensitivity. Dashing between bedrooms on the second floor, he pieced together my outfit in only a few minutes: A sky-blue buttoned shirt, sand-colored khakis, and brown loafers that matched Cody's belt. Everything fit well enough, according to Carson, but I felt like my clothes had been inflated with an inch of air on all sides. It had to be good enough.

Cody and Bea put more effort into their clothes than I expected. Cody's black shirt and gray pants worked better than pastel colors, according to Carson. I wondered if his attention to looks came from his brother. Meanwhile, Bea wore a simple gray dress with lines of stitching that formed waves around her waist.

"Where'd that come from?" Carson asked her when we joined them in the kitchen.

"Oh, the dress? Stole it from one of my 'friends' down the street when they kicked me out. Thought about selling or burning it, but it fit pretty great, so I'm gonna use it awhile first."

"We're still gonna sell it," Cody added, finishing off one last beer.

"*We*? But I'm the one who took it!"

"And I found the phone! But we're splitting the take on that too, right? I can't just live here without a job or anything, and if I can't have any more parties here, we need to figure out something."

"Yeah, I guess."

Bea finished her drink, and we stepped into the hot night air. The whole island buzzed with a slightly different combination of frogs and insects. From the circular driveway of the Welling house, I still heard the crashing waves on the other side of Warley Avenue and the dunes beyond. I wished I could stay there longer and just listen. The feeling of warm air without blistering sunlight relaxed me, which was exactly what I needed to ease the stress of venturing into the unknown.

According to Cody, he sold his old car because he needed cash after arriving in Warley. He didn't say where that cash went, but to sum up his story: Carson's truck was our only vehicle. That meant that he and Bea had to ride all the way to the vigil in the bed of the truck. Neither of them liked that idea, but both of them surrendered to it drunkenly as Carson and I took the truck's only seats.

"Ryan and AJ aren't going," I informed Carson once we got up to speed on Warley Avenue.

"Why not?"

"Ryan's avoiding your brother because of the Tennessee thing that Bea made up. If the police see him, he's screwed, and so is anyone seen with him. And AJ, well… I guess he'd rather spend some time with Ryan."

"Are we still looking out for that creepy fisherman you told me about?"

"I guess. But if he has anything to do with Eliza's death, he'll stay far away from this vigil."

"Unless he does the opposite."

"Careful, Carson. You're starting to sound as paranoid as Ryan."

"Oh, I'm just spit balling. Did that sound good?"

The GPS app on my phone led us to the address from the Facebook event page. Warley Avenue took us all the way south down the island. We passed the watchtower where Ryan and I found Eliza; yellow police tape surrounding the area flapped loosely in the wind. The Murphy family's house was even further, down where the beachfront houses left large gaps of dune grass between one another. The sparse houses grew in size. Wooden stilts lifted them up like all the other houses, but these buildings had more stilts, more garages, and more floors, in some cases. Rather than public beach access paths, these properties had their own private walkways.

"Wow. Good thing we dressed up a bit," Carson mused. I felt increasingly self-conscious, swimming in my clothes.

"Also, Ryan has advised that you avoid flirting with girls at the memorial vigil."

"Oh, c'mon! You know I'm not *that* stupid."

"Even if the girls are rich?"

Carson replied with a muffled squeaking sound, like a child holding in his excitement at the gates of Disney World.

Our blue destination point slid into view on the screen of my phone. Lines of arriving cars on either side of the road stretched toward us like a red carpet of idling and vanishing taillights. The silhouette of the Warley's last house emerged above the flat, wind-swept tip of the island. The three-story building looked more like a permanent mansion than a rental house. Carson could hardly contain himself, and I desperately worked to calm him.

"Just one more reminder: We're here because Eliza is *dead*. It's not a party."

He didn't seem to hear me. We parked at the far end of the line of cars, then disembarked to walk down the sandy avenue that became the house's driveway. Eliza hadn't exaggerated the success of her mother's company; her family's wealth hung in the air like a perfume.

"Oh my gosh. Are we underdressed?"

Carson appeared to short-circuit when we reached the house. Floodlights illuminated its immense white face and tall glass doors. Unlike all the others I'd seen, this house had no name nailed above its door or propped up on the lawn. Several other people—an adult couple, possibly from GRM Development, and two girls our age, possibly from Cody's party—entered the house before us wearing suits and dresses more expensive than anything in Carson's closet. At the door, a tall man in a black suit let them inside. He waited there for us while we stood at the bottom of the house's wide front steps. Carson panicked.

"Rain, what sort of a vigil is this? I thought we'd be outside! These aren't my indoor shoes."

"I don't know. But it's too late to go back, right?"

Cody and Bea gawked at the giant house in silence, but they led our slow charge up the stairs to the front door. When we reached the top, I expected the man at the door to ask for our names, or even maybe ask us for a password, but he just pulled the door open without a word. The four of us cautiously crossed the threshold into what seemed like an alternate universe.

It's difficult to explain just how disoriented I felt. Previously, the white walls and thinly carpeted floors of the Welling family's house made sense to me as the "beach house" standard. That cozy, air-conditioned, practical design comforted me even after Cody's parties had trashed the place. The Murphy house showed no signs of beach life. The foyer's oriental rug, hardwood floor, and chandelier felt alien in a place like Warley Island. The yellow walls, high ceilings, dim lighting, and elaborate doorframe moldings did nothing to ease that effect.

"Bea, I think they have food." Cody sniffed at the air like a dog. His beard twitched.

"Oh my God, yes! I smell shrimp. Let's go. Is the kitchen this way?"

The two of them disappeared hand-in-hand in the direction of the food smell. Other guests floated from room to room through the foyer that neither Carson nor I dared to leave.

"What do we do now?" I asked him before he could ask the same thing.

"Be… *vigil*ant? I don't know. But we can't just stand here."

Carson proceeded forward, and I followed because we both knew I might get lost otherwise. I wished Ryan had come with us. She would have known exactly what to do. I sent her a quick text: *We're at the vigil. House is huge, full of strangers. Could use your advice.*

"Hello," someone greeted, stopping Carson and me as we milled around the house's main floor. We turned to see a woman wearing a black dress and simple beaded necklace. Even without recognizing her waves of blonde hair, I knew her face. After all, her daughter had looked just like her.

Georgia Murphy. Eliza's mom.

"Hi, I'm Rain. I'm sorry for your loss, Ms. Murphy."

"Thank you for being here. And… You are?"

"Carson Welling. My condolences."

"Thank you both. Are you boys lost? We have food over that way in the dining room, and candle ceremony is setting up out back, on the beach."

Of course, the private beach access. Carson and I exchanged a glance agreeing to go that way. I quickly started to retreat in that direction.

"Thanks for telling us. We were actually looking for—"

"Rain? You said your name was Rain, right?"

Uh-oh. I nodded. Carson kept walking toward the back door that led to the beach. He waited for me a moment, but I was a lost cause. For whatever reason, Georgia Murphy captured me, and who would I have been to walk away from a bereaved mother?

"I remember the police officers mentioning your name. You were there on the beach, weren't you? You and that Ryan girl... You two found her?"

I nodded again. There weren't any good words.

"Thank you, Rain. You and Ryan did the right thing by calling the police. Whatever happened to my daughter... We'll figure it out thanks to the two of you. Without your call, who knows how long she might've been there? Just lying in the sand..."

I sensed her tears before they came, and I scrambled around the room for tissues. We stood in some sort of open-floor-plan office. The bookshelf, desk, and table at the wall had no tissue boxes. Ms. Murphy saw my confusion.

"It's okay, they're in here." She opened a drawer in the desk and pulled out a few tissues to wipe her eyes. In the draw with the tissues were pens, several notepads, and... *A gun? No, a stapler.* She shut the drawer. "I know the police will find whoever hurt her. I know they'll bring justice to whoever did this."

The ice in her voice made me shiver for Cody's sake. More importantly, she implied something that the rest of us had only guessed about: *Was Eliza really murdered?* Georgia Murphy already seemed to know that already, which meant that the police did too—or at least they believed that they did. *Will they pin it on Cody? Ryan? Me?*

While I silently panicked, the front door opened in the foyer behind Ms. Murphy. Seeing the man who entered, I panicked even more. He looked much younger than I remembered. He cleaned up nicely; the beard was gone. I met his eyes for the second time in two days, and I searched them for an emotion: Malice, guilt, grief, or pain. Maybe Ryan could have seen through him in that instant—seen all of his secrets like words on a page in a book—but I only saw one thing. I saw the man I remembered from yesterday morning on the beach.

The fisherman.

Ms. Murphy sensed my distractedness and looked to the foyer. The fisherman moved his eyes from me to her. His expression turned even more somber, but he didn't move. Nor did Ms. Murphy. They recognized one another.

"Dean!" Ms. Murphy called in the direction of the kitchen. The man who had opened the front door for Bea, Cody, Carson and me came running to her side as soon as she called.

"Yes, ma'am?"

Ms. Murphy tilted her head in the direction of the fisherman.

"Deal with Lars. And stay at the door awhile longer, please."

"Will do, ma'am."

Dean, the black-suited man, strode into the foyer and grabbed the fisherman tightly on one arm. He pulled him back outside through the front door, and the fisherman didn't resist. That was it; he was gone. Ms. Murphy took one deep breath.

"I'm sorry you had to see that, Rain. Should we go out to the beach now? I'm sure they're almost ready."

"Okay," I agreed, and Georgia Murphy led me outside toward the candles on the sand.

Lars, I repeated to myself. *His name is Lars, and Georgia knows him.*

***
****

There were two, maybe three hundred people gathered on the Murphy family's private beach. A man dressed similarly to Dean handed me a candle from a table as I crossed the dunes. A path marked by shoulder-height torches led me out to the open sand and the crowd of people. They stood with their candles in a loose semicircle that I joined, feeling like a member of a cult with the candle glow flickering over my face. In front of the group, a sand sculpture shaped like a shooting star held a framed copy of Eliza's senior class portrait. The local news article had used the same photo of her wearing a cap and gown.

One by one, the people on the beach placed their candles on the sand in front of the photo. Several people placed flowers, and many of them tucked notes behind the photo frame or into the sand between candles. I thought that someone might speak; that seemed like an appropriate gesture at such an event. Instead, people talked quietly with one another while the candles accumulated. I placed mine at one of the points of the sculpted star in the sand, then I searched around for Bea, Cody, and Carson.

Cody and Bea weren't hard to find. They strayed far from the crowd toward the crashing waves, which looked like waves of ink without the sunlight shining through them. They ran up and down the sand in their fancy vigil clothes, playfully avoiding the waves as they came. They laughed and pushed each other around, but thankfully no one by the candles could hear over the sound of the water.

"Hey!" I called out when I came close enough to them. "Hey! What are you doing?"

"Having fun!" Bea cackled. "Come run with us, it's the best!"

I turned back. I couldn't face them. They didn't care about Eliza. They didn't even care that she was dead. When I watched them running from the waves and laughing together, I wondered if either of them had anything to do with Eliza's death. Cody gave her alcohol, sure... but was there more? In my eyes, he was an asshole and a liar, but an innocent one.

"Let's go," I told Carson when I found him in the Murphys' dining room. He had found the shrimp that Bea and Cody smelled when we arrived. Inexplicably, Bea and Cody pursued me back into the house from the beach, so they too dove into the shrimp platter like moths to a flame.

"Try the shrimp," Carson insisted, but I had no appetite. My Ritz Burger from lunch still sat like a rock in my stomach. A cat jumped up from the carpet and onto the table to join in the feast. "See? Everyone likes the shrimp!" Cody and Bea laughed.

I didn't laugh, because an alarm bell rang somewhere in the back of my head. Some mental voice screamed at me to run for the hills, and I couldn't tell why. Had the strange house driven me crazy? Had Bea and Cody sufficiently pissed me off? Had I become too conscious of my ill-fitting clothes?

No. I had a hunch about what set off the alarm, but I was terrified to find out.

"Hey Cody, can I see your phone?" I extended one hand. Cody held out his phone in its guitar-decorated case.

"What for?"

"The other one."

"Oh."

Cody dug the luxurious secondhand phone out of his pocket. I took it carefully, but my hands shook. I knew what was coming. They had no idea. I tapped the phone's screen to bring it to life, and the cat on the table looked up from her shrimp to scowl at me.

"Oh no. Oh, shit." I threw the phone down on the table and stumbled back against the wall of the dining room. Luckily, I don't think anyone else saw me freaking out.

"Whoa! You good?" Bea laughed. Carson knew something was up.

"Hey! What's that phone? Cody, why do you have two phones?"

"Relax! I found it on the beach. Bea and I are gonna try to sell it. It still works and everything, but we're gonna get it wiped clean first."

"No, you're *not*," I insisted. I stepped directly in front of Cody, hoping to sober him up as much as possible. "Listen. I need you to tell me exactly when and where you found this phone."

"What? Why?"

"Tell me!" My voice rose more than I intended.

"Geez, fine! I found it in the sand. Near the water by that old watchtower, where... On Sunday morning, when... When we... No, I mean... It doesn't have anything to do with that, right?" Three pairs of eyes widened. "No, guys, like... C'mon. It wasn't that close to her. I thought I just got lucky, finding it. I mean, if you found a phone like that, you'd keep it too! Even if it was close to a dead body or whatever."

We all held our breath until I broke the news to him.

"Cody... That's Eliza Murphy's cell phone."

We all took a step away from the phone on the table. We each needed a moment to think, to consider... What if we left it there? What if we just left the phone on the Murphys' dining room table for someone to find, then never talked about it? What if we destroyed it? Threw it back to the ocean? Put it back where Cody found it?

My own phone buzzed, and I jumped. Ryan finally answered my text:

Don't panic. That's my only advice.

"Can't be hers," Cody dismissed with a nervous chuckle. "It has a black case. That's a dude's phone. Rich dude's phone. C'mon, Rain… You're messing with me. Give it up. What's the joke?"

I held up the phone again for everyone to see, then I tapped the screen. The cat on the table purred, and the same cat appeared on the screen of Eliza's locked phone.

There was nothing left to say. We left in a flash, running from the Murphy house. We piled back into Carson's truck, and we sped back toward *All's Well* like our lives depended on it—perhaps they did. Carson drove, Cody cried, and Bea wrapped her arms around him. I held on to Eliza's phone with both hands.

Don't panic, I repeated to myself.

Don't panic. Don't panic.

7: THE EVIDENCE

I placed the phone down in the center of our puzzle table, where only the outer frame of the jigsaw had formed. Carson, Cody, Bea and I sat around the table like Kubrick's astronauts observing a black monolith on the moon. Bea crossed her arms on the table and rested her head down on them. Her neon blue afro wobbled while she shook her head disapprovingly.

"Either I'm way too drunk for this, or I'm not drunk enough."

Cody's eyes glazed over like he'd died in in his chair. I thought we'd get at least some pensive beard-stroking from him, but he froze for at least two minutes before speaking his mind.

"Who else knows about this?"

"Just us," I admitted. "I haven't told Ryan or AJ yet."

"And we're not gonna tell anyone else? Can we keep this between the four of us? Hey, I'm serious. We're screwed if anyone finds out about this, right?"

I agreed. "Yeah. The police think you're in Tennessee. Right now, you're fine, I guess. But if they find out you're here, and *also* that you found Eliza's phone, you're done. Especially after what I heard from Eliza's mom; she doesn't think this was some random accident. She thinks someone killed Eliza, so she's going after them. And with so much money, plus the support of the police—"

Cody stood and grabbed the phone off the table. Carson followed him into the kitchen.

"Wait! What are you doing?"

Cody opened the microwave, threw Eliza's phone inside, and set it to *Popcorn*. I sprung up from the puzzle table with new alarm bells blaring in my head. Cody used both arms to hold his brother back from the microwave, but he couldn't stop me from reaching it and rescuing the phone.

"Cody, you idiot!" Carson growled, but Cody barred him from entering the kitchen.

"I got it!" I held up the phone, which still glowed in my hand when I tapped its screen. Cody lunged for it, and I tossed it to Carson. Before Cody could wrestle it from his hand, he passed it on.

"Bea, think fast!"

Not Carson's best idea—under the circumstances—but it worked. Bea's head popped up from the table, and her eyes locked onto the phone. She caught it with both hands and promptly dropped it down her shirt before resting again on her crossed arms. Cody fumed.

"Fine! I'll just get it back *later*."

"Good luck," mumbled Bea. "You're on the couch tonight, bozo."

"What? This is my house!"

"No!" Carson interrupted. "It's our *parents'* house."

"Well, my bedroom!"

"No, it's not! And that's Eliza's phone!"

"Finders keepers!"

"Shut up!" I snapped, for the second time in one night. That wasn't like me, but no good could come from their endless bickering. "This is why I want to tell Ryan and AJ about the phone. A mystery expert and a treasure hunter! You're all acting like idiots without them here. I didn't think I had to spell this out, but whatever's on that phone might reveal exactly what happened to Eliza. That means it could prove all of us innocent, which we all are! Unless anyone has any objections? Did anyone here murder Eliza Murphy?"

Silence, for a moment, then Cody: "We can't unlock it, so what are we going to do with it, then?"

"I don't know yet. But we are *not* destroying it. Right Carson? Bea? Good. I'll keep the phone safe until we know who to trust with it. Sound good?"

Bea lifted her head again just to glare at me before making her case.

"Rain, you're not in charge here. None of us are. *I'll* keep the phone safe. I don't trust any of you—except maybe Carson—so this phone is not leaving my bra until we all decide what to do with it. I don't care who disagrees; none of you can get this phone away from me."

Carson blushed. I didn't like letting the phone out of my sight, but I had almost no suspicions about Bea. On the night of the party, she drank too much to hurt anyone. Besides, she never left the house. How could she have been miles down the beach at the watchtower?

"Well, goodnight," I gave up, then retreated to my bedroom only a few feet from the kitchen. "Carson, are you driving to work at the same time in the morning?"

"Yup. See you then."

Once safely in my bedroom, my mind wandered just long enough to remember my one daily responsibility—other than being safe and drinking water: Calling my mom. I found her contact in my phone and dialed, hoping only that she'd still be awake. If she wasn't, she still answered on the second ring.

"Rain? How is everything?" She sounded normal. Quiet. Concerned.

"It's… Warmer here. I got a job." *Oh, and a girl was murdered two nights ago.*

"That's wonderful! What is it?"

"Spinning a big red arrow in front of a restaurant." *And solving a murder.*

"Oh. Well, that should be fun."

"Yeah." *When I'm not conspiring to hide critical evidence.*

"Are you sure you're okay?"

"I am." *When I'm asleep.*

"Have you made any new friends?"

"A few." *And they never seem to leave the house.*

"I'm glad. Thank you for remembering to call."

"Can I go now?"

"Yes, you're free. Get some rest."

"Night, mom."

In the morning, after Ryan set up Ritz's umbrellas, I prepared for another day of holding the giant *FOOD* arrow. This time, I applied plenty of sunscreen before leaving the house, and I shielded my head with a bucket hat. As prepared as I was, Ryan wouldn't let me go. She had too many questions, and I found myself more than eager to answer all of them.

"Alright, Rain. Fill me in. What was the vigil like? You said the house was big?"

"Giant, weird, and far down south on the island. A few hundred people showed up, I think. They had us place candles out on their private beach; it was a nice ceremony, but Bea and Cody drank too much before we left, so they acted like complete assholes."

"No surprise there. What about the fisherman? Any sign of him?"

"Um, yeah! He was there!"

"Shit, no way! Who saw him? Did he say anything to you?"

"No. Only I saw him. And first of all, he looked totally different. He shaved off his beard, and about twenty years with it. I almost didn't recognize him. He showed up, and Eliza's mom knew him. She had one of her staff people kick him out. But here's the best part: She said his name: *Lars*."

"Lars? Can't be many people around here with that name. I'll look him up, and I can see if Ms. Roakes has a phone book. You said Eliza's mom kicked him out?"

"Yeah! It's like she knew he was involved. The way they looked at each other… Oh! But that's not the craziest thing that happened. Remember that phone Cody was talking about selling yesterday? Remember how he said that he found it on the *beach?*"

"Yeah. What about it?"

I tried to give Ryan a look that would tell her the full story. After all, I knew Ms. Roakes could probably hear us from back in the kitchen. Ryan reflected my look, clearly not getting my meaning.

"The phone's lock screen is a cat," I whispered. "Eliza's cat."

Ryan recoiled. She fell gently onto her chair behind the register. In that way, she reacted to the discovery just like the rest of us; we all jumped back from the phone when I first threw it down next to the shrimp platter.

"Okay… So, Cody didn't find it yesterday, then. He found it on Sunday, right? He found it by the tower, when he and Carson met us there. Oh shit, I remember him walking down to the water, but I wasn't paying attention to him. I think he was reaching into the sand… That's when he got it! Rain, this is huge. Do you know what this means?"

I shrugged. Ryan tried to keep her voice down, but she was too excited to sort through these new clues.

"Oh, Rain! C'mon, you didn't think about this? Cody found the phone at low tide, far out from where we found Eliza. The waves don't reach the dunes, which means they also don't reach the tower. Now, let's assume Eliza had her phone on her when she died. The water couldn't have washed the phone out to where Cody found it. So how did it get away from her?"

"Someone could've moved the phone, right?" That seemed like an obvious conclusion.

"Of course. But who, Lars? When? And why? Damn, too many questions. I don't know. We need to narrow it down. The phone is locked, right?"

"Yeah."

"No notifications on the screen?"

"Nope."

"Then it's a dead end. Only government agencies have the software to open those phones. We can't get into the phone, so all we have is what we already know. Wait, where is the phone? Who knows about this?"

"Everyone except AJ knows. Bea has the phone now."

Ryan huffed.

"Why *her*?"

"She put it in her bra, and she won't take it out."

"That... That sounds exactly like her."

"What's your issue with Bea, anyway?"

At last, Ms. Roakes heard our ongoing conversation and stepped out of the kitchen. She didn't say good morning to either of us, but it wasn't necessarily a *good morning*, so neither of us said it to her either.

"Eldridge? What are you waiting for? You've got the sign. You've got a hat. Let's go! Ryan, quit *distracting* the boy."

"Lucianne!"

"Am I wrong, young lady?"

I hurried outside into the morning sunlight before I could laugh, blush, or otherwise embarrass myself. Smelling the clean ocean breeze, I wondered if this could still become a *good morning*. Even after the chaos of finding Eliza, Lars, and the cell phone, something felt right about being exactly where I was. After all, the insanity of the past few days gave me plenty of distractions from thinking about Ohio. For the first time since finding Eliza, I felt again that maybe I *had* escaped everything that I ran away from. Warley wasn't the paradise I expected, but maybe I could still be happy as a potential murder suspect.

Maybe all I needed was the right puzzle, I thought. *Or the right person to help me solve it.*

When lunch approached, I walked inside early to escape a few extra minutes in the sun. Ms. Roakes didn't seem to mind, especially since we'd managed to fill most of the tables. If she took any issue with me coming inside early, she had no time to say anything while preparing so many orders at once.

I ordered the Ritz burger again—still without poutine.

"You're lucky you get lunch early," Ryan groaned. "I have to wait until this rush ends so Ms. Roakes can take over."

"Shouldn't be too long. Without my sign, how will anyone find this place?"

Ryan tried not to laugh. Meanwhile, I glanced outside to see Carson's truck pull into Ritz's parking lot. I hadn't checked my phone, so I pulled it out to see a series of texts from him:

When's your lunch break?

Let's go to the Captain Heron Museum during lunch.

Check your phone, dude.

I'm picking you up, so I hope you got food.

I rolled my eyes. I wanted to tell Carson no, but what use would that have been? I already promised to see the museum with him at some point. Thankfully, my lunch order came out just in time, so I grabbed my foil-wrapped burger and returned its plastic basket.

"I'm heading over to the Heron Museum with Carson," I told Ryan.

"Alright, be back in an hour. Text me if you find the treasure or something."

I jogged out to the truck and jumped into the passenger seat. Carson had already queued up his Spotify playlist; I remembered the songs from our long drive on Saturday.

"So, you got my texts?"

"Just now, yeah. Why not wait to see the museum after work?"

"It closes at three, and it's only open on weekdays. I guess I never noticed all these years on vacation because I never had to worry about work. Sucks, right?"

"Yeah," I laughed. "And you don't even have to go outside for work."

Carson drove south down Warley Avenue, back past *All's Well* and toward the watchtower, Eliza's house, and the museum. Endless colorful houses flashed by on the ocean side to our left, plus some others on our right. A lot of the ones on the right sat back from the road in smaller developments, but the narrow island prevented those little neighborhoods from growing too large. Like the houses, those developments advertised with beach-themed names on wood signs along Warley Avenue.

"How far is the museum?" I asked. "I have to be back in an hour."

"Not much further. It's just a tiny place. You'll see what I mean. Look, it's right up there."

Carson pointed. Ahead, I spotted the watchtower, still blocked off by yellow tape. Carson wasn't pointing there. Instead, he turned right onto a small road a few hundred feet before the tower. I couldn't help but notice the closeness of the two sites. At least it helped explain how easily Carson and Cody found Ryan and me on the beach on Sunday; they'd seen that watchtower whenever they visited the museum.

The small road was paved, unlike many others. A sign with an arrow directed drivers: *Captain Heron Pirate Museum: Free Entry and Parking*. Between that sign and the faux wooden windmill at the corner of the parking lot, the museum showed every symptom of a classic tourist trap.

Carson parked his truck at the front of the lot close to the building. The museum itself was tiny—smaller than most houses on the island, and it had no wooden stilts to ride out storms. Pictures of anchors, sails, and swords adorned the sign above the entrance: *Heron Museum: Enter Here*. I already anticipated that the exit would funnel us through a gift shop. I never got the chance to confirm that theory.

"Isn't it great, Rain? After this, you'll know all the clues and historical timelines... You'll be ready to help me and AJ go metal-detecting."

"This is the whole museum?"

"Yeah. It's small. But there's plenty to see. C'mon, I'll show you."

Carson led me inside. Glass cases filled with pictures, letters, and tiny artifacts snaked around the museum's one large room. A long, text-heavy timeline waved up, down, and across three walls of the room. Meanwhile, a single speaker bolted to the ceiling croaked out sounds of screeching seagulls and crashing waves. The whole museum smelled distinctly like sand and salt. We were the only people there.

"Well," I started. "This is… Cute, I guess."

"Start over here, look! Remember everything I told you at that diner? This is that same story all along the walls, but with a lot more detail. You've gotta read that. Oh! And the letters that Captain Heron wrote to his girlfriend in Virginia; those are in the glass case on the back wall. The case next to it has Heron's hat! One of the British ships found it floating in the water after his ship sank. That hat is the most valuable item on display. At least that's what Lars says."

Lars? Did Carson just say Lars?

I stopped breathing and turned around slowly. Carson saw my *Something's Wrong* face, but he didn't see its meaning. I asked one question, just to be sure.

"Carson, what did you just say?"

"I said the hat is the most valuable item on display. What, you think that's a big clue for the treasure?"

"No, after that! You said a name."

"Oh, Lars? He's the guy who runs the museum. Lives in the house next door. He's run the museum ever since his older brother Ned died. Why? Is that a clue?"

Before I could explain, the door to a side room opened, and Lars stepped inside. His beardless face still caught me off-guard, but it was him for sure. He was still the fisherman. He was still the man with the bloody knife, who left the crime scene just as Ryan and I arrived. Now I knew his name. Now I knew how close he lived to the tower where Eliza died. But most importantly, now he knew *me.*

"Welcome to the Heron Museum," Lars spoke before looking up.

"Hey Lars! How've you been? You shaved the beard!" Carson approached him. Lars saw us, and his eyes fixed on me.

"Yes, I did. And… Well, I've been better. Good to see you, Carson. Who's this here?"

"This is my friend Rain. We both just graduated, so we're staying here for the summer."

"Ah, congratulations."

Reluctantly, I shook Lars' hand. I didn't say anything to him, and he didn't say anything else to me. What was there to say? *Hey, I remember you with the bloody knife. And hey, I remember you getting dragged out of the vigil last night.* We stared each other down in the same way; I think we both asked the same question with our eyes: *How much do you know?*

"I should get back to work," I told Carson.

"What? But we just—" I grabbed his shoulder.

"We can come back later. Trust me."

Carson resisted at first, but I pulled him toward the entrance door.

"Take care," Lars waved, and we sped off in Carson's truck.

Needless to say, my best friend was not happy when I accused his favorite museum curator of murdering someone.

"What the hell? You mean *Lars* is the creepy fisherman? You and Ryan saw *him* walking away from Eliza by the watchtower? C'mon, he runs a pirate museum! Why would he murder some teenage girl? What are the odds that he even knew her? Eliza and her mom haven't lived here that long, and he's been here a few years. Just because he was on the beach doesn't mean he killed her."

"I know, but that's not all! When I was talking with Eliza's mom at the vigil, he showed up at the door! She knew him, and she told their servant guy to kick him out. So, Eliza's mom is suspicious of Lars, too. Don't you think that's significant?"

Carson shook his head and tried to focus back on the road as we approached Ritz's Burgers and Fries. He parked his truck in the first open spot. The lunch rush had already died down.

"I don't know, Rain. I've known Lars a long time, and he's never even been rude to anyone in my family. Like I said, I'm on board with whatever investigation you and Ryan are working on, but we're gonna need some solid proof before I believe this whole Lars theory. So just... Let me know whatever you figure out next. Alright?"

"Fine," I agreed, then stepped out into the parking lot and ran inside the restaurant. Ryan blinked in surprise.

"Back so soon? Oh, shit. I know that look. What's wrong?"

She caught on quick. There were a few remaining customers at the tables, so I kept my words as hushed and concise as possible:

"Lars, the fisherman with the knife, owns and curates the Captain Heron Pirate Museum next to the watchtower where we found Eliza."

Ryan linked her hands around the back of her neck and gazed up at the ceiling. She took half a minute just to think that over. After all, I'd dropped two bombshells on her in one day. Nevertheless, I expected her to come out of her trance and conclude—like me—that Lars had murdered Eliza.

"So what?" She asked instead, and I struggled for words.

"So *what*? Lars was at the vigil *and* at the crime scene, which is right near his house. He lives on the intracoastal, and the tower is on the ocean—right across the island from him! How is this not a big deal to you? We have our lead suspect!"

Behind me, a couple curious customers craned their necks to hear. Ryan took notice, and she leaned over the counter to whisper more carefully to me.

"I have lots of suspects. Now we know the name and address of one of them. The rest is assumption without evidence. Where's the connection to Eliza's phone? What about the knife? Eliza wasn't stabbed, was she? We need real evidence before we accuse this Lars guy of murder."

She was right. I knew that, but it hurt me to give in so easily. I felt like I'd made a real breakthrough with the help of Carson, but my conclusions failed to impress either of them. Defeated, I picked up my *FOOD* sign and adjusted my hat.

"See you at closing," I grumbled, but Ryan caught the back of my shirt to stop me.

"I'm sorry, Rain. I know it sucks, but don't give up. I already have some new ideas. I'll tell you later. Okay?"

"Okay."

"Alright, go spin your sign."

I headed back outside, but I didn't start spinning the sign right away. I set it down on the sidewalk facing the restaurant and finally unwrapped and bit into my Ritz burger. The rides to and from the Heron Museum had turned it cold, so I gave it just a few more bites before chucking the remains into a nearby trash can. With a few minutes of lunch break remaining, I called my mom. My early call surprised her.

"Rain? Are you at work?"

"Yup, I'm on my lunch break." *But I threw away my lunch.*

"How's your day going?"

"Pretty good." *I met a murder suspect at a pirate museum.*

"Are your new friends nice?"

"Yeah, they're great." *When they aren't stealing phones and refuting my theories.*

"Good. I hope I can meet them eventually."

"Yeah." *If they don't get arrested by the end of the week.*

"Should I let you get back to work?"

"Probably." *Or else I might actually start telling the truth.*

"Alright. Enjoy the rest of your day."

"Bye, mom."

8: THE WATER

Carson, Cody, Bea, Ryan, AJ, and I returned to the Welling house after work, which seemed almost inevitable. I don't think any of us could handle being alone with our thoughts anymore. Perhaps AJ could carry on alright, but the rest of us carried the burdens of Eliza, Lars, and the cell phone more with each passing hour.

The wind picked up in the afternoon and blew away some of the stagnant summer air. Cody suggested taking out the kayaks on the intracoastal before sunset, so we began setting up the ropes and carrying the three boats toward the end of the dock. Meanwhile, I retrieved the blue-covered notebook from underneath the pull-out couch in my bedroom. It looked the same as always: Unopened, unused, and unwanted. That awful inscription, *Tell Your Story,* replayed and echoed in my head each time I read it from the notebook's cover. Instead of hearing those words in only my father's voice, I began hearing Ryan's voice, too.

"Tell you story," my dad said.

"*Live* your story," Ryan corrected. Meanwhile, in reality…

"What's that book?" AJ asked, pulling my mind out of its abyss. He stood in the open doorway of my room, just as carefree and nonchalant as ever, resting one tattooed arm on the doorframe.

"It's a notebook."

"Sweet. Do you journal?"

"No, I don't."

"You should try it. That can be a great way to de-stress, you know? Helps get all the junk out of your mind and onto paper. Ryan convinced me to start doing it, and I love it now. Has she tried talking you into journaling?"

"Not yet."

"What do you guys talk about? I mean, you two seem to get along real well."

I expected a question like that one to come from AJ, eventually. After I'd spent so many hours around Ryan every day, he could only wait so long before prying into the details of our interactions. How could I *not* expect AJ to be somewhat jealous? Ryan kept the secret of my last name from him, as far as I could tell. She entrusted me with all of her Eliza theories; did she tell him anything? I guessed that maybe AJ and Ryan had their own secrets together, yet I didn't feel jealous of AJ because of that. It wasn't the same situation. But how could I explain all that to him?

"We don't talk much at Ritz's. I'm usually outside with the sign. But I guess it's usually stuff about… Books, since she reads a lot. Mysteries. She thinks I could become some sort of detective."

AJ grinned. "You two gonna solve Eliza together?"

I couldn't answer. He knew that.

"Well, Rain, if you're looking for a *real* puzzle to solve, you should come out metal-detecting with Carson and me on Thursday. There's no buried treasure at the end of Eliza's story, but you can bet there will be at the end of Captain Heron's. I heard that you and Carson went to the museum today, during lunch?"

"Yeah."

"Carson said you think the new curator killed Eliza?"

"Not exactly. I don't know. It might be nothing."

"Well, you gotta go back to the museum before Thursday. See if you can find any clues the rest of us have missed. You're the detective, right?"

"Right." *Ouch.*

AJ held up a *Shaka* sign, then retreated from my doorway, giving me the chance to toss the notebook back under my bed. I couldn't remember why I took it out in the first place.

Downstairs in the garage, I found Carson struggling to release the last kayak from its pulleys on the ceiling. He wrapped the two black ropes around his hands, grunted, and pulled them tight as he leaned his body weight toward the floor.

"This is impossible!" He gasped, throwing the dangling ropes onto the concrete floor. "Everyone else already gave up on this boat. I think they're already out on the water."

I eyed the pulleys that roped the kayak on the ceiling. "Why not just slide the boat out of the ropes?"

Carson thought about it. Without a word, he reached up and tugged the first rope off the kayak's front end. Before I could intervene, the boat crashed to the floor. Its front end hammered into the ground and cracked open like a raw egg. The sound of the impact bounced from wall to wall across the garage bay. Four unopened six packs of beer tumbled out from inside the smashed boat. Carson facepalmed.

"Shit! I forgot about those."

"Well at least you got the kayak down, right?"

Carson rolled his eyes. Leaving the mess for later, we followed the dock behind the garage, past the dumped keg and trash, all the way down toward the covered area over the shallow water beyond the grass. The setting sun reflected a pink glow across the water, revealing shoals of brown oysters, bobs of submerged crab traps, and a silhouette of Cody: Tumbling into the water while trying to sit down in a kayak. Ripples spread softly in all directions, along with the sounds of a splash and his profane shriek.

Carson relished this, of course.

When we reached the platform, Ryan and AJ had already helped Cody out of the water. He sat on one of the benches shaking salty droplets out of his messy beard. Bea held up her phone to take a picture, and Cody whined:

"Hey, no pictures!"

"What? I'm just getting the sunset!" Bea snapped the photo, and the flash washed over Cody.

"That water is too cold. Damn. I'm not going back in there. Oh, Carson, did you get the other kayak?"

Carson and I looked at each other nervously.

"We tried," I said. "It fell hard because of all the beers we hid."

"You broke the kayak?" Cody sounded genuinely upset. Carson knew better.

"Oh, c'mon! You've broken half the things in the house at this point. The glass door in front of Rain's room? The raft on the roof? I mean, how did that even happen?"

"Whatever! But that means we just have two kayaks. So only four people can go."

After seeing Cody's fall, I didn't jump to volunteer. The water did look cold; it was only June. My eyes traced the shoreline south down the island, over many more docks running out parallel to ours. The water seemed to go on forever. *We could just paddle for miles, if we wanted to.*

"Hey, why don't we kayak down to the Captain Heron Museum?" The idea left my lips before I finished thinking it. Five pairs of eyebrows raised, each—I supposed—with a different question. Ryan:

Why should we? AJ: *Who's going?* Bea: *Where's that?* Carson: *Again?* And Cody: *Who's got a towel?*

Ryan voiced her question first, although it came out more like a concern:

"That's just… An awful idea. No offense."

"What's Rain on about?" Bea, following after Ryan, still knew nothing about Lars. Ryan filled her in, along with everyone else.

"Right, right. Some context for those of you who haven't heard: Rain thinks that a museum curator killed Eliza. The evidence: He fished near his *house* when we found her."

I interrupted. "*And* he had a blood knife with him at the tower. And he was at the vigil, and Eliza's mom knew his name, *and* she had him thrown out. He has to be involved!"

With the exception of Carson, three vacant faces betrayed our collective lack of motivation. Like the rest of the island—and like the rest of the people who came to the party on Saturday night—Cody, Bea, and AJ wanted to move on from Eliza. I could tell. But we all knew that wouldn't be possible; the outline of Eliza's phone still made its rectangular outline on the inside of Bea's shirt.

"I'm in," Carson agreed, slapping a hand on my shoulder. That was a relief.

"Me too," said Bea. That caught us all off guard. I think she could tell. One of her hands brushed over the phone in her shirt. Clearly, she felt some responsibility—if only for having plotted to sell the phone—but Bea would never admit that. "What, you guys think I'm too cool to spy on some old dude?"

Leading the charge, Bea climbed down the dock's stout ladder into the green kayak that Cody fell from. She had no trouble with it. Cody handed her one of the double-sided paddles. At the same time, I observed Carson lowering himself into the red kayak; I wouldn't let myself repeat Cody's mistake. I followed after Carson into the red kayak, and he held it steady while I sat down. A puddle in the rear seat instantly soaked through my shorts. *Gross.* Ryan passed me another one of the paddles.

"One seat left! Who's coming with?" Bea prepared to unmoor her kayak from the dock. AJ and Cody played rock-paper-scissors with their eyes, but Ryan unexpectedly stepped forward and started down the ladder. Neither Bea nor Ryan looked enthusiastic about them sharing a kayak.

Ryan sighed. "Rain, I'm only doing this so that I can say 'I told you so' when we paddle three miles and find nothing."

AJ laughed.

"Good enough for me," I shrugged, and we casted off south down the intracoastal.

At first, paddling was easy. I matched Carson's pace, and the remaining breeze helped us reach the deeper waters. Bea and Ryan kept up with us, but they only spoke to instruct each other: *Slow down,* or, *Stop turning!* They tried to say all of that quietly, but voices carried over that water like nobody's business. In fact, their short conversations *were* nobody else's business, yet anyone within half a mile could hear every word.

After ten minutes, once we all got into a rhythm with paddling, my arms felt a bit sore. Behind me, Ryan finally asked Bea a real question. Carson and I tuned in. How could we not?

"Bea, what's the story with your hair?"

"Excuse me?"

"No shade. Really. Just wondering. You mentioned it at the party, and I was curious."

"Oh. Right. I don't know. It was an idea I had."

"An idea?"

"Well… Right before graduation, I had this realization. Long time coming, I think. I was hiding a part of myself… A part that I should've let out. Basically, I'm into women. Guys too. Both, whatever. So, I told Val—one of my closest friends—that I'm bi, and she freaked out. Then I asked myself: Am I just gonna tell everyone else and let them hate me for who I am? Hell no. I'd die. So, then I got an idea: If people are gonna hate me, why not let them hate me for something stupid? Why not give them something else to focus on?"

"Blue hair?"

"Exactly. You know, hair is a powerful thing. For everyone, yeah, but Black women most of all. And I've kept mine natural my whole life, but I left school on my last day, dyed my hair with the most unnatural color I could find, then walked home and came out to my family. And you know what? They couldn't care less about my sexuality. My mom saw the blue and actually fainted."

At first, Bea spoke quietly and tried to keep Carson and me out of the conversation. But by the time she finished her story, her voice reached out to us intentionally. She didn't hesitate anymore. What's more, Ryan changed her tone after that. Not just for the remainder of Tuesday night, but for *always*. If Bea and Ryan were forces of nature, they opposed each other before the kayak trip. Afterwards, maybe their forces didn't move in quite the same direction, but perpendicular, at worst.

"Blue's a good color for you," Carson spoke, turning around to smile at Bea. To my relief, he didn't flirt beyond that simple compliment. Bea seemed to appreciate that too.

"Thanks, Carson."

The wooden windmill near the Captain Heron Museum served as our landmark, illuminated by its small spotlight shining up from the ground. Without that windmill, the short dock behind the museum could have belonged to any restaurant, rental house, or other local attraction. Aside from the light at the windmill, there were no others nearby. The museum and Lars' small house hid behind layers of shadow. Luckily for us, that meant Lars had to be either asleep or away.

We approached with caution, not only because of my suspicions about Lars, but also because we couldn't be caught trespassing. Near the dock, only one of us paddled each kayak—Carson and Bea, respectively—and we kept our phones locked to maintain the cover of darkness. As the dock drew closer, I recognized the lapping sound of water on the sides of a small fishing boat. At the dock, Carson read the name on the side:

"*Saint Olga IV*. Captain Heron's lead ship was the *Saint Olga*, patron saint of revenge. That's such a cool—"

"Shh!" Bea hissed.

My heart beat harder than usual in my chest. I felt little sense of risk by the time we moored ourselves to the dock, but the adrenaline rush continued anyway—maybe because I knew this had been my idea, or maybe because I sensed what was coming.

"Are we gonna walk on the dock?" Carson asked in a harsh whisper. Ryan had already climbed up onto it.

"Yeah, how else can we get over there? The water stops where the grasses start. Here, I'll help you up." Ryan held out one had to lift Carson onto the platform next to her. I looked around all sides of the dock's platform, but I found no ladder. After all, the *Saint Olga IV* sat high enough in the water that its deck met the dock without any ladder.

Once we all mounted the platform, I expected Ryan to lead the charge, but she pushed me toward the front of the pack. It was my plan, after all. Stepping as quietly as possible, we crept all the way up to the shore where the dock met the house's porch.

"Go around the building first?" I suggested quietly, to which everyone else either nodded, shrugged, or thumbs upped. In an episode of Scooby Doo, we might have split up and walked in opposite directions around the house, but instead we travelled together toward the side facing the museum. In that narrow twenty-foot gap between the buildings, we struggled not to step on a wide blue tarp staked across the ground.

"What's under the tarp?"

"Mulch? Rocks?"

"Why not check?"

"It's staked down!"

"Yeah, but just pull it up here."

Ryan lifted part of the tarp between stakes, but there was no pile, just more dirt and a large rock. They tarp must've been for the boat. I felt like an idiot.

"Ryan? Anyone? What should we look for?"

"He's a museum curator. Are you expecting the skeletons in his closet to be literal or figurative?"

Before I could laugh, before I could come up with ideas, and before we could even begin a real search of the property, a car pulled into the museum's parking lot. Its headlights washed quickly over us, just once, and we scrambled over one another to get back behind the house.

"Shit! Is that Lars?"

"No, look!"

Out in the parking lot, three more vehicles rolled up behind the first one. They parked in a single straight line, screeching to a halt with no regard for the lined spots on the pavement. In the chain of headlights, all became clear: *Two police cars, an ambulance, and a black armored van.* Inside the small house between us and the cars, a light flickered on.

"Go, go, go! Move!" Carson pushed me out of the way, leading our mad dash back to the dock. We couldn't afford to step quietly this time, and there was no need for any discussion of a plan or strategy. I began to believe my plan had failed, but then something else occurred to me: *Four police vehicles? They're not here to catch trespassers.*

We reached the platform in a matter of seconds. Bea jumped straight down into her kayak, and Ryan right after. Carson was next, but he hesitated.

"No ladder!" He exclaimed.

"Just jump in! You'll be fine!"

Poor choice of words, on my part. Rather than carefully landing down in the kayak, Carson lunged past it and landed in the water with a noisy splash.

"Carson, you idiot!" Bea shouted, wiping splashed salty water from her face.

I began to lift the kayaks' mooring ropes off of the dock when I heard pounding footsteps behind me. I turned, horrified to see the form of a man running toward me at a full sprint, carrying a knife.

Lars.

I crossed my arms and braced myself.

At the last second, when he reached the platform, Lars turned and jumped into his boat. He fumbled around in his pocket, then pulled out a key and jammed it into the boat's ignition. The engine of the *Saint Olga IV* coughed once, then once more. Lars looked up from the controls at me, and although I expected to sense his malice, anger, or murderous intent, I saw only the same fear and timidity that he showed at the vigil. For that moment, I almost understood him. I glimpsed whatever piece of the puzzle I'd been missing. Like Ryan might do, I read the lines in the book that gave away his secrets—but only for a second. Then the *Saint Olga IV*'s engine roared ferociously, and Lars cut the mooring lines with two swipes of his bloody fishing knife.

Lars and his boat sped away from us, leaving only a pair of waves that rocked our kayaks in the water.

"Rain!" Ryan's voice dragged me back to reality. "Get in the kayak! We have to go, *now*!"

We had to, and yet we couldn't. Even as I lowered myself down into the remaining empty kayak, I knew our time was up. The police officers saw Lars leaving in his boat, so they swarmed around the house and museum with flashlights. They wasted no time, and neither did we.

"Under the dock," I whispered to Bea, Ryan, and Carson. Where else could we go? Paddling away, we'd be seen. Not to mention, Carson still clung to the red kayak with his feet and legs down in muck and water. Ryan and Bea ducked down and floated their green kayak underneath the mildewed planks of the dock platform. Carson and I did the same, although he remained in the water, shivering.

More heavy footsteps echoed up the dock. We held our breath. Salty droplets slipped from our idle kayak paddles and struck the water with rhythms like our heartbeats. Ryan lowered her paddle into the water on one side of the kayak to stop the noise. Bea and I followed suit; Carson's paddle was already submerged. Every motion of my feet or hands *clunked* or scraped along the plastic body of the red kayak. My low-leaning position under the dock hurt to hold, but I kept as still as I could. I had no choice.

The beams of flashlights shot across the water like lightning, barely missing us or shining only through hairline cracks in the dock. Carson held our two kayaks close together, himself between them. Inevitably, the voices of the officers drifted within our earshot.

"...the wake. Just missed him." *Officer Lee, maybe?*

"Is the Coast Guard aware?" That voice I knew. The carefully enunciated syllables of Chief Fitz jumped out to all of us. We met each other's eyes, one by one. Even amid the terror of hiding from the police under a stranger's dock, I found small joy in one thing: If Fitz came to the museum, then Lars had to be important.

"The Coast Guard? Well, not yet. Should I—"

"Make them aware, yes. We need to set a perimeter around the island before he makes it to the open water. Did you send someone into the house?"

"Yeah, right here..."

More footsteps. Someone else, maybe even a few people rushed out to the dock. Right above us, Fitz continued her endless line of questioning.

"Well, did you find the box?"

Box? What box?

"We got it, Chief."

"And the contents?"

"It's what you expected."

"Damn. Whenever I think I know this island, something like *this* comes along, right when we are up to our necks in underage drunks and noise complaints. We need to bring this under control. Take pictures of everything inside his house. I am not sleeping tonight until I review every piece of evidence in that house, and in the museum too."

"You got it, Chief." A radio beeped, and the officer repeated Fitz's instructions back for the others at the house. Fitz paced up and down the platform above us, and the creaking wood planks sent dust down on our heads. Carson's eyes widened. He didn't have to say anything; I knew he was about to sneeze. We had seconds to act. I leaned forward and shoved his head down underwater. He sneezed, and a stream of bubbles quietly broke the water's surface.

Not quietly enough for the officer standing by Fitz.

"You hear that, Chief?"

"Hear what?

"Water, something under the dock. Should I take a look?"

"Sure, after you call up the Coast Guard. Get state on the line, too. Keep the DEA out of this if you can; the last thing we need is a squad of federal grunts arresting teenagers by the dozen. We need to focus on finding Lars. That is our priority."

"You got it, Chief."

Several pairs of feet retreated toward the house, but Fitz remained out on the dock. For a minute, I wondered if she would shine her light down and find us, but she did nothing. As far as we could hear, she stood motionless for an uncomfortable time. Without warning, she began talking again, but there was no one else for her to be talking to.

Phone? Ryan asked her question by holding a *Shaka* sign to her ear. I nodded. As we listened, Chief Fitz dropped her all-business tone. Her voice sounded like someone else's, and I could hardly believe that the same person still stood above us.

"Hey, honey. Oh, everything's fine. I just wanted to call to say I'm gonna be home late again. Sorry, I know. Yes, I know. I promise it'll be better after this week, but something came up, and I need to get ahead of the paperwork. Oh, don't worry about that. I'm really sorry. I'll make you dinner tomorrow? No, you're right, you're the better chef. But hey, this'll all be better soon. Soon we'll be done with this island. Living somewhere quieter, with mountains… Alright, well I should say goodnight now. See you in the morning. I love you too!"

Fitz hung up. She waited another minute, then followed her fellow officers back to the house. I had so much to discuss with Ryan, and with everyone. I had so much to think about: Eliza, Lars, the phone, the *box*, and now Chief Fitz's love life, apparently. In our predicament under the dock, we couldn't discuss anything.

We waited, and when the police flashlights stopped panning out over the water, I helped Carson back into the kayak. In silence and in darkness, we began our journey back to *All's Well*. The return trip felt a million times longer, but we eventually arrived to find Cody and AJ still waiting impatiently for us on the dock.

"What the hell took so long?"

"Oh, we stopped for ice cream," Bea answered without hesitation. "You bums missed out."

9: THE EMERGENCY

I dreamt of his funeral—not for the first time, and not for the last. This dream began like the others; I arrived with my mother in the funeral procession. We stepped from the dark car into the bright sun that washed over the cemetery. It didn't rain. For early April, the air was too warm. The sky glowed a vibrant, cloudless blue. I began to sweat through my suit immediately, and not just because of the weather.

They buried him between his parents' graves. Like me, he had no siblings. That meant no aunts or uncles for me—not on his side of the family, anyway. Seeing his casket between two *Eldridge* headstones, I wondered where mine would rest someday. They couldn't bury me between my parents' graves, not if they buried him between his.

The dying act of his big, fat ego.

Then the dream changed. Time shifted into overdrive. My mother vanished, and the other mourners too. My dad's casket dropped like a stone into the abyss below. Heaps of dirt flung over it until the ground leveled out. The sun slipped away, and the air turned dark. My eyes struggled to adjust so quickly.

"Hey!" I called out. "Hey! Come back!"

"Shh!" Someone hissed, and I glanced over my shoulder. It was Ryan. Behind her: Carson and Bea. All of us stood close against a wall. I remembered the place… Lars' house! Only this time, the side on his house turned into smooth gray stone. It stretched high up into the sky like a monument, and the museum opposite the house did the same. As I looked, the two parallel buildings became the headstones of my grandparents. My father's parents.

Between the headstones, in the space between the buildings, a blue tarp covered something.

"Take a look," Carson suggested, and Ryan lifted the tarp. Instead of the gray rock we saw between the museum and the house, the tarp covered a giant plaque—the one from my father's grave:

Hunter Mason Eldridge
January 7, 1971 - April 4, 2019
"Tell Your Story"

A phone rang, and I awoke. I sat up in my bed—disoriented; nothing new there—and the phone rang again. I grasped for the nightstand a few feet away and snapped my phone free of its charger, but the ringing came again from elsewhere. *7:05 AM,* said my phone, and the desperate desire for more sleep crawled up from my feet and into my head. But the phone outside my room rang again, pulling me another step further from whatever dream I left behind.

The funeral, I remembered. *Something about the funeral.*

I slid out from under the bedsheets and followed the sound of the phone. I didn't have to go far. On the kitchen counter just beyond my bedroom door, a landline chirped its incessant song for the fifth time. I checked the caller ID on the white handset's display, but there was none. Who still had a landline, anyway? If only to stop the ringing, I picked up the phone, making possibly the worst or best decision of my entire summer.

"Hello?"

"Oh, Carson, is that you?" A woman's voice. Not unfamiliar. My groggy head took an extra second to identify: *Carson's mom.*

Shit. I couldn't believe my own stupidity. Why did I pick up the phone? One more ring, and it would've gone to voicemail!

"No, sorry. It's Rain. I think Carson's asleep."

"Well, you tell him to wake up. He won't respond to my texts, not since last night. Do you know if he saw them?"

"Oh, probably. Was it something important?"

"Well, I had some questions for him."

"Questions?"

"The *police* called me. Warley Island Police. Something about a wild party at my house? Do *you* know anything about that, Rain?" Her tone dropped. My sleepy brain couldn't fabricate a denial fast enough. "I guess it doesn't matter now. I caught the red eye, and I'll be at the house in an hour. I hope Carson is ready to answer all of my—"

I dropped the phone into its cradle. The Earth stood still for five to ten seconds while I wrapped my head around the magnitude of our imminent emergency. At the end of those seconds, I ran through the living room and up the stairs. I pounded my fist on the door of Carson's room.

"Hey! Have you checked your phone?"

Nothing.

"Carson, c'mon! Your mom just called."

The bedroom door sprang open, and there Carson stood, half-naked and fully alert.

"Whah?"

"Your mom just called. I answered. Check your phone!"

"Rain, I can't!"

"What? Why not?"

"Because I jumped off Lars' dock with my phone in my pocket, doofus! It's drying out in a bowl of rice on the puzzle table."

"Oh shit, that means… Okay, I'll just say what I know: Your mom called, and she knows there was a party. Police called her. She said she's on her way here. Wait, wait! Don't panic yet; it gets worse! She said she'll be here in an *hour* because she flew in overnight!"

Carson shoved me out of the way and leaned into a sprint down the upstairs hallway. He charged at Cody's door, which I supposed had also become Bea's door.

"Cody!" Carson shouted and pushed through the unlocked door, wasting no time knocking. He walked straight into the darkness of the master bedroom. I stayed out and listened in, but I could only hear Carson's side of the conversation: "Cody, get up. She's coming! What do you mean, 'who?' Mom! No, I don't know why; I just found out. We have to clean up. Everything, all of it! We have one hour! No, you have to. Get up! I'll just blame it all on you! Yeah, that's what I thought. Where's Bea?"

She moved back to her room, I realized.

The blinds clattered in Cody's room, and sunlight rushed in like an orange wave. Carson flew back into the hallway toward Bea's door, and I stopped him before he could barge in.

"Knock!" I insisted. He huffed once, but then he obeyed.

Bea peeled her door open and squinted out at the two of us. It felt like our arrival all over again: Carson and I standing outside a door, scared out of our minds, greeted by Bea's tired face framed with blue curls.

"Is the world ending?"

"Yes!" Carson and I answered in unison.

"Well, it's about time. Can someone grab me a Red Bull? I need to put on my apocalypse socks."

Cody emerged from the master bedroom carrying a hastily gathered ball of linens and the duvet from the bed. He flung them from the top of the staircase, then slid down the railing and picked them all up. I think he sensed Carson and I staring at him.

"What are you looking at? Laundry, assholes! We gotta wash anything that smells like jizz, piss, or beer! Strip the beds!"

Carson turned back to his room and obeyed. I rushed downstairs to clean up my room, but I was in the clear: No alcohol, no weed, and nothing else to freak out Carson's mom. But looking into my bedroom, the dream, the tombstones, the plaque, the museum… All of it returned at once.

"Tell Your Story."

I pulled my phone charger out of the wall by the nightstand and shot Ryan a text: *Carson and Cody's mom is coming to Warley in less than an hour. We're cleaning up the house. Please help if you can! If not, see you at work.*

Across the foyer, in the first-floor bathroom, Carson added his laundry to the washing machine, which Cody's linens had already filled. The pile of fabric bulged outward, which made me nervous.

"Is this all gonna fit?"

"It has to. We don't even have time for one wash cycle, and definitely not two. Where's Bea? Bea! Do you have your sheets?"

Heard through the ceiling above us: "Yeah! Do you have my Red Bull?"

Carson grabbed a can from the fridge.

Thanks to the Police Chief's visit, the party trash had already vanished, but it wasn't r*eally* gone. Bea just threw the trash can off the back porch with the empty keg. That solution worked for the police, but something told me it wouldn't be good enough for

Mrs. Welling. I put on my running shoes and hurried down the steps from the back porch. Through the muggy air and ten feet of marsh grasses, I spied the trash and keg not far behind the garage's back door. I pushed my way through the plants and gathered the debris as fast as I could, but my sneakers sunk two inches into the mud with each step.

The garbage bin was heavy, but the keg was heavier. Inside the garage, I dropped the keg into the big green trash bin and poured the kitchen trash on top of it. Everything stunk and dripped with a mix of beer, fruit punch, and intracoastal muck.

At the back of the garage, I also gathered up the bits and chunks of the smashed kayak. From inside the wreck, I pulled the unopened six packs of beer. I knew Cody would want those eventually, so I stowed them under a nearby workbench behind a leaf blower. With those out of the way, I began disposing of the kayak. Most of its pieces fit in the house's big green trash bin, but the remainder of the kayak stuck out three feet above the lid. I had no other option—with all my strength, I lifted the large piece over my head and threw it back down on the garage's concrete floor. That worked, certainly, but the enormous shattering sound drew Bea and Cody down into the basement.

"Oh, good!" Cody exclaimed. "I thought you died or something."

"I'm fine. It should fit now. But what about this trash can? Won't your mom look inside it?"

"Damn. Yeah, probably."

Bea downed the last of her energy drink, then interrupted us by stomping her foot to flatten its can on the garage floor. She chucked it into the garbage on top of the kayak bits.

"Woo! Alright. Cody, get the kitchen trash can back upstairs. We need to clear the water balloons and plastic bags from the driveway. Rain, where's that broken baseball bat? Oh! I need to grab my jeans from the railing on the porch. Carson, where is he? Tell him to bring the kayaks back in from the dock. And didn't that garage door have a dent? Yeah, there it is!"

Bea pointed at the one garage door still slightly off the ground. She ran at it, jumped into the air, and kicked hard with one foot. She popped the dent back out in one smooth stunt, and the garage door settled into place. After she kicked to door, I glimpsed the Buffy quote on her apocalypse socks: *"If the apocalypse comes, beep me."* For the first time since my harrowing phone call with Carson's mom, I began to believe we might still clean up in time. Bea saved us all when the police came, so maybe she'd do it again. She knew how to take charge, when needed.

"Rain! Get out to the driveway and pull the pink shirt off that cactus! But don't rip it. I want that shirt."

"Will do!"

I headed for the circular gravel driveway and approached the cactus at its center. The *Warley Island Gal* t-shirt stuck on hundreds of prickly thorns. On closer inspection, the cactus wasn't wearing the shirt; someone just wrapped it onto the front of the cactus like a Lost Dog poster on a telephone pole. Grabbing the loose sleeves with both hands, I ripped the shirt slowly off the cactus. Pink shirt in hand, I looked back to the house, and that's when I saw it:

The raft on the roof.

"Bea!" I called out.

On the front porch, Bea collected her jeans and the other clothes left behind before and after Saturday's party. She peered down at me from the porch.

"Oh good, you got the shirt!"

"Yeah, but there's still a raft on the roof above you."

Bea angled her head up.

"Well, shit. I forgot about that."

"How did that happen, anyway?"

"For the sake of my spotless reputation, I'd rather not say."

"Oh. Alright. But how can we get it down?"

"That's the real trick, isn't it?"

Fortunately for us, someone else had been thinking about the raft on the roof, too. The repaired garage door opened with a whirring sound, and Carson stepped outside. He carried out the old leaf blower that I'd spotted when I hid the beers. With one hand, he pulled the starter cord, and the cobweb-wrapped machine rattled to life. Bea leaned over the porch with excitement when she heard the sound.

"Yeah, Carson! Now we're talking!"

Unfortunately for Carson, I don't think he could hear her compliment over the torrent of the leaf blower. He carried it up the steps from the driveway to the porch, then angled the flat end up the roof at the crumpled rubber raft. Its edge fluttered once, then the whole thing lifted, flipped, and fell down over the porch onto the driveway. Carson shut off the leaf blower, and Bea gave him a high-five. At least he noticed that.

When the leaf blower's engine slowed to silence, another rumbling sound took over. This one came in slower thumps, oscillating like the heartbeat of a whale running a marathon.

"What the hell is that?" Carson asked. The sound came from everywhere all at once. Before I could move the raft into the trash with the kayak, the growing sound ended in a massive metal *bang* that visibly shook the front porch. In seconds, Cody emerged from the front door.

"Guys, I think we have a problem."

Bea, Carson and I ran inside after Cody. A thin puddle of water and soap bubbles covered the foyer. I quickly traced it to the bathroom across from my bedroom, where we'd all put our sheets into the laundry machine. That machine, needless to say, had leaked everywhere and nearly shook itself apart before dying with the *bang* that we all heard.

"Shit!" Bea cried, tiptoeing through the soapy water and opening the door of the ruptured washer. The oversized pile of linens, socks, comforters, pants, and other garments spilled out onto the slick linoleum floor in a sopping heap. "Damn, now I wet my apocalypse socks."

"Bea, are those all your clothes?" Cody splashed his way into the bathroom next.

"Yeah, and?"

"*All* of your clothes? There was no more room!" Cody sounded frantic for the first time.

"We didn't have time for another load!"

"Funny, you said the same thing last night."

"Oh, you asshole…"

Bea grabbed a wet sock and used it to slap Cody's face. Droplets of water rained across the mirror over the sink. Neither Carson nor I dared to intervene.

"Gross!" Cody shouted, wiping detergent bubbles from his cheek.

"Oh, that's gross? No, you're gross, Cody. Seriously! When I met you on Friday, I thought: 'Wow, a musician with his own house who throws great parties, I must be in *looove*,' but no! You haven't picked up a guitar in months, you're squatting in your parents' vacation house, and you haven't even asked what my last name is!"

Bea paused. We waited. Cody opened his mouth, then he closed it again. She was right.

"McCoy," Bea answered for him. "Beatrice McCoy. Now if you don't mind, I'm gonna go and throw myself out with the rest of your trash. I'm done here."

Carson and I stepped aside. Bea, in her water-logged apocalypse socks, opened the front door to leave. Before she could, we watched the gnarled trees of the driveway sway and rustle. An engine hummed, and four wheels crackled down the gravel toward us.

Oh no, I thought. *She's here early.*

An old beige Winnebago with orange stripes on the sides pushed its way through the foliage. All of us, now hypnotized by the spectacle, floated onto the porch again. The beast of a vehicle lumbered into the driveway's open circle. Its horn blasted once, playing what sounded like the opening notes of The Beach Boys song "Surfin' USA." Suffice to say, the Winnebago did not belong to the Wellings.

When all four wheels slid to a stop in a cloud of dust and leaves, both doors opened.

"I heard there's some parental emergency?" Ryan called up to us, jumping down from the driver's side.

"Sweet!" AJ shouted, looking over the house like a piece of artwork. "Cody, man, you cleaned up this place fast! Wait, that was probably Bea. Never mind. Looks great though."

"Where'd you get that thing?" Carson asked, gesturing to the orange-striped monster in the driveway. AJ smiled.

"Oh, this beauty? She's ours. Driven her coast to coast and back again twice. Cheapest way to travel is to take home with you, right?"

I finally understood why we hadn't seen AJ and Ryan's Warley house yet. There wasn't one! Even after Ryan told me about her year of cross-country trekking with AJ, I hadn't considered their mode of transport.

"Right on!" Carson agreed, and he held up the *Shaka* sign.

"Let's go, c'mon! Bea, what's the plan here? What's left to be done?" Ryan marched up the wooden stairs, finally ready to cooperate with Bea after their heart-to-heart in the kayak. Bea just shrugged and moved down the stairs. As she passed Ryan, Bea reached into her shirt and handed Eliza's cell phone to Ryan. Still down at the Winnebago, AJ hardly noticed, thankfully; we still hadn't told him about the phone. Ryan accepted it from Bea.

"Here, just take it. I'll come back for the rest of my stuff whenever. Carson, can you give me a ride to my friends' house?"

None of us knew what to say.

"Um, sure, I guess?" Carson jogged down the steps toward his truck, where Bea already sat in the bed. He looked up to us for approval, but we said nothing. Bea could leave if she wanted, but it hurt to think that she chose her old friends over us. A few days earlier, she wanted to slash their tires. If Bea suddenly preferred them over us, who had we become? I knew it was Cody's fault for being a jerk toward her, especially after all the times she'd helped us out: The party, the police scare, and even with protecting Eliza's phone. Still, Bea's departure hurt, and I knew it hurt Carson worst of all.

Despite that, he drove her—just like she asked—down the driveway and out of sight.

**

Only half an hour remained before Mrs. Welling arrived, so we kicked our cleanup into overdrive. We moved the wet laundry into the dryer, soaked up the water on the floor using beach towels, and threw those in the dryer with everything else. Cody figured out that the trash truck wouldn't come until Friday, so we tied the big green trash can shut and bungeed it onto the back of the Winnebago. Ryan disapproved of that, but she still helped set it up.

AJ dug around in the Winnebago for some good air fresheners. Unsurprisingly, the vehicle had plenty of its own clutter to deal with. Some small pillows, a ring of keys, empty Amazon boxes, and worn-out books—many with my father's name on the cover—spilled out into the driveway from the Winnebago's open door. I tossed all of that back inside, trying not to make matters worse.

"Found it!" AJ yelled from inside. He tossed me a jumbo-size can of Lysol, saving another one for himself. Together we sprayed the mist of artificial freshness around the garage, up the stairs, around the kitchen and living room, then thoroughly in every bedroom. By the time both cans of Lysol ran dry, the house smelled as clean as a newly opened hospital. With the help of Cody and Ryan rearranging the furniture, the house looked neat enough to match.

"It almost feels wrong," Ryan said. "This house actually looks livable. It's like we've cheated the system somehow."

"We did it!" Cody laughed. It was hard not to. With minutes to spare, we did the impossible. Behind us, the front door opened, and we shared a collective heart attack. Luckily, that was just Carson returning. He nodded uncomfortably to greet us.

"Wow. This looks… Different. Geez, how much Lysol did you use?"

"All of it," AJ confessed. Ryan clapped her hands, bringing everyone back to the present.

"Okay, time to get out? Only Carson and Rain can stay, right?"

Cody hardly had anything to bring; he kept all his stuff in a giant black trash bag. Ryan opened the front door for him. Cody, AJ, and I followed her down to the Winnebago, and I help Cody pile himself and his trash bag into the cramped house-on-wheels. I pretended not to notice the Ziploc bag of weed sitting on the center console.

"Nice place," Cody mused. "I should get myself one of these. You guys got any food back here?" Cody asked while rooting around in the cabinets of the mini kitchen. "I skipped breakfast, so I'm dying here."

I shut the Winnebago's door, and the beast dragged itself around the circular driveway. Just like before, the branches on either side scraped violently across the Winnebago's side panels. Carson and I watched them leave, probably both hoping that Mrs. Welling wouldn't notice all the tree damage.

I retreated back into the house, where Carson continued marveling at how clean everything felt.

"Honestly, I think we got everything. I guess we just need to explain the broken washing machine somehow?"

"Just say it broke when we tried to use it," I suggested. "And that's the truth, really."

A few minutes later, the garage door shook to life underneath us. An unseen car pulled into the garage bay, and the door shut again with the same sound. Carson and I sat in the kitchen next to the unfinished puzzle and his bowl of dry rice, trying to look busy.

A door opened, and we turned to greet Mrs. Welling, but it wasn't the door of the garage stairs. Instead, the front door opened once more, and Cody burst into the foyer panting, sweating, and confused. Carson nearly jumped out of his skin, and I remained stupefied as Cody darted into the kitchen, exhausted.

"I ran... From the van thing... Because... Forgot my Swiss Rolls!"

Swiss Rolls. Of course.

"Cody! No! You have to leave!" Carson yelled, but it was futile.

"I need my Rolls!" Cody pulled the oven open, then threw the Swiss Roll packets into his pockets. Carson tried to pull him away and push him back out the front door.

"Go! There's no time!"

"There driveway is empty, see?" Cody pointed out the front door at the circle of the driveway, still clear of all but Carson's pickup. Carson shook his head. He looked pale. I shouted over them, desperately trying to explain:

"Cody, you don't understand. A few seconds before you got here, your mom parked in the *garage!*"

Before Cody could run or hide, the door to the garage stairwell opened. Mrs. Welling stepped forward and gasped, seeing her sons frozen like deer in headlights. Cody screamed, but as always, he didn't drop the Swiss Rolls. He jumped out the front door and made a run for it.

Mrs. Welling—without a word to me or Carson—turned around, returned to her car, and drove away to chase him down.

10: THE DELIVERY

"So… Their mom is just gone now?" Ryan laughed and finished turning on the lights inside the Ritz.

"I guess? I don't know. I had to leave the house to get here on time. Maybe she caught up to him? He didn't have a car, and she did, but I think we both know how sneaky Cody can be. Then again, Bea's gone back to her friends now. Cody's on his own."

"Serves him right, don't you think?"

"Probably."

I remembered the way Cody acted at the vigil with Bea. I remembered the horrible things he said to her just an hour ago, and I reminded myself how long he'd lied to his family about everything. Even then, I felt sorry for him. I once thought Cody would drift away thanks to his fame, but without even a taste of success, he still broke apart from his family, friends, and reality. It was a different means to the same end. I felt that in a few years—unless I made some drastic changes—I could end up just like him: Washed-up, broke, and trapped in a web of my own lies.

I picked up the *FOOD* sign and adjusted my hat. Before I could head outside, Ryan gently set Eliza's phone on the counter between us. My shoulders tensed.

"Should we have that out in public?"

"Rain, there's no one here. Mrs. Roakes is in the kitchen. And I think I might have a new idea." Ryan pushed her palms down onto the counter and lifted herself an inch off the ground. She floated there for a second, smiling knowingly over the cell phone.

"Okay, what's the idea?"

"So, it's a fancy smartphone, see?" She tapped the screen, and the closed-lock icon presented itself over Eliza's cat. "There's a six-digit passcode."

"You want to guess it? We have no information. We'll just get locked-out."

"I know. I think Bea already tried that because the phone was locked-out when she gave it to me earlier. We can't guess Eliza's passcode, or at least not yet. But the passcode is the phone's backup security. There's another way in."

"Fingerprint scan?"

"Nope. This is the newer model. *Face scan.*"

My stomach lurched.

"No, that's a horrible idea! You want to go to Eliza's funeral, and just wave the phone over her open casket? If there even *is* an open casket? You didn't even go to her vigil!"

"That was before I knew we had the phone! And I wouldn't do that at her *funeral*. This whole thing is about finding justice for Eliza—but also about proving us innocent. We can't risk someone seeing us with the phone. We can't risk waiting while Lars is on the loose, either. We have to do something, otherwise this whole situation might fly even further off the rails."

"So, what's your idea, then?"

Ryan pulled out her own smartphone, then unlocked it to show me a map of Warley Island and the mainland county nearby. I traced out the bridge, Warley Avenue, and the other familiar places on the island. A red pin on Ryan's map marked an inconspicuous spot a few miles inland from us. I couldn't place it in my memory. Ryan zoomed the map in to reveal the title over the red pin: *Williams Mortuary and Crematory.*

Not for the first or last time, I wondered if Ryan might belong on my suspect list after all.

"Are you crazy? What's your plan? We just walk right in and ask to see the body?"

"No!" Ryan scoffed, putting away her phone and Eliza's. "I've looked at the satellite imagery of the building. There's a side door, and I know how to pick locks. There shouldn't be much security, since it's just a family-owned business. We go in, find Eliza, unlock the phone, and get out. No one will ever know."

I couldn't believe how easily Ryan explained such a daunting and dangerous scheme. I couldn't think of a valid response; she seemed completely certain that this was the only way to investigate further. Maybe she was right about that, but she wasn't right about everything.

"I can't tell you one more reason this is a bad idea: If we went to that mortuary, we'd be disappointed. Eliza won't be there."

"Why not? It's the only mortuary within thirty miles. There's nowhere else for—"

"Not a mortuary," I insisted. "Mortuaries don't perform autopsies. What's today… Wednesday? Four days after they found her, they'll be doing an autopsy soon if they haven't already. We'll find Eliza's body at the county medical examiner's office."

Ryan glared at me in the same way I'd glared at her moments ago. Suddenly, I became the crazy one: The one who seemed to know too much, who had a dark and twisted master plan.

"Alright, thanks for the tip. But I have to ask, how did you know that?"

"Oh, um… My dad, you know?"

"I thought you never read his books?"

"I didn't. What I meant was that because of what happened to him, they had to—"

"Right. Sorry. God, I'm stupid. Forget I said any-thing."

"It's okay."

Under the scorching sun in front of Ritz's Burgers and Fries, while I spun the *FOOD* sign and watched beachgoers cross the island's busiest intersection, I thought only about how to break into a morgue. That's not the best brain fuel at ten in the morning, but I found it hard to think about anything else. So much could be decided by the success or failure of this plan. We could discover some critical evidence to incriminate Lars, or we could fail completely, and all be arrested.

When Ryan and I found Eliza's body on the beach, I wanted to just walk away. I didn't even want to call the police. Ryan slapped sense back into me. Now, only four days later, I wanted to dive as deep into the mystery as possible. In just four days, I'd seen so much: The vigil at Eliza's house, the cell phone Cody found, Lars at the museum, and then his escape dur-ing the police raid. Stepping away felt impossible; I could only throw myself deeper into the puzzle of Eliza's death.

What's more, I knew time was running out. Eve-rything began with Cody's party, and most of the guests came because of beach week. All those gradu-ated seniors would be gone in a few more days, back to their hometowns anywhere across the country. If one of them—some anonymous grad, another face at the party—had something to do with Eliza, they'd be gone soon. In a couple days, they'd get away with it. If unlocking Eliza's phone was our only possible move in this bizarre chess game, we couldn't just pass our turn.

Shortly before the start of my lunch break, a gray sedan screamed over the bridge, past me, and into the Ritz's parking lot. The frantic driver parked, jumped out, and scrambled into the restaurant. Although I didn't recognize the car at first, I knew the driver instantly.

Cody.

"Hey!" I shouted, but he was already inside. Carrying my sign, I followed him into the restaurant to find Ryan equally shocked.

"Whoa, what happened? Whose car is that?"

Cody sunk into a chair by the window. A few our lunch-rush customers glared at him, and so did we. His hair stuck flat to his head with sweat, and his patchy beard skewed to one side. Cody pointed to the car.

"It's my mom's."

"Why do you have it?"

"She chased me down. I hid in a gas station. When she got out of the car to beat my ass, I left through the back door and stole her car." He paused. We took a second to process. "Hey, why do you two do that? You always give each other that 'you're-thinking-what-I'm-thinking' look. What's that about? I'm right here; talk to me!"

Ryan began quietly, hoping not to alert the curious customers around us, "The police are looking for you. Your mom is looking for you. You stole a car. And now you're here, in public, where Chief Fitz could just walk in and arrest you. Why? What do you want from us?"

"Food," he breathed. "I'm starving."

An idea struck me: Something so obvious that it felt stupid. I raised my hand to alert Ryan.

"Can I talk to you for a sec?"

"Yeah Rain, let me just—"

I stepped behind the counter with her. Cody tapped his foot anxiously. Before I could explain my master plan, I let loose a few deal-breaker questions.

"Can you take your lunch break now? With me?"

"Well, I guess. But Mrs. Roakes won't like—"

"Great. Can you just throw some cheap stuff into a to-go order?"

"Rain… Okay, I see what you're thinking. I like this. Mrs. Welling's car, our uniforms… This could actually work."

Ryan dove into the kitchen. After a minute of muffled bickering with Mrs. Roakes, she returned with two white to-go bags and slid them across the counter to me. I opened the map application on my phone and plotted out our course—a twenty-minute drive inland. At my request, Cody started up his mom's sedan, but I didn't tell him about our destination. Even he might have flipped out. Ryan and I buckled in with our forged to-go order; Mrs. Welling's car became the unofficial delivery vehicle for Ritz's Burgers and Fries.

"The Ritz does delivery?" Cody mused while he reached for one of the bags. Ryan opened it to grant him a fistful of fries.

"Today only, we deliver. You just drive."

The bridge carried us off the island, but not out of trouble. My phone led us down a mainland street through miles of sandy coniferous forests. Unlike the island, the houses here appeared one by one. Each grew more moss on its roof, and each looked less and less welcoming.

"Where is this place?" Cody wondered aloud, but we bit our tongues. "You two are supposed to be the chatty ones. Should I be worried?"

"Just turn at the next light," I reminded him.

Minutes later, we approached a wide eggshell-colored building. I don't know what I expected—maybe a bright red sign saying "morgue" in sans-serif text—but the facility could have been a small home if not for its small lot with two handicapped parking spaces. My phone buzzed to affirm our arrival. Cody pulled into one of the available spaces, which put us next to the only two other vehicles: An unmarked white SUV and county police cruiser. Cody bristled.

"My turn to have an idea! We leave. Like, now?"

Ryan and I stepped out of the sedan with our white to-go bags and matching RBF shirts.

"Wait here," Ryan told Cody. "Seriously, don't leave without us."

"Or what, you'll call the cops? News flash: They're already here! What even is this place?"

"County morgue."

"What the—"

Ryan and I pulled open the building's tinted glass door and strolled inside. I tried to act bored, like a real food delivery guy, but my eyes darted around the room. A leafy plant, dark blue carpet, and two ripped chairs adorned the uncomfortably small waiting area. I supposed that the office of a medical examiner wouldn't often accommodate many *living* visitors.

A window on the back wall showed us an abandoned desk, complete with a bell marked *"Ring for assistance."* I took an extra moment to breathe.

"Ready to go in?"

"Quit stalling, bud."

I rang the bell. The tinny chime echoed briefly. I rang it again, then one more time. I wondered if maybe the staff left for *their* lunch break, too. If so, shouldn't they have put up a sign?

The door to the room behind the window eased open. A uniformed police officer leaned in to survey us.

"Can I help you two?"

"Delivery for… Doc?" Ryan pointed to the receipt on her bag. "Just says Doc, at this address."

The officer did not seem impressed, but he met us at the window for a closer look. The receipt was authentic, except that Ryan placed the order herself.

"RBF, that what I think it is?"

"No," I explained. "Ritz's Burgers and Fries." The officer nodded.

"Damn, I could go for a good burger about now. You said that's for Doctor M? Let's see here…" He searched the desk for notes, papers, or something important. "Receptionist went out for lunch. I'm trying to find the little buzzer thing, so I can call him out. Sorry about this, I'm only here a couple times a month. Uh… Here we go!"

The officer finally clicked a button on the desk. A door on the left side of the room swung open. He sighed.

"Dammit, wrong one. I was trying to get… Ah, you know what? He's right back there. You, go and bring those bags to the second door, right after the window. You, stay back here. What's your name?"

"Ryan." She handed me the second bag of food. Underneath it, the cold glass of Eliza's phone slid into my palm. I had no choice but to go in without her, like the officer asked. She wished me good luck with her eyes, or maybe it was more of a "please don't screw up." Either way, the hallway door began to close itself, so I rushed through while the officer carried on:

"Ryan? Funny, I always hear that as a boy's name. But my name's Leslie, so I get the same crap all the time…"

The door clicked shut, leaving me in a silent hallway. A week earlier, at the same time of day, I sat with Carson in my school's cafeteria, scrolling through Instagram. Now, a week later, I stood alone in the secured hallway of a Carolina morgue with two bags of greasy food, a dead girl's cell phone, and absolutely no one to guide me forward.

Second door on the right, I reminded myself. *After the window.*

One foot at a time, I inched down the smooth linoleum floor. The first door was unmarked, but I tried it anyway. Locked. The window after that first door showed me nothing; a wall of closed blinds let out only a few beams of light from the room within. After the window, I read the placard on the second door:

"Examination Room."

I wished Ryan could have knocked for me. Her hands wouldn't have shaken like mine. When we found Eliza, she kept her cool, and I willed myself to calm down like her. Nothing changed. I cradled the bags and phone with one arm, then raised one fist to tap twice on the door.

"Autopsy in progress," a voice called out. *Shit.*

"Food delivery for… Doctor M?"

The door sprung open without delay. A man dressed in white, roughly my height, held a bowl of soup in one hand. He wore scrubs from head to toe.

"Well, I am Dr. Moridi, but I didn't order any delivery. Did Candy let you back here?"

"No, an officer did. I have your receipt here." I pulled the slip off the bag, and he set down his soup bowl to examine it.

"I was kidding, before, about the autopsy. I say that to keep people out during my lunch. Which I already have! See, soup? And by the smell of those bags… not Halal, I'm afraid."

"Halal?" I took the receipt back from Dr. Moridi.

"Never mind. I didn't order this! Maybe there was a mistake?" He tried to shut the door, but I stood close enough to stop him. I felt my opportunity slipping away, so I dug in as firmly as possible.

"I'm sorry, I don't know. I'm new to the job. We drove awhile to get this delivery to you. My coworker, Ryan, she's out in the lobby. You could ask her about sending it all back, maybe."

The doctor scratched his head.

"Alright, fine. Wait right here."

Dr. Moridi weaved around me and jogged toward the lobby at the end of the hall. I held the examination room door open with just the toe of my shoe. If the doctor looked back at me, even for a second, everything could fall apart.

He didn't look. He vanished out into the lobby, suspecting nothing.

Ryan, you better stall like hell.

I flung open the door and dumped the grease-soaked bags near the doctor's soup. The exam room was bigger than the lobby by a factor of five. A pair of metal tables, each stacked with metal instruments and plastic bins, stood at opposite ends of the long room. Another similar table at the center of the room glowed under the rays of two bright lamps above. To my relief, the table was empty. I turned my attention to one of the room's longer walls, fitted with a dozen square metal doors.

Coolers.

I shivered, but not because of the cold air in the room. The doors had no labels, so I had no choice but to try them all, starting at the upper left. Perhaps there was some chart or paper that could have helped me, but I couldn't rely on Ryan to stall forever.

Empty. Empty again.

When I opened the third door, I recoiled at a pair of bare feet inside. I stood high enough above that I couldn't see more, but I didn't need to; the feet were too big. A man's body.

Another, empty. Empty. Empty too.

The sixth door was closer to my eye level. Instead of seeing only feet, I saw all the way up the nude corpse of a woman—still not Eliza. Until that moment, a part of me forgot that corpses don't wear clothes. When I found Eliza—if I found Eliza—she would be completely naked in one of the cooler drawers.

There's not time to think about that. It doesn't matter.

I opened the seventh door. I saw her, but I didn't really see her. A part of me closed my eyes, so I can't say exactly what I saw in the seventh cooler. I grabbed the drawer handle and pulled Eliza into the open air of the examination room. I think I remember stitches, somewhere around her neck. Her autopsy was over. Eliza had already told her story to Dr. Moridi, and he'd tell the same story to Chief Fitz, but Eliza had one last story to tell me. I was the last step in her autopsy. I would be the last person to uncover her secrets.

I searched my pockets for Eliza's phone. It was gone. *Shit!* I ran back to the counter with the soup and bags of food. Under one bag, I found the phone and rushed it back to Eliza. I held it over her, facing down, and tapped the screen. The image of her cat appeared, and the phone buzzed.

Locked.

I hissed. The bag left grease all over the phone's screen and camera. I grabbed the waist of my shirt and rubbed the greasy phone across it. With every swipe of my shirt, I knew the doctor came closer to returning. I held the phone up again, closer to her face this time. Another buzz.

Locked.

One attempt left before another lockout. I couldn't imagine why it didn't work. We knew the phone belonged to Eliza. We knew her face. I held it close enough. There was no more grease on the camera. I put the phone down and looked at Eliza's face one more time. It was the same face I saw when I met her at the party.

With just one exception.

Using two fingers, as carefully as I could, I pulled up Eliza's eyelids to reveal her watery blue irises. I held up the phone one more time.

Unlocked.

I stared at the screen in disbelief, letting Eliza's eyes close for the last time. I opened the phone to its home screen, then launched the *Settings* application to stop the phone from locking itself again. With that taken care of, I pushed Eliza's drawer back into the cooler and shut the door. Taking the two food bags, I dove out of the examination room and finally let the door close.

A second later, Dr. Moridi stepped into the hallway from the lobby.

"C'mon out here," he motioned. "Officer Jackson bought your food."

With my heart pounding at a thousand miles per hour, I entered the lobby and offered the bags to the officer. He had joined Ryan and Moridi on the outside of the front desk window. I wanted to scream, cry, or maybe jump for joy. I wanted to tell Ryan that we'd done it, we could leave and be done with the morgue, but I couldn't even smile. All I could do was sweat and hand Officer Jackson his food.

"Still warm. Perfect."

"You look pale," Moridi noted, pointing to me. "Never been around an ME's office before?"

"I'm always pale," I choked out. "Comes with the red hair." Ryan saw me drowning and dove underwater to save me.

"Alright, well it's been great talking with *y'all*. Leslie, I hope your daughter manages to keep her scholarship. USC is a great school. And Dr. Moridi, you go enjoy that soup. Rain and I have to get back to work."

"His name is Rain?" The officer asked, but I led Ryan outside before I could introduce myself properly. Ryan pushed me toward the car, and I fell into the backseat like a sack of potatoes. Ryan took the passenger seat.

"Geez, you guys took forever!" Cody whined, then started the engine.

"Rain?" Ryan reached back to me. She poked my cold cheek, and I flinched. "Did you get it? Did it work?"

I pulled Eliza's phone from my pocket, almost expecting it to be locked again. That would have matched our luck: Finding a body, accidentally stealing a victim's phone, and getting caught in the middle of a police raid. I couldn't look at the screen; I let Ryan discover whether our luck had finally changed. I pointed the phone in her direction, and a smile peeled her lips apart.

"Cody, get us out of here. Lunch break is almost over. Rain, you go have a look at that phone first. I think you've earned it."

Sprawled out in the back seat of Mrs. Welling's car, I began my search.

In the meantime, Cody carted us back to Warley Island. This time, when we crossed the tall bridge into the fray of the party-trashed beach town, I knew the risks. I knew exactly how dangerous paradise could be. Nonetheless, I knew I could survive all of that—with a little help.

As we rode over the bridge, a swath of gray clouds rolled out toward the ocean. A few heavy water droplets fell on the sedan's windshield. Cody started up the wipers. Ryan peered into the sky outside her window.

"Looks like the fringes of that storm coming in. We could use some rain, right Rain?"

"Island Rain," I laughed. "That sounds like the title of a book."

"You gonna write it?"

"Hell no."

11: THE SUSPECT

I don't know what I expected, but diving into the gigabytes of information on Eliza's phone made me dizzy. Until I actually saw the thousands of texts, photos, emails, posts, and notes, I never fully grasped that Eliza had lived a life as rich and complex as any of ours. Reading and understanding all of that information would take years. At best, I had four more days until the end of senior week. At worst, I had a couple hours before accidentally locking the phone again—forever.

Cody delivered Ryan and I back to work, but at our request, he spent the rest of the day at the beach. We didn't want to risk the extra attention he always drew from the police, Mrs. Roakes, his mom, or even the random customers at Ritz's. Besides, Cody liked the beach. I wondered if he'd enjoy it as much without Bea there with him.

"Found anything yet?" Ryan asked after checking the clock on her phone. We made it back from our "lunch break" with minutes to spare. I couldn't pull my eyes away from Eliza's phone screen. "You look like a zombie, Rain."

"Hm? Oh, yeah. There's a lot here. I don't even know where to start."

"Start at Saturday night. What was she doing? Where did she go? Who did she talk to?"

"Well, the recent texts are from group messages. A bunch of her friends, all pretty upset. It's… Tough to read. And I'm having trouble finding messages that Eliza has sent, not just received since she died."

Ryan took over for Mrs. Roakes at the register, so she stopped listening to me. There were too many customers waiting to order. I carefully pocketed the unlocked phone and brought my *FOOD* sign and hat back out to the rain-dotted sidewalk. Instead of spinning it, waving it, or holding it over my head to keep my hair dry, I held it steady under one arm and returned to Eliza's phone.

Even as I held the phone, a few friends and relatives sent new messages that floated to the top of Eliza's inbox. They weren't meant to be read, and certainly not by me. Most of the messages sounded like the notes left by visitors at the vigil. People wrote about their fond memories of times spent with Eliza, and about how much they missed her. I read these messages and wondered if they helped people to grieve. Looking back, I couldn't remember writing any notes like those for my dad.

A few minutes into reading the newer messages, I felt chills—even under the midday Carolina sun. My face turned hot, so I knew something was wrong. A terrible thought dawned on me:

Read receipts.

I clicked and swiped my way into the *Settings* app as quickly as possible, but I was too late. In my rush to find information, I'd already sent read receipts to eight grieving strangers. If any one of them looked back at their message thread, they'd know that *someone* had seen their message.

One slip-up was enough for me. I began a search for any of the phone's security settings that might tie the device back to me, Ryan, or any of us. Phone tracking stood out to me as the elephant in the room, but thankfully, Eliza had never finished setting it up properly. That explained why the authorities never came looking for Eliza's phone while Bea carried it.

Next, I set the phone airplane mode. I didn't need any more buzzing, texts, Snapchats, group messages, or social media updates. Plus, I couldn't risk sending out any more read receipts, whether in texts or in any other application. I needed become Eliza's ghost: An invisible observer, seeing every clue above and below.

Deeper in Eliza's messages, I found a thread from Saturday night. As far as I could tell, those were the last texts that she sent. I began reading at the top; there weren't many messages.

Hey, you still at the party? Eliza began the thread.

Checked out early. Why? The other person had no contact name, just a phone number.

Need to talk.

We talked already. I told you, I'm done with last summer.

Next, Eliza sent a picture: A dark blue surface, which looked like hard plastic. In the center of the frame, a partially removed sticker spread its papery tendrils out from one corner, where the last hint of a yellow sticker remained. It didn't mean much to me. There weren't any words in the photo, and Eliza didn't bother captioning her text. Whatever she meant to show with the picture, the other person understood.

Delete this, they replied.

Thought you were done? I could hear the harshness of Eliza's voice in that one message. The other person didn't respond, so she ended the thread with one final text:

Meet me at the tower.

I almost fell over, and not because of the hot air outside. Eliza wasn't alone at the tower; her last message confirmed that. She never named the mysterious contact in her phone, but I already knew who owned that phone number. I could feel myself reaching the end of the puzzle. Everything came full-circle, and with Eliza's last text, I had more than enough evidence to confirm my theory about her killer.

Lars.

Only one step remained, and it was easy. Soon I could tell Ryan what I found, and we could send an anonymous tip to the police. Chief Fitz would find Lars and lock him up, then Ryan, Carson, Cody, Bea, AJ, and I would never hear about the case again. All I had to do was confirm Lars' phone number.

I took out my phone, copied the ten digits with my own keyboard, and dialed.

First ring. My heart raced.

Second ring. What would I say? Nothing? Just hear his voice and hang up?

Third ring. Would he look up my number? Could Lars find us? Would he—

"Hey," a male voice picked up. "It's AJ."

I don't know how long I waited to talk. It felt like hours. All around me, the puzzle expanded. All the clues changed. Pieces that once fit together flung apart and tumbled into the air like popcorn. Whatever I thought I knew about Eliza, Lars, and Saturday night vanished. Instead, I returned to square one. I knew nothing. I was finding Eliza's body all over again. Only this time, my suspect list gained a new name: AJ.

"Anyone there? I gotta get back to work."

I didn't have time to think everything over. One way or another, I needed to act. AJ wouldn't wait on the line for ever, and soon he'd get worried. Could I hang up? Hell no. He'd figure out my number, thanks to Carson. I had to speak. I had to hold a conversation, just like normal, and pretend everything was okay.

"Hey. It's… Rain."

"Oh, Rain! How's it going, man?"

"It's good. You?"

"Yeah, all good here," he trailed off. "So… What's going on?"

"Oh, right, yeah. Um, Ryan gave me your number. I just wanted to ask…"

"…About?"

"Oh, Thursday! The, uh, metal detecting trip? Are you still doing that?"

"Hundred percent, yeah. Plan is to start up by Carson's place after work, then make our way down the beach. Ryan's gonna pick us up in the Winnebago near the inlet once we're finished. Sound good to you?"

"Sure."

"Sweet. See you later, Rain. Say hi to Ryan for me."

"Will do."

Click.

I dropped my sign and rushed past the outdoor tables and open umbrellas. I wrenched open the front door of Ritz's, ready to announce my emergency to Ryan. But as soon as I found myself standing face-to-face with her, I couldn't say a word. I couldn't tell Ryan that her boyfriend might be a suspect. I couldn't show her the messages he sent to Eliza. Ryan kept her emotions out of our investigations, but how could she do that after knowing what I knew?

"Rain? You good?" She laughed at me with wide eyes. I must've looked ridiculous, running inside the restaurant just to freeze like a statue.

"AJ says hi," I muttered, and that was all.

*
**

I remember years ago, when my dad published his third book. It wrapped up his first trilogy, *The Dugrave Series*, and generated national buzz. For the third time, H.M. Eldridge climbed the bestseller lists. For the third time, news outlets fought for an interview with my dad, and they paid big money for his time—or so I've heard.

This madness unfolded in the summer after I finished third grade. Back then, I knew almost nothing about the wild world of media, publishing, and fan culture. I spent more time worrying about which Silly Bandz to collect than about how many boxed collector's sets of *The Dugrave Series* sold every week. Nonetheless, as the son of America's favorite new author, I inevitably fell into the spotlight.

That summer, my dad spent weeks at a time travelling on his book tour. His first book tour happened while I was too young to come along, and the second one happened at a season when I was still in school. The third book tour gave me—and also my mom—an opportunity to leave the house and come along.

Again, as a rising fourth grader, I barely understood what a book tour entailed. I wouldn't have enjoyed the crowds, the noise, or the question-answer sessions about my dad's imaginary friends. I just heard the frequent murmurs about "New York" or "San Francisco," so my excitement came only from curiosity. But I still felt the sting of disappointment when my dad shook his head and insisted that he travel alone—again.

If that upset my mom, she never spoke up.

In late June, my dad packed up his bags and loaded crates of autographed books into a trailer. He rented a trailer for every book tour after the first one; the libraries and bookstores never had enough copies for each town's Eldridge fans. Each tour, the trailer grew larger, putting more strain on our aging SUV.

I sat on our house's front porch waiting for my dad to finish loading up the trailer. Carson rode his bike up our driveway to stop by. He pointed to the trailer.

"What's that for?" I did my best to explain.

"My dad's leaving to go sell books everywhere."

"Even in Hawaii?"

"I think so."

Carson joined me on the porch. He didn't ask why I looked so glum, but I told him anyway.

"I want to go sell books too, but he said I have to stay here."

"Why?"

"I don't know. It's stupid."

"I wanna sell books too."

Carson and I wandered down to the street and looked inside the trailer. The crates of books almost reached the ceiling. I wondered how long it took my dad to sign all of them. While my dad fetched the last few crates inside the house, my tiny brain coughed up a neat little idea.

"C'mon!" I shouted. I pulled myself up and into the open trailer bay.

"What? You'll get in trouble!"

"We'll hide in here and go with him when he leaves!"

"Me too?"

"Of course!" I grabbed Carson's hand and pulled him up into the trailer with me. "We just have to be quiet. Shh! He's coming back."

I led Carson closer to the front of the trailer, behind a stack of book crates. Sure enough, a minute or two later, my dad piled on the last two crates of autographed copies. With them safely inside, he closed the door, which clattered downward and clanged shut at the back of the trailer. The key rattled for a few seconds while he locked up the trailer, then we waited for the rumbling of the car's engine starting.

We waited for a while. I never anticipated how dark the trailer would be with the door closed. Back then, neither of us had phone flashlights ready in our pockets. Our game of hide-and-seek played on, but the trailer never moved. Carson turned impatient.

"Is he going?"

"Soon."

"Are you sure? I have to pee."

"Just stay quiet. We'll all leave soon."

Little did I know; my dad had planned to leave the next day. He just loaded the trailer in advance.

Hour by hour, the darkness closed in on us, and the stale air became hotter. The stacks of crates left little room for the two of us, not to mention for breathable air. Either by heat, boredom, or oxygen deprivation, Carson and I passed out inside the trailer. I nearly died while literally surrounded by my father's success.

Within an hour of the door locking, my mom started searching for me. Carson's parents did nothing; they assumed he arrived safely at my house to hang out. My parents turned our whole house upside down. Finding Carson's bike in the driveway, they called up the Wellings, who drove to our house and joined the search. In the early evening, my dad finally unlocked the trailer, and a roaring rush of cool air woke us up. Carson and I had each wet our pants by then, but we made it out alive.

My dad went on the book tour without me, as planned. He threw out dozens of autographed books that smelled like urine.

Year after year, Carson and I hung out at my house whenever my dad left for business. Elementary school turned to middle, and middle to high. Our cross-country book-selling road trip never came to fruition. We never spoke of the dreaded book trailer incident, but we both remembered.

Years later, our real road trip—to Warley Island— somehow turned out even worse.

For the first time since our arrival in Warley, Carson and I found ourselves alone at *All's Well* after work. Even stranger, the house was both clean and quiet. With Bea gone, Cody hiding out on a rainy beach, Mrs. Welling stranded at a far-off gas station, and Ryan with AJ, the house felt dark—perhaps because of the gray clouds outside, too. We could hear the clicking of raindrops on the back porch behind the living room. No one came bursting through the front door, no one fought for the TV remote, and no one made a mess in the kitchen. For the first time, Warley Island almost met my initial expectations.

Carson took a seat at the puzzle table, and I joined him after leaving Eliza's phone to charge in my room. I couldn't tell Ryan or Cody about my discovery regarding AJ, but I thought that I might be able to tell Carson. We trusted each other all through high school, anyway, and I owed him for letting me borrow clothes for the vigil. Unfortunately for me, Carson struck up a conversation almost immediately while we scavenged for puzzle pieces of blue sky.

"You know what I learned today at Ron's? Boogie boards have to be propped up nose-down because the tail damages more on the ground. I've been doing it wrong for years! Can you believe that?"

"Which one is the boogie board again?" I knew what he meant, but I knew that playing dumb could force him to give up teaching me. He shook his head like a disappointed father.

"Ah, young Rain. So much to learn."

"I'm three months older than you. Have you found the piece of cloud from that corner up there?"

"Not yet. Anyways, how's the Ritz?" He handed me a perfect opportunity to break the news. I seized it—and the missing cloud piece, across the table.

"Well actually, today was kinda crazy. Cody showed up, and he helped me and Ryan unlock Eliza's phone."

Carson laughed out loud. "Wait, Cody? First of all, didn't our mom catch him? And how the hell did he manage to unlock that phone?"

"Oh, he didn't do it himself. He just drove us. In your mom's car, which he kinda stole."

"That doesn't sound like real life, but please keep talking."

A bit thrown off, I waited and tried to shove together a few blue pieces. They all looked the same, but none of them fit together.

"Ugh! First of all, this is top secret. Okay?"

"Yeah, I won't tell. So, what happened?" Carson grabbed a piece that I'd tried, then fit it smoothly between three others.

"We went to a morgue. I mean, Cody drove us. We faked a food delivery. I went to the examination room while Ryan distracted people. I found Eliza. I had to hold her eyes open, but her face unlocked the phone. Then I spent some time at work just reading everything, especially her texts. I found something that... Hey, you good?"

Carson stood up from the table, wide-eyed, just to stare at the carpet and grip his chair with both hands. I could hardly blame him. I could barely believe my own story.

"Are you insane?" He wheezed. "You used her *face*? In a *morgue*? This is some next-level shit, Rain. You could go to jail! Do you think you're Tom Cruise or something?"

"It worked though! We got the—"

"Why didn't you invite me?"

The house fell silent again. Of all the reasons for Carson to be upset, I never guessed he'd feel left-out. Regardless of the stolen car, frozen corpses, and fake deliveries, Carson still wanted to stay involved. Looking back on my lunch break, I had no good reason for not inviting him. We had plenty of room in the car. I wanted to explain why I never texted him during the day, but I couldn't even explain that to myself. Carson just sat back down at the table, looking for more pieces.

"Yellow corner, blue top. Some tan near the yellow. Seen that one?"

"No."

"Okay, like, I know I jumped off Lars' dock when the police came. I know I'm not fast. I know I can't just *solve* things like you and Ryan do. To be honest, I do know I'm a little obnoxious sometimes. I know I'm probably not gonna be a hero or whatever, but I want the chance to try. We survived high school together, and if there's any way to survive this week without being arrested, killed, or scarred for life, that way is together. Plus, like… I invited you here. Technically, I think I can kick you out."

I smiled. He was right. I reached one hand over the table to point out a yellow, tan, and blue puzzle piece. Carson snatched it up.

"You're right," I nodded. "I'm sorry I didn't tell you about our plan earlier. I will next time, I promise.

Starting now, actually. What I was gonna say before… I found something in Eliza's phone that I think you should know about."

"What is it, her nudes?"

"Carson!"

"Kidding! Go on."

"Wait here. It's probably better if I show you."

I left the table and rushed to my room. To my relief, once again, the phone remained unlocked. Even better, the battery icon showed a full charge. I unplugged the phone and brought it out to the puzzle table, then opened the *Messages* app to show Carson. He read all eight texts once, and he read them again. He tapped on the photo Eliza sent to get a closer look. I saw nothing more than the first time.

"I called this phone number. The one she texted. Do you know who it is?"

"Well, maybe."

"Whoa, what? Who? How do you know?"

"The picture. Look closer."

Carson zoomed in on the picture again. The scraped-off sticker looked no different. The blue surface behind it still resembled nothing specific.

"There," Carson pointed. "The sticker has a little bit of yellow at the corner."

"What does that mean? I thought you were no good at 'solving' things?"

"Well, yeah, but I see that sticker all the time. That's a Ron's Surf Shop sticker. We sell tons of them. See? This is why you need me! I know stickers. And whoever Eliza sent this to, they know that sticker too. Which means they probably work at Ron's. So… Either Ron or AJ. And Ron doesn't like texting. So, it's gotta be AJ. But that makes no sense."

"But it's true. I called the number, and it was AJ. Even if he didn't meet her at the tower, he knew where Eliza went after the party. And he didn't tell any of us."

"But Rain, c'mon. I know AJ pretty well now. He's not perfect, but he's also not a murderer. Like, he sells pot, but he's not like a *drug dealer*, you know? He doesn't have a gun or anything. AJ is a chill guy. You've seen how he is."

I read the texts again on Eliza's phone. I could barely hear AJ's voice in his few brief messages. There wasn't enough there to build a case against him. The mention of the tower sounded significant, but from only eight texts, I couldn't understand his connection to Eliza. *Why aren't there more messages?* I thought to myself. *Where is the rest of it?*

Scrolling to the top of the short thread, I glimpsed the next piece of the puzzle—not on the table, but in the phone.

"Look," I spun the phone around to Carson. "Why is this the first message?"

"'Hey, you still at the party?' Sounds like a good way to start a conversation."

"Not just any conversation. This is the absolute first text between them! You see what I mean? They know each other, clearly. So why haven't they texted before?"

"Maybe they used Snapchat?"

"Maybe. Or?"

"Or what? I'm not Ryan! Just tell me the damn thing already!"

"Right there, AJ told Eliza to delete the photo of the sticker. What if he's asked her to do that before? What if he asked Eliza to delete their older messages? To hide something?"

Carson took the phone and scrolled up again. Still nothing new. His other hand wandered over the table and linked together another piece of the jigsaw's blue sky. He shook his head at the phone.

"That… That *kinda* makes sense. But what would AJ be hiding?"

"I don't know. You said he sells drugs, right?"

"Yeah, but everyone knows that already."

I flashed back to our encounter with Chief Fitz, when she searched the house. Before we let her inside, AJ flushed something down the toilet. Then when Fitz introduced herself, she looked at AJ to say, "Long time, no see." Carson had a good point: If Fitz already knew about AJ's side business, so did Ryan, Cody, and everyone else.

"I don't know," I admitted.

"You didn't tell Ryan about this, did you?"

"Not yet."

"Well, don't. This shit could stir up some serious drama. Let's just keep it between us until we know more. Top-level secret. You know, like the trailer full of books?"

"Don't even go there."

12: THE BEACH

I set no alarm for Thursday morning. Carson drove to work without me. I knew that missing a day of my new job might have consequences, but how could I spend all day keeping such a major secret from Ryan? One way or another, she would rip the truth out of me. Even worse, I didn't know what Eliza's texts really meant. I could only guess how Ryan would interpret them. Rather than risk the fallout that Carson predicted, I slept past ten and missed my shift.

A different sort of alarm woke me up anyway. My phone buzzed against the glass surface of the nightstand near my bed. In the quiet room, that simple buzz echoed like a chainsaw engine. I flipped over and grabbed my phone to shut it off.

Phone Call: Mom.

I groaned and sat upright, then cleared my throat before answering.

"Hey, mom. Sorry I didn't call yesterday." *I was busy breaking into a morgue.*

"Well, good morning. How are you? Busy at work now?"

"Yeah." *No.*

"Okay, I won't keep you long, but Mrs. Welling called me last night from a hotel. She said Cody took her car? And something with the police? Do you know what's going on?"

"Oh, right. Um…" *The police are after Cody because someone died after his party.* "The neighbors had a party, and I think the police wrote our address by mistake, so they called her. But I thought Cody was in Tennessee?"

"So did I! I don't know what's going on; I'll try calling her again later."

"Can I go now?" *I'm busy hiding from work.*

"Alright. Call me later, okay?"

"Okay, bye." *No thanks.*

"Bye."

I ended the call. My phone screen glowed with the time, date, and a reminder: *"Treasure hunt later today."* A huge clump of puzzle pieces snapped into place in my head. *Captain Heron's treasure!* All at once, I knew what to do. I couldn't ask Ryan for help this time, but I already knew what she would do in my shoes. I could explain everything to Carson, but first I needed to get out of bed.

I opened the blinds once again. The morning sunlight didn't burn like usual. Instead, it rolled in with a softer white glow. Over the front porch, yesterday's gray clouds crawled out further across the ocean. The bugs and frogs in the nearby trees chirped more quietly than usual. The overnight rains had dulled them somehow. Luckily for the sake of my morning plans, those rains abated for the time being.

The first part of my new plan scared me, but it had to be done. I already saw everything I needed to see in Eliza's phone. I'd spent hours snooping through all of the phone's apps, but nothing looked as significant as her texts with AJ. No one else sent anything suspicious on the night of Cody's party. Friends, her mom, her dad, and dozens of people messaged her within days of her death, but I found no mention of Lars—not even on Facebook. I screenshotted the AJ texts, then dropped those screenshots and the photo of the sticker to my phone. I deleted the screenshots from Eliza's phone, reset her wallpaper from her cat to the sticker photo, then locked her phone for good.

Locking the phone took a lot of nerve. My finger waited gently on the button for a whole minute before I finished the job. I really wanted to keep the evidence open and available for later, but excluding Ryan and AJ meant I needed to protect the phone's contents. Otherwise, I'd sacrifice the safety of my plan—and perhaps my only chance to catch Eliza's killer.

After a quick breakfast of Cody's Captain Crunch, I changed clothes and threw on one of my two pairs of shoes. After my first trip to the beach on Sunday morning, that one pair held enough sand that I could never wear them anywhere else. I slid my phone into my right pocket and Eliza's phone into my left. I still needed her phone, even locked.

As I walked down the driveway toward the beach, Ryan texted me.

Hey, where are you?

Sick, I lied. *Can you let Mrs. Roakes know?*

Suuure. How's the phone? Find anything?

Maybe. Not sure yet.

Next, she sent me a link to an article from the Warley Gazette. Alarmed by the headline, I clicked it and opened the full webpage. I read while I walked.

Unnamed Suspect Flees Drug Bust

WARLEY ISLAND — On Tuesday night, Warley Island police raided the property of a local resident. According to WIPD Chief Marie Fitz, the officers found "...a significant supply of illegal substances." Fitz explained that her team acted on information from an anonymous tip. "We are dedicated to protecting the safety of everyone on this island," she went on.

"Threats like this one can often be mitigated by local authorities. If you see something, say something."

During the raid, the property owner fled the scene by boat. Although the man is a suspect on drug possession charges, police have refused to name him or show his face to the public. This bizarre move opposes the department's history of transparency. However, when asked about the decision to conceal the suspect's identity, Chief Fitz answered: "The current decision to hide our suspect's face arrives from our need to protect this delicate investigation. We expect to have our suspect in custody soon, and there is no immediate danger to the public."

Warley Island has a history of minor drug crimes, but the scale of this event stands out. A press release confirmed that the substances confiscated in Tuesday's raid included large volumes of prescription pills. Ron Fredericks, a long-time island resident and local business owner, voiced his concerns about this news.

"You might hear about this stuff further south, but never up here," Fredericks claimed. "Just thinking there might be some big drug operation here in Warley, that scares me."

This new investigation begins at a tense time for the island police department, which recently opened a separate investigation into the sudden death of

Eliza Murphy, a 19-year-old island resident. This week's pair of alarming events marks the start of Warley Island's busy summer season, which has historically shown higher crime rates.

Expect further coverage of these cases in coming days as more information becomes available.

"Pills?" I exclaimed out loud, not at anyone but myself. "They raided his house for drugs?" I could already imagine the smug look on Ryan's face. She called it from the start.

He could still be involved w/ Eliza's case, I texted her once I finished reading and cursing under my breath. *What if the police just don't know yet?*

If he's involved, they'd know by now. And if they knew, they'd say something.

Are you sure? They didn't even name him.

More proof that he's nobody to them. Just keep looking at the phone, and if you don't find anything, I'll take a look next.

Ryan could never take a look. Not anymore.

I pocketed my own phone before crossing the street to the public beach access path. For a second, I flashed back to Sunday. I imagined Ryan pushing past me again, ready to run on the beach at blistering speeds. I remembered how everything began that way. Everything started when I called out to Ryan, and we ran together. If she never led me so far south, would I have seen Eliza's body? If she ran alone, would she have glanced up at the tower to see a fluttering lock of blonde hair? Maybe if we never ran together on Sunday, no one would have found Eliza.

Maybe she'd still be out by the tower, four days later, waiting for someone to come along.

No one ran up behind me on the beach access path, but someone waved to me from the edge of the waves ahead. I knew that scraggly beard.

"Hey, Cody," I waved back and stepped down onto the sand.

"You not working today?"

"Not really. Needed a break."

"Yeah, with that Ryan chick, I get it. Bitches be crazy, right?"

I resisted the urge to groan—or maybe it was an urge to punch Cody in the jaw. Either way, I ground my teeth hard enough to mill flour. I thought we saved ourselves by banishing Cody to the beach, but I needed the beach, at least for a little while. Even though I tried to walk south and get away, Cody tagged along.

"Did my mom show up yet?"

"Apparently she's at a hotel somewhere."

"Really? She couldn't just get an Uber back to our house? I mean, I knew I'd slow her down by taking the car, but a hotel? That's just a little stupid, you know what I'm saying?"

I held my tongue and kept walking down the beach, but Cody stayed close behind. I sensed how lonely he felt, having nowhere safe to stay and no friends to keep him company. Then again, he brought that situation on himself. No one made him lie to his family, trash the house, or lash out at Bea. Cody walked his self-destructive path alone.

Not for the first time, I feared ending up like him. Where would I go without college? What job could I find without a degree? I couldn't force myself to write, so I could never earn a living like my dad. At the very least, Cody could play guitar, somewhat. Me, on the other hand… What did I have? How could I stop myself from becoming Cody Welling in another five years?

"Have you seen Bea?" Cody asked. He tried to sound nonchalant.

"Not since she left the house, no."

"She'll come around. She will."

I wondered whether Cody wanted to reassure me or himself.

Further down the beach, where the waterfront houses grew taller and squeezed closer together, a collection of chairs, towels, and umbrellas marked someone's sandy territory. Few people bothered to see the beach on such a cloudy morning, but some didn't care. As we approached, a few girls floated up and down the wood plank stairs between their rental house and their beach claim. Cody walked ahead of me, and soon I saw why.

"Hey," he called out. Each of the three girls sitting on the beach looked our way. One looked back down immediately: Bea.

Shit, I spoke in my head.

"How are you?" Cody asked her once we came closer. The other two girls scrutinized him.

"This the one?" asked one girl.

"Mm-hm." Bea answered without looking up from her phone. I thought about just walking away, if only to spare myself. Cody ignored their exchange— or maybe he didn't catch the subtext.

"What're you scrolling on?" Cody craned his neck to see her phone. "Is that Tinder?" Bea huffed and flipped the screen to show us.

"Pinterest, asshole. I'm learning how to make shell necklaces."

"Oh, cool. You gonna sell those back home?"

"Yes, actually. You know, I make jewelry? I polish and set stones for necklaces that I sell on my website?"

"You have a website?"

"Oh, right… You wouldn't know that, because you never *asked* me about it. The world revolves around Cody and his guitar, which he never plays unless someone's paying to hear it. Because you're just perfect, so everyone bows down? You just—"

One of the other girls nudged Bea to cut her off. Cody stepped back. I let out the breath I'd held by accident.

"That's your cue to get lost, hipster," said the one who nudged Bea.

"Thanks, Carmen," Bea lay back down to study more necklaces.

"I'm not a hipster," Cody muttered. He finally broke away to follow me down the beach, but not fast enough to dodge the sand Carmen kicked at him. Then he rushed away faster.

"You really know how to pick 'em, Bea," Carmen snickered once she thought we couldn't hear. The third girl chimed in too:

"You got with *him*? Wait, aren't you playing for the other team now?"

The splashing waves smothered whatever they said next. Now I pitied Bea far more than Cody; something about her friends bothered me. Maybe it was the way Carmen cut her off. Maybe it was what she told Carson, Ryan, and me during the kayak trip: Bea thought her friends hated her. Even at the party, she mentioned that they kicked her out. She wanted to key someone's car! Just days later, she sat with those same friends, like nothing ever went wrong. I couldn't stomach that. Carefully hiding my phone from Cody, I sent Bea a text.

Are you ok with your friends now?

She started typing, stopped, and then started again. Seeing her reply, my heart sank.

Better I'm with them than alone.

I carried on down the beach, now led by Cody, although I never told him where I was going. Maybe he knew, or maybe he didn't care whether I followed him or not. As ever, he kept trying to make conversation.

"You got a girlfriend, Rain?"

"No."

"Boyfriend?"

"No."

"Did you, like, date anyone in high school?"

"Nope."

"Damn. Never been rejected, then. Good for you."

I never told him about my burned-up college rejection letters, but I don't think he meant that sort of rejection anyway. The rest was true, though. I never dated anyone in high school. With those years over, I wondered if I made a mistake by staying single all that time. Did I miss some critical rite of passage? I witnessed Carson's intermittent series of short relationships. He always seemed to have more fun finding a date than having one. Maybe I lived vicariously through him? Maybe I just never took the time to meet someone new? Whatever the truth, high school slipped past, and I stayed single. Less than a week after graduation, those four years felt like ancient history.

I might've continued reflecting for the rest of the walk, but Cody kept trying to talk.

"So, no dates. Hookups, then? It's cool; I mean, I've been there, dude."

"No, I never did that. What's your interest in my love life?"

"I dunno. Just trying to understand, I guess. You don't talk about that shit too much, so I guess I wanna know what's going on in your head. Like, are you into Ryan? And don't worry, I won't tell AJ if you are. But that's not my point. I just wanna understand how you..." He motioned with his hands, but not in any familiar way. "I dunno."

"Why would you think I'm into Ryan?" I shook my head. I already knew this line of questions. AJ asked similar things before the kayak trip. Did some cosmic force want me to be with Ryan? Did everyone but me see the two of us as a couple? I knew I should text Carson about it, but I couldn't interrupt him during work.

"Well, you spend a lot of time with her. You guys work together, but not just at work, like you and her *work*. Like, the whole morgue thing yesterday was seriously badass. Creepy, but badass. And you guys smiled a ton afterwards. It's like you and Ryan are two guitars harmonizing. Music to my ears! And hey, harmony in the streets means harmony in the sheets. You know what I'm saying?"

I almost gagged.

"Oh my God! C'mon. I feel like... Don't you think it's possible that Ryan and I are just good friends? Can all that 'harmony' be... Platonic?"

Cody chuckled like a wise old man. I thought he might even try stroking his beard, but he just kicked at a receding wave.

"Rain, Rain. Let this be a life lesson: That platonic stuff—at least, with a straight dude and a straight girl—it *always* changes. Either you both fall out, or you both fall *in.*"

I suspected that I shouldn't take any sort of relationship advice from Cody, under the circumstances, but something in his philosophy rang true for me.

Carson never had any long-term female friends. Like Cody said, they always either fell out or fell in (then fell out a few weeks later). Ryan liked me, even if only because of my last name. I liked her too, but not in *Carson's* way. I didn't want our new friendship to change. I wanted to walk that thin line—the line between the fall-out and the fall-in—for as long as possible.

"I just want to stay friends with her," I told Cody, which for some reason prompted his next question almost instantly.

"Do you jerk off?"

"*What?*"

"Okay, never mind. But like, do you think you might be asexual?"

"Asexual? Like a fern?"

"Ha!" Cody stumbled and nearly fell onto the wet sand. "No, not like a plant! It's a real thing. Asexual, aromantic… I met a girl after a gig in Tennessee once, and she said she was asexual. I could tell she liked me, in a way, but she's just, like, not interested in anyone like *that*. Got better things to do than screw around, I guess."

"Doesn't everyone have better things to do?"

"Oh, Rain… Spoken like a true virgin. No offense."

"None taken."

The sudden turns of my conversation with Cody nearly distracted me from my plan. I only remembered when I noticed the approaching watchtower on our right. A fluttering ribbon of yellow tape, held up on stakes around the tower site reminded us: "*PO-LICE LINE DO NOT CROSS.*" Cody bristled.

"I shouldn't be here," he mumbled, glancing back north up the empty beach. "Getting caught by my mom would suck, but getting arrested might be worse."

"I don't see anyone here," I assured him.

For the second time, I arrived at the tower and stopped. To anyone else, the new scene meant nothing. Before reading the barricade tape, anyone else might walk on without a second thought. Only those who knew about Eliza knew the tower's new, dark story. At the very least, we knew there *was* a story, and we knew its ending. In fact, from the moment I spotted Eliza's body, I only saw her story's ending. To find the beginning, I needed my new plan. I needed to travel back in time.

"I was going to do this myself," I told Cody, "but since you're here, you can help me." I pulled Eliza's phone from my pocket.

"Dammit. Not that thing again."

"Don't worry, just take it. Here."

"Yeah, now what?"

"Bury it."

Cody squeezed his face together. At first, I didn't like the plan either. Cody didn't need to know all my reasons for returning the phone, but I gave him some anyway.

"I know it's weird, but we can't keep this phone forever. We need to put it back where we found it. Where *you* found it, actually. To move forward, we need to move backwards. I think it makes sense for you to do the honors."

"Whatever, dude. As long as we'll be done with this thing."

Cody picked a spot in the dry sand halfway between the water and the tower. He used his feet to scoop out a shallow hole, maybe a foot deep. Never one for fanfare, he dropped the phone straight into its sandy grave, then pushed the sand back on top. In our own way, I suppose, we held a miniature funeral for Eliza. But instead of playing somber, Cody perked up.

"One less thing I'm getting arrested for, right?"

Cody and I returned up the beach. To my relief, he gave up on small talk. In the meantime, I wanted to text Carson and keep him involved in my new plan—like we agreed—but his phone never woke up from its bowl of dry rice.

A slow whirring sound broke through the rhythm of waves. It grew louder behind us when we came up on Bea's friends' house again. I looked toward the noise first, and my pulse kicked into overdrive.

"Cody, *run!*" I grabbed his shoulder. He looked back to see the beach patrol vehicle bearing down on us from the south. Even worse, I recognized Officer Lee closing in. I hoped for a second that he'd looked past us; maybe he saw only two nameless losers walking up a beach, but the wheels of his ATV kicked up plumes of sand. Cody saw them too. He launched into a sprint, me right after him.

"Shit, shit! Where do we go?" Cody shouted across the beach like a madman.

"Up there!" I aimed for the wooden steps of Bea's friends' house. "Run right through! Let's put some distance between us and him." One of the girls from the house jumped up from her towel on the sand when she heard me.

"Hey, assholes! What are you doing?"

I think she knew exactly what we were doing. I led our charge up the steps. Not far behind, Officer Lee parked his ATV and pursued us on foot. At the top of the steps, Bea grabbed the porch railings with both hands, blocking our path. The lasers of her eyes grazed my shoulder to bore into Cody.

"Rain, you go." Bea ordered. She lifted one arm. I hesitated.

"Rain, listen," Cody panted. "It wasn't me. I swear, I really know nothing. I screwed up with the party. I screw up Tennessee, my family, my life… Everything! Bea, I think I screwed us up most of all. But listen to me, just one time. I never hurt Eliza. Whatever the police decide, you have to believe me. It's all I have left."

"I believe you," I said as I crossed the threshold of the porch. I couldn't negotiate with Bea, and neither could Cody. I couldn't wait; there was no time. I across the porch and through the open door of the rental house. Inside, five pairs of eyes sized me up from all corners of a posh open-plan living room.

Back on the porch, Bea held her ground. Officer Lee stomped up to Cody, then pulled his wrists behind his back. Bea never moved; she just watched, and so did I, along with everyone in the living room. Two girls whipped out cell phones to film the scene for their stories.

"Cody Welling, nice to meet you." Officer Lee read from a paper card in his hand, speaking loud enough for everyone to hear. "You have the right to remain silent. Anything you say can and will be used against you in a court of law. You have the right to an attorney. If you desire…"

Bea stood there for everything, and she never turned around. I wondered if she really relished the moment. I wondered if she could really hate Cody that much. After all, Bea knew hate. I couldn't imagine her passing that on, not even to a jerk like Cody. The way she stared at him, it looked wrong—until she turned her head, just a bit. I don't know if her friends noticed, but I did: Bea blinked away tears.

She's not looking at him, I realized. *She's hiding her face from us.*

My time ran out. Officer Lee didn't show signs of wanting to chase me, but I took no chances. Before introducing myself to Bea's friends, I rushed through the house to their front door. Cody's cause would have to wait.

"I believe you." That was what I told him. *Soon everyone else will, too.*

13: THE HUNT

I set my phone down on the puzzle table and opened up the picture of the yellow sticker. Thanks to Carson, I knew where the sticker came from, but that left so much to be explained. How could a surf shop sticker matter so much? Why would AJ ask Eliza to delete the picture of it? Did he try to scratch of the sticker, leaving it almost unrecognizable? My whole understanding of AJ's involvement hinged on a tiny patch of yellow pixels on a screen.

I needed to map things out, so I picked apart the puzzle. I stole the first *A* from *CAROLINA*, the eye of a fish, and the *E* from a *BEACH*. I moved AJ's *A* and Eliza's *E* onto the puzzle's unfinished watchtower, then I dropped Lars' fisheye near the Heron Pirate Museum.

I read my unfinished map of the crime.

AJ left the party early; Cody told us that. Whether or not he met Eliza at the tower, she never deleted the photo like he wanted; I found the photo, duh. Maybe he let her keep the photo. Then again, why did she fall from the tower? No one kills people over pictures on cell phones—not even nudes. What could be so important about a scratched-up yellow sticker?

My map of the crime turned out less simple than I expected. Meanwhile, the fisheye piece waited far off at the museum, disconnected.

He came to her funeral. Her mom kicked him out. She suspected him too, but why? Lars must be connected. Did he come to the tower? Did he see something through his window, far across the street? The police raided his house; they found pills—

That jogged my memory.

When we hid in the kayaks, Chief Fitz made a phone call on the dock. She sounded like a different person, all warm and informal... No, before that. She talked to the other officers. What did she say?

Whatever tiny detail I needed, it vanished somewhere into my frenzied memories of the kayak trip. I wished I had recorded something from that night. In front of me, the puzzle pieces held their positions. Like a movie director, I changed the scene, moving the *A* to a surfboard and the fisheye to the tower. My new conclusion came easily.

Okay, suppose AJ never went to the tower. What if she came too close to the museum? Maybe Lars moved his drugs at night. She could've seen something. What if Lars needed her quiet? What if...

I moved Lars back to the museum and AJ back to the tower. I slid the *E* piece down lower.

What if Lars pushed her off the tower, then AJ showed up, and he never saw her body down below? He might've thought she ditched him. What if he did see her, but couldn't call the police because of his record? What if he ran away from her body, just like I wanted to the first time? Ryan never came along to stop him. Unless...

I snagged the *R* in from *CAROLINA* to represent Ryan. I dropper her next to AJ at the top of the watchtower.

Say that Ryan and AJ both went to the tower. Why not? They share a house-car-truck thing. Ryan knows about AJ's drug habit; they trust each other. What if they both saw Eliza and said nothing? Even worse, what if they killed her and pretended not to know? Maybe Ryan had a reason to run down the beach on Sunday morning. Maybe she kept calm around the body because she'd seen it already. What if she used her knowledge of my dad's books? What if Ryan, the biggest fan of murder mysteries, led me on a wild goose chase to cover her tracks?

I couldn't accept my new theory. Even worse, I couldn't ask for Ryan's advice. For days, I dismissed her as a suspect because she wanted to find the truth. Every trail of evidence led in a new direction, but none of them led toward her.

A perfect crime.

My mind raced to poke holes in my new theory, but the idea stuck to my brain like maple syrup. I grabbed the *R* away from the watchtower and set it back into place in *CAROLINA*. I wanted to find more letters, bring in more suspects, and wash away the idea of Ryan's guilt. Who could I bring in? Cody did plenty of stupid shit, but he and Bea never left the house after the party—or so Carson *heard*. Having sex made for a solid alibi. I needed more suspects, but I hardly knew anyone else on the island. Eliza's mom, Mrs. Roakes, Officer Lee, and Chief Fitz all had good reasons to be presumed innocent. The rest, hundreds of nameless drunk teenagers, blended into their own crowds.

I never read my dad's stories, but I assumed they ended happily. I always assumed that people loved the books for their good endings. No matter who killed Eliza, I saw no happy ending for the rest of us. Ryan's warning rang true more than ever: "Real life isn't an Eldridge novel."

I put away my phone and the image of the sticker, then picked up the fisheye piece and spun it around in my hand. Somewhere off my map of Warley, Lars walked free.

I hope it's all him, I thought. *Please, let this all be Lars.*

✼
✼✼

Several hours after I gave up on the puzzle, Carson returned from work alongside AJ. I expected them, but the rattling of the front door's lock still caught me off guard. One day after the next, someone surprised us through that door. For once, the only surprise was the lack of one.

"Who's ready to find Heron's treasure?" Carson pumped his fists and darted toward the pantry. "Man, I'm starving."

"How are you feeling, Rain?" AJ scrutinized me. "Ryan said you called in sick."

"I'm better. Ready for the beach, at least."

Carson led us to the garage below. On one of the back walls, four metal detectors hung from hooks. They almost resembled short crutches because of their handles and arm supports. Below each handle, a small digital display ran its wire in a spiral to a flat antenna at the bottom. Carson lifted one down from the hook and powered it on.

"AJ, have you used this model before?"

"Nah, these are the good ones. Mine's something cheap I bought years ago in Cali."

"Well Rain, this is for you. Here, take one of these. The power button is right there, and they should all have plenty of power. You'll see numbers on the little screen. I have it muted, but you can turn on the alien sounds if you want to feel like Indiana Jones or something. Just, yeah, you got it. Be careful not to smash the search coil into anything. Cody's done that twice."

The metal detector felt powerful in my hand. I sensed it like an extension of my arm, like a sixth sense grasping at the underground world. I waved the search coil from side to side. Numbers jumped on the display whenever I floated across scrap nails near the wall.

"I see why you guys like this," I admitted, letting myself smile for once.

"Alright, we all ready? Gotta get out there ahead of this weather." AJ powered up his detector and pushed through the small door at the front of the garage. Carson and I waited inside for another moment.

"What's your plan?" Carson whispered.

"This is my plan. Just follow AJ and go dig up some treasure."

Carson gritted his teeth and trusted me. I thought things through carefully, after all. I wouldn't allow a repeat of the third-grade book trailer incident.

Our archaeological expedition found the beach mostly empty. Some of the beach-weekers left for dinner, and others ran from the darkening clouds. The wind whipped the waves back, and they rushed in faster than usual. Like me, the beach tensed up somehow. Only the idiots, the danger junkies, and the treasure hunters remained. I represented all three groups.

"So, Carson, have you read all the letters?" AJ asked while panning his coil over the sand.

"Most of them. The handwriting sucks."

"Damn, true."

"What do you mean?" I interrupted. Carson filled me in.

"Remember, at the museum? I know we left early because you flipped out, but—"

"Hey!"

"Well, it's true! But anyway, at the museum, they have a glass case on the back wall. It's full of these old letters that Heron wrote to his girlfriend, Margaret. Mostly just old-timey poetry and romantic bull-shit. Here's the interesting part: He couldn't risk signing his name on the letters because they'd be intercepted, so he signed each letter with a drawing of the last coastline he saw. So, in theory, she knew where he was, sorta."

AJ took over as our storyteller. "And now, with Google Earth and everything, people have been trying to match up Heron's signatures with real places. Not because of history, though, just cause the east coast is full of treasure-hungry assholes."

"Dude?!" Carson laughed and kicked some sand at AJ. "You're here too, Cali bro."

"Caught me red handed, you win."

The towels and umbrellas of Bea's friends' house no longer decorated their narrow stretch of beach. Whatever anyone had left on the beach, the wind took before we passed by. A few minutes later, Carson's metal detector whined. He stopped to focus on a small area, so AJ and I watched. Carson laid down his detector to sift through the sand with his hands. After a few seconds, a silvery metal object glinted in his palm.

"Lost earring," he announced. "Just one."

AJ snapped his fingers. "Damn. It's never the pair, is it?"

Further down the beach, AJ dug up a rusty screw. Carson got lucky with more jewelry: A simple bracelet and another earring, but it didn't match the first one. AJ found a thin chain necklace, although he said it looked like a cheap one. The two of them picked up more and more bits of metal trash or lost little things, but I got nothing. I kept my eyes on the numbers of the detector's screen, but nothing changed. Rather than waste time, I turned off my detector and walked a few paces behind them. I decided to break their silence.

"So, with those letters, did they find all the places Heron drew?"

"About half of them," AJ shrugged. "The tides and storms change the shorelines every year. So, like, about two hundred years later, it's tough. But some of the drawings are easy, like two of them where you can see the old lighthouse at... Uh, where was that."

"Cape Lookout," Carson reminded him.

"Right, that one. So, the old buildings help, but some drawings are just tiny patches of grass. Like, just a clump of oysters at the shore or a couple rocks with some trees. A lot of people think one of those drawings is the location of the treasure, but I think that's bull. Like, why bury a treasure if you're just gonna send a letter telling someone where it is anyway? If he wanted Margaret to have the treasure, he could've just sent it to her."

"No way!" Carson shook his head. "Not with the whole Royal navy looking for him. They would've intercepted the treasure and taken back the gold he stole."

"Yeah, probably. It just sucks for us that he hid the treasure so well."

"I don't understand," I puzzled. "Where did the letters come from? I mean, how did the museum get the letters?"

Carson laughed.

"That would be a great question for Lars, wherever he is. You still think he killed Eliza?"

I fought the urge to watch AJ's face. I wanted to know what he knew; I wanted to see if it bothered him to talk about her. Carson knew the risk of mentioning Eliza around AJ, but he did it anyway. Instead of waiting for a better moment, I set my plan into motion.

"Actually, I'm not sure it was Lars. I read an article in the Gazette today, and they said the police only came to his house for a drug bust. He lives close to the tower, and he did break some laws, but he might not have killed her."

"Well then who did it?"

Carson struggled to ask that question without raising some alarm. I think he started to understand my plan. All the while, AJ just kept waving his metal detector over the sand, listening in silence.

"I don't know who did it, but they're probably still on the island. The police will catch up to them."

"Do you think they'll kill someone else, next? Like a serial killer?"

"Well, I don't know. They'd have to be a real maniac, right?"

"Yeah. Someone who doesn't feel any sort of guilt."

AJ finally spoke up, but not in the way I needed. I thought he might snap, change the subject, or even defend himself by mistake. Instead, he dove right into our discussion.

"How do you all know for sure that she got killed?"

The phone, I thought. *Ryan knew that immediately. Cody found it too far from her body. Someone moved the phone away from Eliza, and that's how we know. But I can't tell you that, AJ.*

"I guess we don't really know. What do you think happened?"

"Oh, geez. I don't know either, guys."

"C'mon, man," Carson prodded him. "Everyone has a theory now. Let's hear yours."

"Alright, um… She was at the party, probably drunk. Maybe a little blazed, who knows. She leaves the party, then starts walking home. It's a long way though, so she gets tired. She thinks she'll take a break by the watchtower. So, all drunk or whatever, she climbs to the top to see the waves better. The top of the tower doesn't have railings or anything, so she loses her balance. She falls, breaks her neck. I guess that's a simpler story."

I liked his theory, but I also liked hearing him work so hard at lying. AJ texted her! If the texts meant nothing, he could've told us. Instead, he made up a story to leave him uninvolved. Carson held his tongue while AJ walked straight into my trap.

"I like that theory," I told him, "but what if someone just wanted her death to look like an accident? What if someone snapped her neck, then set her up that way to look like she died accidentally?"

AJ huffed.

"Listen, Rain. I know you and Ryan love murder mysteries, but you can't just turn Eliza's death into one. We all read that article on Monday; the police don't suspect foul play. Now I get that the police aren't always right—trust me, I know that more than anyone—but there's no way any of us can do their job better. We're not living in an episode of Scooby-Doo. To be honest, I think we all just need to calm down, shut up, and let the right people tell us the truth."

AJ's metal detector whined. Keeping with our routine, we all stopped walking so he could dig up his new find. AJ's eyes focused on the ground, eager to behold some tiny new treasure. If he looked up, he might have noticed the south tower above the dunes on our right. I saw the tower, of course; I had watched it drawing closer for ten minutes. Carson saw the tower too. As AJ plunged his fingers into the sand,

Carson grinned. He nudged my shoulder and held up a *Shaka* sign.

Awesome.

AJ brushed the sand off Eliza's cell phone. He stayed low to the ground, not ready to show off his score to us. His eyes darted up once toward the tower, then back down to the phone. AJ held the phone low enough that it never left the hole Cody dug. His right thumb hovered over the phone's side button. As soon as he pressed it, he threw the phone back down into the hole and stood up.

"No way," AJ muttered, stepping back quickly. He turned around to see me filming him on my phone, and he stopped in his tracks. "Rain, put that away. The hell are you doing?"

"I'm taking your advice. I'm letting the right person tell me the truth."

"Whoa, what? Rain, just put your phone away." AJ moved closer to me, but Carson held out his metal detector like a spear between us.

"AJ, don't come any closer. I don't want to break this thing's search coil, but I will."

"So, tell me," I insisted. "Tell me the truth about what happened at the tower."

AJ backpedaled and held up his hands innocently. "I told you, I don't know! Why do you think I know?"

"You can cut the shit already. We saw your texts. We know she told you to meet her at the tower." I kept filming him with my phone. Hearing his confession would help, but recording it would seal the deal. "We know you told her to delete that photo. The photo of the scratched-up sticker from Ron's. We have proof of everything, so tell us what happened on Saturday night."

"Dude, stop! I don't know what you think you saw, but you're making a mistake. If anyone killed

Eliza, it's gotta be Lars! You know, the legit criminal? The one with a tackle box full of pills in his house?"

Box! That's what I forgot. When we hid under the dock in the kayaks, Chief Fitz asked the other officers if they found a box. They said they had, and they said that the contents matched whatever she expected. Thanks to the latest news article—and thanks to AJ—I finally knew why the box mattered.

"Wait, wait," Carson interrupted us. He put the puzzle pieces together before me. "AJ, you stayed back when we went out in the kayaks. You never heard Fitz talk about a box, and that article didn't say anything about a box. You can't know about that, unless Ryan told you… But even if she did, no one ever said it was a *tackle* box. Only *you* said that."

AJ crossed his tattooed arms and let a deep breath hiss through his teeth. We won. He couldn't run anymore.

"Tell us the truth," I told him. "Or I'm going to show Ryan this video."

"Son of a bitch! You would do that, wouldn't you? Hell, I knew it. I knew this was your game, the whole time. You'll do whatever it takes to get Ryan away from me, won't you? You're gonna use *this* as… As what? Some messed-up trick to steal my girlfriend? You know, when Ryan told me what happened to your dad, I actually felt bad for you, but now I'm hoping you end up just like him!"

I don't know exactly what happened next. For once, I shut off my brain.

I remember handing my phone to Carson and dropping my metal detector. My feet jumped in front of one another, over and over. I heard a scream; I think it came from somewhere in my chest. I lifted off the sand and then crashed back down, taking AJ with me. I never thought I could tackle someone to the ground—especially not someone as strong as him—so I guess he never thought I could either. With the element of surprise on my side, I threw my punches blindly and hoped for the best until AJ flung me away from him. I stumbled to my feet. My brain rebooted itself.

"We can cut out that part of the video," Carson suggested. He returned my phone to me.

AJ got back on his feet. His cheeks glowed red, but I hadn't drawn blood. His voice sank and quieted.

"Dude, back off. You can't show Ryan this video. You can't tell her about the texts. Okay?"

"Why not?" I held the phone closer to him.

"Because... She already knows what happened last summer."

Carson and I waited. No one needed to ask him. AJ gave in.

"When Ryan and I first got settled on the island, I got too comfortable. I started selling some of the stuff I bought in California, you know? It made good money. Hell, I even got Ron to help out. Then Eliza moved to the island, a little while after us. She bought from me. We met on the beach at night; it was the same for everyone who bought. Right here, by the tower. My spot. After a few weeks, Eliza and I started smoking together. Then, somehow, I guess it became more than that.

"I knew it was wrong. Ryan and I, we need each other like you wouldn't know. You don't drive across the country for just anyone. I came clean, told Ryan I cheated on her. And I thought that would be the end of it, but guess what? She said 'fine,' as long as I kept away from Eliza and quit my side business, I got a second chance. So, I stopped seeing Eliza, stopped selling to her and everyone else. I told her why, but she never got over it. She never… She never *really* understood, so she told everybody, of course. Her mom, mostly. The cops came knocking, searched the Winne, but I cleaned everything out by then. That Fitz woman… She's still after me. But Ryan and I are good now. We got better. *I* got better.

"Now, if you tell her what you know, that's all gone."

AJ's voice softened. He choked up, but he didn't cry.

I ended the video on my phone. AJ's story explained a lot, but not everything. Now I knew why he and Ryan avoided the vigil: Eliza's mom knew them from last summer! For better or for worse, Ryan and AJ had deep connections to the Murphy family. I wanted to pry deeper. I wanted to finish the puzzle, but I could barely keep track of all the new pieces dumped into my open hands. I tried to speak delicately without giving up on our interrogation.

"If you don't want us to tell Ryan, then you should tell her first."

AJ shook his head. He leaned down and scooped up Eliza's phone from its grave.

"Hey, what're you doing with that?" Carson held out his metal detector again.

"You aren't gonna tell Ryan anything," AJ insisted. He used his hands to break apart the halves of the waterproof case on Eliza's phone. "You know enough to upset her, but you still don't know enough about Saturday night."

AJ took a long step, held one arm back over his shoulder, then lobbed Eliza's unprotected phone toward the ocean. The wind carried it up, spun it around like a leaf, and dropped it into the swirling waves. I couldn't even hear the splash.

When Carson and I looked back, AJ had already started up the stairs of the nearest beach access path. Neither of us chased him.

"Holy shit," Carson wheezed. "You're a genius. How did you... When... What?"

"I buried the phone on the beach this morning. Well, actually, Cody buried it for me."

"How did you know AJ would find it?"

"C'mon, let's keep walking. Ryan is picking us up further south."

"Wait, did you say *Cody* buried the phone?"

"Yeah. Also, this might be a good time to tell you he got arrested."

"*What!?*"

14: THE STORM

Carson and I walked far down the beach to a parking lot on the barren stretch of dunes. I could almost see the Murphy mansion further south, poking through the gray of mist and clouds. I hoped that Ryan would be at the parking lot when we arrived, but we arrived there early. After AJ ran off, neither of us could go back to real treasure hunting. Carson carried his detector while I carried the other two. All the way to the parking lot, he kept freaking out.

"Arrested? You saw all of this happen, and you just did nothing?"

"What could I have done?"

"Intervened! Created a distraction! You just let Cody get arrested?"

"Not exactly," I told him for the third time. I couldn't admit to him that it was Bea's doing. "I thought you'd be glad about this! He trashed the house, blackmailed you, mouthed off to Bea, and dragged your mom all the way down to the island! Don't you think it might be good to have Cody away? At least for a little while?"

Carson pushed my shoulder, but not in his usual friendly way.

"Away in a *holding cell*? Rain, you really don't get it. You don't have any brothers or sisters. There's always fighting, messes, and stupid shit, but Cody is still my brother! I can't let him get arrested, no matter what he did."

"You're being ridiculous. What if Cody killed Eliza?"

"We already know it was probably AJ! *You're* the one being ridiculous!"

Carson kicked a heap of sand at the edge of the parking lot. I knew he aimed for me, but the wind ripped the plume away toward the ocean. I kicked another pile of sand into the wind, hoping to strike back, but it blasted back into both of our faces. Carson spit sand off his tongue, and I rubbed it out of my eyes.

Meanwhile, the orange-striped Winnebago squealed to a crawl on the road. Ryan turned into the lot, wind rocking the tall vehicle. Ryan pressed the horn, and the opening riff of *Surfin' U.S.A.* echoed into the wind. Once she rolled up closer to us, she lowered her window.

"Just in time," she said. "The rain should start any minute. You guys find anything cool? Chests of gold, maybe another dead body? Sorry, too soon. Where's AJ?"

Shit. I didn't plan an excuse. I never planned on lying to Ryan. Carson flipped out about Cody's arrest, but what would Ryan say about AJ? What would she say if he knew about the box of pills? What would she say about his texts with Eliza? Perhaps worst of all, I feared what would she think of my role in exposing his past. I filmed the video. I left Eliza's phone for him to find. I kept the screenshots of the texts and the sticker. With Carson already pissed at me, I couldn't afford to upset Ryan too.

My mind raced to fabricate some believable story about AJ. Judging by Carson's silence, he did the same. When enough seconds passed, I opted to stay quiet and hope for the best. Ryan noticed, of course.

"Ah, stunned silence. Well, that's not worrisome! Hop in; we should get back before the storm."

Carson and I piled into the Winnebago and dropped our equipment in the mini kitchen. One of us could have faced the tension of sitting up front with Ryan, but neither of us did. Instead, we sank down onto the side-facing couch ten feet behind her. Outside, the wind howled. The sun, somewhere behind the clouds, dipped low enough to darken the whole sky.

"Should I wait for him?" Ryan asked. She adjusted her rear-view mirror to meet our eyes.

"No," I confessed. Ryan turned off the engine.

"Okay, going by the looks on your faces, shit went down. AJ must have a good reason for ditching, since there's a storm coming, and he literally lives in this thing. So, are you going to tell me, or am I going to figure this out myself?"

Carson opened his mouth, but I shook my head. Ryan began.

"Rain, where's the phone, bud? You have it? Looks like you're all healthy now; that's great. Not even a cough. So, you called in sick to avoid me all day, and now you won't give me the phone. You're hiding something, but I already knew that. You're hiding something that's on the phone. Or you lost it? Broke it? Locked it by accident? No, I see your face. You found something, didn't you? Carson, you know about it too; I can tell you do. Does AJ know? Is that why he left? What the hell is it, Eliza's nudes?"

I couldn't take it anymore.

"Assumptions," I interrupted. I remembered what she told me almost a week earlier, when we met at the party. "H.M. Eldridge would remind you to separate your *assumptions* from *deductions*."

Ryan waited, fuming.

"Okay," she quieted. "No more assumptions, just evidence. AJ isn't here, and he hasn't texted me. You won't let me see Eliza's phone. All of you are really obviously hiding something! I don't get why you're doing this now."

"AJ told us," Carson whispered. I shoved him.

"What?" Ryan turned around in the driver's seat. Once Carson spoke up, I couldn't stop him.

"Rain, knock it off. You didn't tell me about Cody, and now you're not gonna tell Ryan about AJ? That's a sucky way to treat your friends. Either you tell her what happened, or I will. Because unlike you, I think the truth matters—even when it hurts. So, what's it gonna be?"

I cringed and dropped my face into my hands. Carson caught me. I couldn't escape, hold my tongue, or change the subject. It was third grade all over again. The door to the trailer locked, the books closed in, and each of my silent breaths stripped the oxygen from around us. I knew that Carson made the right choice for me, but I hated the risk of telling Ryan. I hated the pain of being honest. I hated the island and everyone on it. I wanted—of all things—to run away back to Ohio.

After one painful gulp of air, I came clean to Ryan.

"Cody found Eliza's phone. Bea, Carson, and I found out at the vigil. Ryan, I showed you the next morning because I didn't know what to do. But that whole time, no one told AJ about it. Not even you. You could have told him, I know. Hell, you told him almost everything else we discovered. He's your boyfriend, so you trust him. But you didn't trust him with Eliza's phone, and I never understood why. None one suspected him of anything, right? Well, I found something in Eliza's texts. Wait, Ryan, please listen. I wanted to show you first! I really wanted to, but…"

"But what!?" She stood up, always taller than me, but even more so now. "You wanted to go behind my back to question my boyfriend? Because you thought

I'd get in the way? Rain, get over yourself. I've interrogated AJ more than once. If anyone has a right to—"

"I know! I know that now! I was wrong, Ryan. I was wrong. AJ told us about last summer."

"I don't care!" Ryan shouted, gripping the headrests of both front seats. "You said so yourself: He's my boyfriend. It was my business before it was yours. Pretty soon, I'm sure I'll be pissed at AJ over whatever you found in Eliza's texts. Right now, I'm pissed at you for lying to me. Not just Rain, both of you!" She stepped back to the Winnebago's door and opened it. A gust of mist entered like a ghost. "If you're all so eager to solve this puzzle without me, there's the door." We hesitated. Ryan tilted her head toward the open door. "I need to go find AJ. You two, get out."

Carson and I left our equipment behind to save it from the weather, but we couldn't save ourselves. Only a minute after Ryan pulled into the lot, the storm grew heavier and colder. A few thick beads of water slashed across the sand. The dark haze of twilight lowered around us like a candle burning out. Ryan shut the door behind us and backed out of the lot. In a few more seconds, her giant rolling house slipped away into the fog.

"Well, that sucked," Carson mumbled as we started up the road. "Do you have any more surprise secrets? Can we just get those out of the way, so this doesn't happen again?"

I shivered. "Alright. Well, Bea kinda let Cody get arrested."

"Oh, it was her? I thought you did that."

"No, she let Officer Lee catch him. I thought you'd be mad at her."

"Nah, that's actually better. Means she's really over him and ready for someone better." He pointed at himself with both hands. The rain soaked through his Polo shirt, and I laughed.

"Are you serious?"

"I still have a chance with Bea. But you and Ryan, not so much now. Sorry about that, man."

"For the millionth time, I'm not trying to date Ryan!"

In the howling wind, I couldn't hear a car approaching behind us. Instead, I only saw flashes of red and blue shimmering on the wet pavement ahead. Carson and I halted helplessly as a Warley Island Police cruiser slowed down next to us. I considered running away again, but I couldn't run far. Over and over, the cops found their way back to us. Whether out of exhaustion or plain emotional defeat, Carson and I stood still. The passenger window of the car rolled down. Chief Fitz leaned from the driver's seat to examine us.

"Carson Welling, Rain Eldridge. You two are far from home. What happened?"

Thankfully, Carson kept his mouth shut this time. Fitz parked her car.

"Mr. Welling, I heard that your brother returned from Tennessee. Apparently, he stole your mother's car, too. Officer Lee found him strolling up the beach with Mr. Eldridge this morning." She sent me a stink-eye. "You should have called us first, Rain. Are you familiar with 'Aiding and Abetting?'"

"Yes," I frowned. I decided not to try some lame excuse.

"Then consider this your warning. I have more important things to take care of, which seems to now include driving you two home. Yes, go ahead. Get in the back, both of you. I do not want anyone outside in this storm."

Trust me, I thought. *We don't want to be out here either.*

Carson jumped inside the squad car and slid across the backseat. I sat down next, then closed the door and freed us from the rain. Even so, our clothes were already drenched. Fitz noticed the damp smell when Carson shook water from his hair onto the backseat. She flattened her lips together, maybe regretting her decision to take us home.

"I hate rain," Carson grimaced. "With a lowercase 'r.'"

We buckled out seatbelts, and Chief Fitz returned her eyes to the road. Her car's wipers danced across the windshield to fight the downpour. As she drove, the water fell fast enough to distort every road sign and wood-carved house name. Fitz picked up her corded radio microphone and called to the other officers:

"Unit 1, 10-13, all units be advised. High winds and rain, Warley Avenue near 1200."

Carson grinned. Outside my window, the familiar watchtower approached. Some of the yellow ribbons surrounding it fluttered wildly at one end or broke free to entangle themselves in the dune grasses. I imagined Eliza waiting at the top of that tower, texting AJ. Even after hearing some of his story, I couldn't imagine him pushing her off that tower. When I tackled him to the ground and punched him, he never fought back. I couldn't see AJ turning so violent, no matter how much suspicion he raised.

"What's that light?" Carson asked. He pointed out his window at a soft white light in the distance. Fitz looked too, and she slowed the car to a crawl. I didn't understand why she cared until I glimpsed the white glow fracturing through raindrops to our left. It shone from the edge of the intracoastal, behind two buildings and a small wooden windmill.

"I knew he might come back," Fitz thought aloud. Hand over hand, she spun the steering wheel and pulled us into the parking lot of the Captain Heron Pirate Museum. She shut off the cruiser's headlights so that only the mysterious glow remained. When we halted close to the museum, I saw the source of the light. The glistening beam from the water wobbled atop a small boat moored at Lars' dock.

"The Saint Olga IV," Carson whispered to me. "Lars is back. Why would he come back?"

"What was that?" Fitz twisted around in her seat to eavesdrop.

"Nothing," I lied. Her eyes drilled right through me, but Fitz wasted no more time with us. She pulled out her radio microphone and sent out another message:

"Unit 1, 10-20 at 988 Warley Ave. Stopping for 10-40."

The radio clicked and a man's voice replied over the static. "10-4 on that, Chief. Is it him?"

"10-12 on that." Fitz put down the radio microphone and glared at Carson and me. "You two stay in the car. I have to finish some business here, and then we can be on our way."

Carson and I nodded but continued craning our necks for a better view of the museum. Fitz stepped outside and locked the car behind her. In any other vehicle, we could've unlocked the backseat doors ourselves and followed her down to the museum. Instead, after days chasing Lars, we found ourselves locked in the back of a police cruiser, squinting through sheets of rain for an obscure view of the tense situation.

"Look!" Carson pointed. I saw nothing.

"Where?"

"Between the buildings! He's coming around… Do you see him? Right on the side of the museum, coming up from the dock. Fitz went around the other side. Oh, she's got him. He hasn't seen the car yet. Is he… Oh, he's getting out his keys. He's gonna go into the museum. Wait, no! He saw us. Okay, he's going back down. Look, he's so scared! Oh! Fitz came out in front of him. Holy shit! She's got her gun out. Is he gonna run? Wait, no. He's got his hands up. That's insane. She actually got him!"

Carson laughed like a rocket scientist after a perfect launch. In the shining white light from the Saint Olga IV, Chief Fitz pushed Lars up against the side of the museum. They stood near the spot where Carson, Bea, Ryan and I fled on the night of the raid, next the blue tarp between the house and the museum. Almost two days since that terrifying night, Chief Fitz finished her mission of arresting Lars. Carson's favorite curator, Warley Island's unnamed drug suspect, Ms. Murphy's undesirable guest, the fisherman with the bloody knife… Lars, the mystery man of many monikers, crossed his arms behind his back to accept Fitz's handcuffs.

"She's walking him back toward us," I announced. Carson wiped his nose.

"Dude, I can see."

"So can I, but you narrated everything a minute ago. What was that about?"

Fitz led Lars across the watery lot toward the police cruiser. A few wet locks of his hair dangled halfway in front of his eyes. Lars stumbled across the pavement, his feet splashing water as if pulling him back toward his home. Fitz pushed Lars up against the hood of the car, leaning him over so his eye level matched ours.

I met his gaze for the first time since our brief encounter at the dock. Again, I searched for some hint of villainy in his trembling face. I wanted to unmask Lars like a monster from Scooby-Doo, but more than ever, I sensed that he wore no mask. After the revelation of AJ's role in Eliza's death, I might've placed more faith in Lars' puppy eyes—if not for the whole drug-bust situation and the handcuffs on his wrists.

Even if Lars never met Eliza, I was right not to trust him, I thought. *Even if I got everything else wrong, I was right to go after Lars.*

Carson's door unlocked and swung open.

"Hop out," Fitz barked. Neither Carson nor I moved. "Move it. I have limited patience right now. Both of you, step out of the car. I need to give him a seat." Fitz gestured to Lars.

"You can't just let him sit up front?" I pointed to the dry, empty seat in front of us. Fitz shook her head.

"All passengers ride in the back."

"Wait, you're gonna kick us out because of him?" Carson scoffed at the idea and narrowed his eyes at Fitz. "There's enough room for all of us! Even if no one can ride shotgun, all three of us can squeeze back here!"

Fitz took a deep breath. "No one is squeezing anywhere. This vehicle has a third rear seat to be used in emergencies only. I told you boys that I have more important things to take care of, and *he* is the most important one. I would love to continue providing you with a free taxi ride, but I need to transport my suspect. Now both of you, get out of my car before I have to drag you out!"

"No thanks, bitch," Carson shrugged, turning to me. "You think she has another pair of handcuffs? I doubt it."

"Carson, are you nuts?" I wanted to slap him.

"C'mon, it's fine. Do you really think she'd drag me out—"

Fitz reached over Carson, unbuckled his seatbelt, then wrenched him out of the car using only one hand on his shoulder. He fell into a muddy puddle with a loud splash. Fitz immediately rolled him over and started placing handcuffs on his wrists.

"Ouch! Geez, do you know how hard it'll be to wash the mud outta this shirt? Oh, looks like you did have another pair of handcuffs. Don't get out of the car, Rain! There's no way she has another pair of them."

"Please remain still," Fitz groaned, but only out of annoyance. "For the record, I do have more handcuffs. Carson Welling, I am arresting you for delaying an officer. You have the right to remain silent..."

Chief Fitz recited Carson's rights while I promptly exited through the open door. I stepped back from the car in disbelief. In one day, I'd witnessed three arrests but none in direct connection with Eliza's death. Carson caught me wringing my hands several feet away.

"Don't worry, Rain. At least I'll get to say hi to Cody at the police station."

"Dammit, Carson! Are you trying to make me feel worse?"

"Is it working?"

Fitz shoved Carson back into the car. Meanwhile, I almost forgot about Lars. He whistled to catch my attention.

"Hey you. Rain, right? I left my boat running. Can you go get my keys for me?" Lars waited a second but kept talking when I ignored him—or at least tried to. "Please, I left my keys on the boat. Hey, I need your help. I'm innocent! The tackle box wasn't mine. It was locked. Hell, I didn't know what was in it! She brought it here; she said it came in the mail for me. Don't you get it? I've been framed! I did nothing, okay? Just run and get my keys, will you? I need someone to make sure she doesn't—"

"Stand up. Stop talking. Time to go." Fitz called out to Lars, cutting his speech short. "This side. Watch your head. Sit down." She shut the door behind him, leaving Carson and Lars together in the backseat. I watched from nearby, still drenched in rain and dreading the long walk back to *All's Well*. In a strange and rare display of human compassion, Fitz checked in with me before leaving me behind.

"Will you be okay walking home, Mr. Eldridge?"

"I guess." I shivered. Fitz waited another moment, perhaps weighing the risk of letting me sit in her passenger seat. She decided against it.

"Alright, be safe. Stay out of trouble."

I almost nodded, but even the lie of that silent promise felt obvious in front of Fitz. Instead, I turned away and pretended not to watch her car drive off with Carson and Lars. Once the red taillights vanished north into the storm, I gave up every intention of walking back to the Welling house. My legs already ached from my day of walking up and down the island. My mind ached from trying to understand Cody's arrest, Bea's isolation, AJ's confession, Ryan's anger, and Carson's bizarre self-sacrifice. Everyone turned away from me—and from one another. Eliza's death remained a mystery, and I remained a loser standing alone in the summer rain.

*
**

"Hi, mom." I began. For once, I made the phone call.

"Well, hello! Thank you for remembering to call me. What's going on?"

"Not much." *I'm just squatting in an abandoned museum that I opened with the keys I stole from a suspected drug dealer's boat.*

"Of course. It's never much with you. But Mrs. Welling called me today."

"Oh, what did she say?" *Uh-oh.*

"She told me that the police arrested Cody. She told me he stole her car. And she told me that she can't seem to reach Carson. Sounds like a lot more than 'not much,' doesn't it?"

"Yeah…"

"Rain, talk to me. What is going on down there? What's all that sound?"

"It's a storm. The wind is loud."

"Are you safe? Where are you now?"

"Actually, Mom, can I call you back tomorrow?"

"No, Rain. You're going to talk to me now. You're going to tell me the truth about what's happening on that island. You're going to tell me about your new job. You're going to tell me about all your new friends. You're going to tell me what all this madness with Cody means. You're going to tell me why no one can reach Carson. You're going to talk to me now because you promised that you would call me while you're gone. That was our deal, and if you break it, I will drive down to that stupid island and drive you home. Do you understand?"

I stared around the darkened glass cases of the Captain Heron Pirate Museum. Pictures, letters, and small wooden objects filled the silent chamber. Heron's dusty hat drooped on its metal wire pedestal. The elaborate timeline of the pirate's tragic adventure encircled me and all the room's artifacts. I stood in a tourist trap. The museum was a lame excuse to build a gift shop, a twisted shrine to an all-American crook, a dying business for an arrested fisherman, and a pitiful monument to Warley Island's first unsolved mystery: Heron's lost treasure.

Over two hundred years, I realized. *For two whole centuries, bright-eyed tourists like the Wellings have come here trying to solve one stupid, simple mystery. All that time, no one's found a single gold coin. Two hundred years, and millions of people have never found Heron's maple chest.*

Somehow, I let Ryan convince me that we could solve a new mystery in only a week. I believed I could be better than my father. I thought I could solve a real mystery and prove how worthless all his books turned out to be.

"Okay," I spoke into the phone. "Come drive me home, then. I'm done here."

"Rain, are you—"

Before she could say any more, I hung up my phone and set it to airplane mode. Only the sounds of pounding rain and howling wind remained. My tears were silent.

15: THE NIGHT

In high school, many days of my life passed without fanfare. Hundreds of burnt-out school days slipped away, forever unremembered. As unpleasant as that sounds, I liked my routine. I woke up, rode the bus to school, learned as little as possible, and rode the bus home for dinner and another night's sleep. I swam in a circle like a goldfish in a bowl, resetting my brain each morning for a clean slate. Without any memorable events, my day-to-day memories withered.

On one of those unremarkable weekdays, a Wednesday, I left school in high spirits. After the bus ride home, Carson and I walked to my house. The warming spring air tasted more and more like freedom every day. Each morning, I felt the thrill of graduation inching closer to push schoolwork aside forever.

"You started studying for calc yet?" Carson asked, and I shrugged.

"I didn't think we had a test this week. Is it on the new stuff?"

"No, Rain! There's no test this week. I meant *finals*. Have you started studying?"

"Right. Forgot about those."

We rounded a bend in the street to see my house, complete with a new trailer hitched to my dad's SUV. As we approached, he stepped out from the house carrying a box of signed books and posters. I took a deep breath but couldn't quite let it out. When I left for school, there was no trailer out front. Dad only arrived a few weeks earlier, so I had hoped for him to stay longer. He strolled down the front lawn smiling at

Carson and me. Maybe he was happy to see us, or maybe smiled at the thought of getting away for his next book tour.

"New trailer?" Carson asked, and I nodded.

"More books, more posters, more banners. Soon he'll need an eighteen-wheeler."

"Wow. Sometimes I forget he's so famous. Like, I see news articles and tweets and everything… And my mom still runs that Facebook group for his fans in the neighborhood… But I forget that he's still your dad, too. Another classic suburban guy. Does he mow the lawn on Saturdays?"

"Nah, he pays someone to come do it."

"See? Lifestyles of the rich and famous."

I led Carson inside through the two-car garage. My family's other car belonged to my mom. It was no late model, but she didn't care; she only needed a car for errands. When I turned sixteen, I asked my mom for a car. She laughed and asked what I needed one for. After all, I rode the bus to and from school every day. I never left the neighborhood on week-ends. A couple years later, I still had no car to call my own. I still had nowhere to drive one, anyway. She made a good point.

"Oh, Rain! And Carson, hi. How was school?" My mom greeted us in the living room. A half dozen open scrapbooks surrounded her on the couch and coffee table, so she didn't try to stand up.

"It was good," we agreed in unison. Mom laughed. She often joked that Carson and I might be twins—if not for my saffron hair, of course.

"What're those for?" Carson peered over the photo albums.

"Well, a while ago Rain asked me to look for something, and when I remembered to break these out today, I got a bit carried away. I keep scrapbooks by the decade, plus one for older photos. See, these two have all the pictures of Rain. He wanted me to find an old baby picture for your yearbook. Is it too late now?"

"Yeah," I sighed. "I think they stopped collecting class baby photos in March."

"Shoot. I should've remembered during the winter. Oh well. But I found this one… Here, Carson. Show Rain."

She handed a four-by-six photo to Carson, who passed it to me. In the picture, a younger me sat on the kitchen floor with a hardcover book open between my hands. I couldn't see the cover, but I made an educated guess.

"Is that Dad's second book?"

"Yup. *The Oxnard Investigation.* I don't know how much you really understood in kindergarten, but you enjoyed that one. You wanted to dress as Dr. Dugrave for Halloween."

I couldn't believe the photo I couldn't recall reading that book or any of my dad's other ones. Carson seemed equally surprised; his eyes grew.

"Whoa, you read his books back then? In kindergarten?" *No way. That's impossible.*

"Oh, of course he did." Mom gave me no time to disagree. "Rain first learned to read because of Hunter's books. I was so proud… I used to think he was fake-reading just to mimic grown-ups like kids all do, but he would read aloud sometimes. I loved that. Rain, don't you remember reading with me?"

I shook my head. "That must've been a long time ago. I can't remember reading any of Dad's books. I just know the names and when they hit the market because of his book tours."

That was true, almost. I knew as much about Dad's books as anyone knew from the advertisements, reviews, and chatter among fans. I knew characters like Dr. Dugrave, the expat American doctor who investigates psychic phenomena. I knew just enough to play my character: "Son of the Author." But that old picture flew in the face of everything I knew. It disagreed with *my* story, the one I always told. I told everyone—even myself—that I never read my dad's books. Feeling sick, I handed the picture back to my mom. She picked up another.

"Anyway, I thought you'd want to see this one, too."

I took the second picture. It was smaller, blurrier, and even more perplexing. In the picture, I leaned on the hood of a small black car in a short driveway. I recognized neither the car nor the driveway. Carson looked too.

"Whoa. What are those white shoes? You gotta wear those more."

"I don't understand," I told my mom. "When was this taken? Where was I?"

She grinned. "That's not you. It's Dad, around the time when we met in college."

I squinted my eyes at the photo. If I really focused, I could almost imagine that familiar face growing to match its current shape. His smile glowed with the same self-assuredness I saw outside, minutes earlier. Still, the young man in the photo wore an unexpected mop of red curls over his head. *My* red hair, grown out to match the style of the '80s.

"Dad's hair is brown. That can't be him."

Mom took back the photo and nodded. "Sure is. You have his old hair. Give it a few more years, and your crown of flames will burn out too."

I tried not to shudder. I pictured myself in five years, ten years, then more. I wondered if I might look exactly like him after long enough. If I grew up to be a clone of my dad, I could only hope to be a better version. I wouldn't let myself follow in his footsteps; I would find a different path or pave my own. Maybe I would have to dye my hair red someday.

Carson and I planned to work on homework. We always planned to be productive, but instead spent four hours discussing the invention of saxophones, why carrots are orange, and how the United States could have prevented both world wars. Admittedly, Carson led the discussion. In fact, it resembled a lecture more than a conversation. Regardless, I enjoyed learning about saxophones more than I would've enjoyed my calculus homework.

My mom told Carson he could eat dinner with us, but his mom wanted him home. As Carson left, the sun dipped behind our neighbor's maple trees. With the trailer fully packed, my dad saw this as a cue to get moving. Mom wrapped a bowl of soup for him to bring on the road, and we began our usual goodbyes on the front lawn.

"I'll be gone for your birthday," he announced softly. I guess he saved that news for the last moment. "First time I've missed one. Sorry, kiddo. I'm in San Francisco that day; my media escort says it can't be changed. I got you something in advance this time." He reached through the open window of the SUV and pulled out the notebook. I took one glance at his mantra inscribed on the cover and started counting the seconds until he left.

"Thanks," I told him.

Fewer than a hundred seconds later, the tail of his stuffed trailer swung out of sight at the end of our street.

"You hungry now?" Mom pointed back to the house.

"Maybe later," I hoped, but my appetite vanished for the day. I retreated upstairs to the safety of my bedroom, where I fell asleep before the light left the Ohio sky.

I woke to the sound of four knocks on my door. *Shit, I overslept,* I thought, since I never set an alarm for the morning. I blinked into the invisible space around me. If the lack of morning sunlight didn't surprise me enough, the *12:31* on my nightstand clock sure did. Mom never knocked past ten. Hell, she never knocked after dark on school nights, and never with four loud raps on the door—often two, maybe three. I rolled out of bed and onto my feet, then searched my floor for some sweatpants and a t-shirt. By the time I answered the four knocks, she gave up waiting for me. I squinted down an empty hallway.

"Mom?"

No answer. Her voice echoed up the stairs from the dining room. In my sleepless state, I couldn't catch enough of her words from so far off. *She's on the phone,* I knew; only her voice drifted upstairs to my sleepy ears. I left my room barefoot, irritated but curious to know why she knocked.

"Mom? Mom!"

She sat on the hardwood floor near the mail table, squeezing her cell phone between her shoulder and her cheek. Her two hands shook as she hopelessly tried to lace up her sneakers. Her head snapped upright when I spoke, and her phone tumbled onto the ground. The redness in her eyes and the rivers on her cheeks sent a shot of adrenaline to my head. Finally, I woke up.

"Keys," she wheezed. One hand lifted a key ring in my direction. I took it and sunk to her eye level.

"Mom? What's wrong? Where are you going?"

She lifted her phone up again and pointed toward the garage.

"Start the car. I'll be right there."

My bare feet bristled against the ridged pedals of my mom's car. I became aware of every sound, light, and sensation while I rolled the car out to the driveway. My mom jogged through the car's headlights with one shoe tied. She slid into the passenger seat and kept the phone glued to one ear.

"Scottstown Road," she whispered away from the phone's mic. "Rain? Do you know where Scottstown Road is?"

"What? Mom, I... You said Scottstown? Near Aunt Crystal's house?"

"Yes. The way we normally go, but keep driving past her development."

Any other day, I might've wasted ten minutes with questions. On that night, I followed my mom's instructions without a word. She cried too much to drive; seeing her in that state, I felt responsible. For once, I had a reason to drive somewhere. I didn't need to understand the reason to accept it. I didn't need to understand my destination. I sunk my bare foot onto the gas pedal and rushed us from our neighborhood to the main street.

"I don't have shoes," I reminded her once she hung up the phone.

"That's okay." Her gaze grasped tightly onto the empty road ahead.

"I don't have my license with me, either. If we get pulled over—"

"It's okay. Just keep going. You know the next turn?"

"Who was on the phone?"

"It's okay," she said again and blinked more water from her eyes. "It's okay. It's okay."

Scottstown road swam like a snake through the woods south of us. By the stroke of one in the morning, we cruised past my aunt's house with no sign of stopping. Thin wisps of gray fog danced between the car's headlights. Bitter, smoky air flowed inside through the vents on the dashboard, so I shut off the fans and slowed below the speed limit. Between the shadowed trunks of a thousand trees, red lights flickered toward us from ahead. A few seconds later, some of the blue lights slipped through the trees too.

My mom made a sound like she'd been stabbed in the gut. It sounded light a gasp, a sob, and a shout of pain rolled into the space of a single second. Her hands wrapped like shells over her face, and she pulled her head down to her knees near the dash.

"Mom! What—"

My bare foot stomped the brake pedal. A hundred feet ahead, a police car blocked the road. Flares hissed on either side of the road like candles of blood. Further, an ambulance and two fire trucks glowed with a hundred flashing points of orange and red. Every light cut a new hole through the heavy gray clouds around us. I jammed my mom's car into park and walked into the road without closing the door. The thickening smoke choked my lungs, and I coughed it back out.

"Excuse me, sir," a police officer spoke when I approached her car. "Is that your mother in the car? Are you next-of kin?"

"What?"

"Is that your mother in your car?"

"Yes, she's… What's going on?"

The officer turned once toward the other vehicles, maybe hoping for someone to help talk to me. No one came to help her. My mom stayed back in the car with her head between her legs. The officer stepped closer and faced her empty palms toward me.

"There's been an accident. We had to close the road. We've notified next-of-kin."

"*Whose* next-of-kin? Who?"

She glanced at my mom's car, then back to my face with solemn purpose.

"I'm very sorry to tell you this, sir. We were unable to rescue the driver of the vehicle. We're still working to open the doors and confirm I.D., but there was a fire…"

My ears rang and blocked the rest of her speech. The ground tipped like a seesaw. I didn't run; I *fell*. Gravity pulled me into the smoke. I floated past the flares, the nervous officer, her car, the ambulance, and the first fire truck. I wiped my eyes to discover the scene. A heap of smoking, smoldering wreckage filled the drainage ditch on the left side of the road. Black, ash-filled water bubbled and rolled off into the grass. Half-behind and half-beneath the larger wreck, an SUV nosed down into a tall gray face of rock. The overfilled trailer had crushed it down to half its size.

A pinch of pain rose from my left foot. I looked to find a small glass shard buried in my heel. Stuck to it: A page of a book. All around, everywhere, cream-colored leaves of text decorated the street. Their remnants spun in the air like joyless confetti. I stood in the ashes of my dad's final story, watching his count-less words burn and wash away. H.M. Eldridge sat unseen in his car at the bottom of the rock face—crushed, buried, and scorched to death by ten thousand autographed books.

The rest of the night unfolded in pieces, scattered like the shards of glass that sliced my feet. A firefighter grabbed me from behind and pulled me back toward the vehicles. Mom finally left the car, but she refused to walk closer to the scene. My aunt arrived and cried over her lost brother-in-law. One of the paramedics bandaged the cuts on my feet. I watched the firefighters cut their way into the SUV, then the nervous police officer walked closer to block my view.

No matter how hard I tried, I couldn't make myself cry.

I dreamt of his funeral—not for the first time, but maybe for the last. This dream began like the others; I arrived with my mother in the funeral procession. We stepped from the dark car into the bright sun that washed over the cemetery. It didn't rain. For early April, the air was too warm. The sky glowed a vibrant, cloudless blue. I began to sweat through my suit immediately, and not just because of the weather.

I stared for minutes at the flat stone that bore his name. Still, I couldn't force a single tear. After the people at our county morgue finished their autopsy, they sealed his remains in his coffin. No embalmer in the world could powder the life back into his face—not after the fire. In the end, Mom and I were the last people to see my dad as we all remembered him. That was the funny thing: I hardly remembered his face once I knew he was gone for good.

"Tell Your Story," said his gravestone. My notebook echoed the phrase. They lowered his coffin into the earth at the foot of that smooth stone plaque. *Strange,* I thought, *that he's been buried twice at the base of a dull gray rock.*

Then the dream changed. Time shifted into overdrive. My mother vanished, and the other mourners too. My dad's casket dropped like a lead weight into the abyss below. Heaps of dirt flung over it until the ground leveled out. The sun slipped away, and the air turned dark. My eyes struggled to adjust so quickly.

His gravestone grew and spread and ripped across the grass. His parents' stones widened and stretched up, becoming the Heron Museum and Lars' house. A blue boat tarp unfurled itself over the flat rock between the buildings, completing a scene I now knew so well.

"The tarp's not for his boat," someone spoke. I spun around. Eliza stood in the darkness of the empty parking lot, holding her hands on her hips. She approached me with her eyes fixed on the unseen rock. Words froze in my throat; I could only watch. Her smile broadened and filled with life once more. "Look at yourself, Rain. You're trying too hard to solve the wrong puzzle. Stop it. I'm already dead, and you know that. There's nothing you can do for me. You keep trying to tell my story, but you can't even finish telling yours."

She leaned down and began to lift the tarp from the rock. Eliza's eyes locked themselves on mine. Under the tarp, the rock and the gravestone merged into one.

"Finish the story, Rain Eldridge."

*
**

I wrenched my body upright and stumbled back to the wall. Glass cases surrounded me like walls in a maze. Captain Heron's hat pointed toward me on its pedestal. I disembarked from the rollercoaster of my dreams, and the strange reality of the museum returned.

Shit, I actually slept here. Gross.

I slid my phone from a pocket. The time read *4:39*, but hazy daylight slipped inside through the museum's front windows.

Oh my God, it's the afternoon. I missed work again. People must be looking for me. Oh, Mom! Is she on her way? Ugh.

I peeled my hand from its grasp on the last of the glass cases. Inside the case, a creased yellow paper bore lines of tight, illegible handwriting. I only understood the signature. Back on the beach with AJ, Carson told me about the letters that Heron sent to his girlfriend, Margaret. He told me they ended with drawings of the last coastline Heron saw. I would've ignored the letter and moved on from the museum forever, but the last letter's tiny ink drawing caught my eye. I looked, then looked again

Oh my God.

I didn't rush at first. I held my eyes on the drawing to make sure I understood. Even with more than a week to gather the lost pieces, I could never solve Eliza's puzzle. The jigsaw of clues spread across Warley Island never formed a clean rectangular border around Eliza's death. Her story mattered, but it was never the only one. Since the start of my journey to the island, Carson shared every legend about Captain Heron. He, AJ, Lars, and half the people on Warley Island seemed obsessed with every detail of pirate history. Since the start of our road trip, I tuned out each mention of Heron and his long-lost maple chest.

I picked up all the clues, and I tossed them back into the ocean like seashells. I could never solve Eliza's puzzle because half of the puzzle pieces belonged to a different one.

You're trying too hard to solve the wrong puzzle.

I finally moved away from the letter and started toward the door. The words of Eliza from my dream carried too much weight for me to understand all at once. With each step I took toward the door, her words meshed together and laid a path in front of me.

Finish the story, Rain Eldridge.

I wondered for a moment how Eliza could know so much, but then I realized those words never really came from Eliza. Everything in my dream came straight from my own mixed-up head; I couldn't take my subconscious thoughts as gospel. Nonetheless, I felt like the connections made too much sense. Something about the dream, my dad, Eliza, Lars, Heron… It all connected at the same place.

Outside the museum, the air smelled like rainwater and salt. The image of Heron's drawing seared itself into my retinas. With both hands, I ripped the first stake from the ground where it held the blue tarp. I pulled up the second, the third, and the fourth. Finally, I flipped and crumpled the tarp away from its longtime spot between the two buildings. The flat rock, like a giant gravestone, whispered to me in Eliza's voice:

The tarp's not for his boat.

I followed the dusty path down to the muddy shoreline, then I ran out onto the dock where we hid from the police. The *Saint Olga IV* bobbed in the water uncrewed. I turned away from her and back to the shore. With the tarp cast aside, the flat gray rock stood out among the dense grasses and short bushes of the island's inner coast.

Inside the museum, in a glass case, the faded ink of Captain Heron's letter showed similar patches of tall grass and brambles. The descendants of those centuries-old plants now stood in front of me growing from the same soil. In the center of the tiny drawing, Heron outlined a large flat rock. Standing at the same distance as Heron once stood, I gazed out at the *same* rock, unchanged after two hundred years.

All this time, no one noticed, I thought to myself with a laugh. Hiding in plain sight, no one noticed the answer to Warley's greatest mystery. Carson said that people spent ages searching for the location from Heron's last drawing, but someone built a museum right next to it. With just a waterproof tarp and a few cheap stakes, Lars hid the truth from everyone.

And so did his brother before him, and whoever curated the museum before him...

I ran back up the dock. I ran across the parking lot. I ran up Warley Avenue toward Carson, Ryan, Bea, and everyone else. I felt no pain or soreness in my legs; I felt invincible. The final piece of the Heron's puzzle had risen from beneath the museum's grave-stone rock and fallen into my hands.

At a quarter to five on that fateful Friday, Warley Island's wildest night began.

16: THE TEAM

Warley Avenue led me faithfully back to the dusty driveway that sunk down into its tunnel of brambles. At the street side end of that tunnel, next to the Wellings' mailbox, a green plastic garbage bin faced the road. While catching my breath, I took a look inside: No kayak pieces. Before everything with AJ happened, Ryan must've returned the empty bin on her way to pick us up from the beach.

I thought about skipping *All's Well* and running into town toward Ron's Surf Shop, but it made no sense not to check the house first. Besides, I had a hunch about what went down after Carson got himself arrested. Ready to prove that hunch, I jogged down the freshly cleaned driveway, past Carson's red truck and Mrs. Welling's gray sedan, and up the wooden stairs to the house's front door.

After one knock, Mrs. Welling peeled the door open.

"Rain, where on Earth have you been? Why are you so sweaty?"

"I… Well, I've—" Mrs. Welling raised a hand to cut me off.

"Your mom called. She says you aren't answering your phone, and now she's thinking about driving you all the way home. Where were you last night? I can't even imagine what's been going on all week, aside from my sons becoming *felons!*"

She shouted her last words back into the house, and Carson's echoing reply proved my hunch.

"Obstructing an officer is a Class 2 misdemeanor, Mom!"

"So is mine! Providing alcohol to minors!" Cody's voice followed.

"Boys, enough! I don't care what the charges said. I posted *both* your bail money from our vacation savings. You two might not go to prison, but you'll be wishing for a ball and chain after one week in Mom Jail!" Both brothers fell silent. Mrs. Welling turned back to me and smiled. "Come on in, Rain. Do you need a snack? Gatorade?"

I stepped into the cool air of the house but declined the Gatorade. Mrs. Welling retreated to the kitchen's reading nook and began flipping through a magazine. Carson and Cody sat at the kitchen island with two pens, a stack of paper, and dozens of empty envelopes. They stared with pained expressions at a mixing bowl in the sink, where the house's Wi-Fi router bobbed up and down in milky water.

"Baking soda and vinegar," Carson whined. "She turned our internet into a science fair volcano."

"There's no Wi-Fi in Mom Jail," Mrs. Welling sang.

"What are all those for?" I pointed to the envelopes. Carson sighed.

"Mom's making us write letters to everyone who we hurt with our 'lawlessness.'"

Cody held up a stack of unfinished papers.

"Carson got off easy. Just one letter to Chief Fitz, and he's done. I have to write one letter to each person who showed up at the party, plus one to *each* of their parents! Do you know how hard it's gonna be to track down all those people?"

"That's not all," Carson reminded him. "Mom said you have to write one to me, Rain, and Bea." Cody gulped, and Carson sneered. "Anyway, Rain, what's your deal? Where were you? It's been almost a whole day! Did you go to work, or what?"

"No, I didn't. And actually, I stayed overnight in the, uh…" I glanced at Mrs. Welling across the room. Even with her nose in a magazine, she'd hear every word between me and Carson. I grabbed a blank paper from the stack on the island and took one of the spare pens. As quickly as possible, I scratched out a message to explain everything: "*Slept in museum. Found rock from last letter. Need metal detectors + shovels.*"

Carson's face lit up. He dropped his pen.

"Rock?" Cody puzzled at my message.

"The letters! Remember?" Carson waved his hands trying to explain. "Heron's letters. Remember the last one, with that rock?"

"Oh, *those* letters. Wait, you mean Rain found the… Shit, you serious?"

Mrs. Welling stirred.

"Language, Cody."

"I'm a legal adult, Mom."

"No, you're inmate number one. Mom Jail has rules."

Carson folded my paper message in his hand.

"Rain, are you sure? People have been looking for ages. There's no way you just randomly uncovered the most historically significant hidden secret in the Carolinas. Where is it, anyway?"

I shook my head. I needed to say so much, but I couldn't let Mrs. Welling hear most of it, so I tried to speak in code. "I know I've made a lot of mistakes this week, but I need you to trust me that this isn't one of them. I'm sorry I left you out when we did the 'food delivery.' I'm sorry I ran away when Cody got arrested. Sorry to you too, Cody. And Carson, I'm sorry I didn't tell you my whole plan for the beach with AJ. I don't know what I was thinking. I know we don't always agree, but everything always seems to turn out better when we're there to help each other. So, if I can help you right now, will you help me with whatever's under that rock?"

I held out my right hand.

"Aw," Cody murmured while writing out another apology letter. "You're a real one, Rain. How do you spell 'inebriated?'"

"Of course, Rain! This is Captain Heron we're talking about." Carson agreed and shook my hand. "But how?"

Time for some theatrics, I decided.

"Letters!" I spoke louder. "I'll stick around and help you write some of your letter to Fitz. But first, Mrs. Welling, have you checked the railing on the master bedroom porch? I think someone at the party broke part of it."

"Oh, isn't that lovely. Let's have a look." She slapped her magazine down on the table and followed me through the living room. We proceeded upstairs and through the bedroom that Cody had commandeered. I opened the sliding glass door, and she stepped onto the sunny porch. Truth be told, I never saw anyone break the railing on that porch; I just needed an excuse to send Mrs. Welling up there. Unlike the living room porch below, the master bedroom porch connected to nothing else. No stairs, no other doors. While Mrs. Welling inspected the unharmed railing, I shut the glass door and locked her out. She whirled around with fire in her eyes.

"Rain, what are you doing?" She stepped closer and pounded one fist on the glass. "Unlock the door, Rain. Rain? Rain!"

I wasted no time running back downstairs to the kitchen. Carson and Cody stood up in surprise. Through the floor above us, we could hear the faint sounds of hands banging on glass.

"Dude, did you just lock my mom outside?" Cody laughed in mixed awe and fear.

"Yeah. Sorry."

"No sweat. Kinda badass, if you ask me."

"Now what?" Carson threw down his pen and paper. "She's gonna kill us! What about—"

"Not if we get out of here," I interrupted. "Did Ryan bring back the metal detectors?" Carson shook his head. "Damn. That means we need to go find her. Probably at Ritz's, right? Do you have the keys to your truck?"

"That's what I'm trying to tell you: My mom took them! If she's locked out on the upstairs porch, then so are my keys. We'll have to walk."

Shit. I'm an idiot. To my surprise, Cody provided a backup plan before I could.

"Walk? Hah!" Cody pulled a different set of keys from his pocket. "You know, after the first time I stole Mom's car, I thought she'd keep her keys in a different spot. But nope, she still just drops them right into the middle pocket of her purse. When she got up to answer the door, she put her purse on the table. I couldn't help myself."

I laughed out loud, but Carson just seemed disappointed. Regardless, we abandoned the apology letters and headed out to the driveway. Outside, we could still hear Mrs. Welling's shouts from the opposite side of the house.

"Let me in, Rain! Your mother will hear about this, and you'll be in deep shit when I'm—"

"Language, Mom!" Cody cupped his hands and called to her over the house. "There's no cursing in Mom Jail!"

✻
✻✻

After piling a few rusty beach shovels into the sedan's trunk, Cody drove Carson and I north up Warley Avenue. The lingering haze of the storm kept most of the normal beachgoers indoors, but the empty intersection of Warley and Turner was deceptive. All around the island, the many nameless guests from our fateful party prepared to celebrate the last Friday of beach week.

While Cody raced up the road, Carson's mouth moved even faster.

"But Rain, how do you know it's *that* rock? There are a lot of rocks. It could be any rock. And how did you find it, anyway? Where is it? You still haven't told us! Are you gonna tell Ryan? What if she tells AJ, and he finds the treasure first? Does he have shovels? Oh God, what if it's not there. You locked my mom on a porch for this, so you better be right about this rock. If we come back to the house and we aren't millionaires, we'll be on *death row* in Mom Jail."

"Dude, chill," Cody laughed. "I trashed a house and stole a car. Twice! Treasure or not, I'm basically there already."

Ritz's Burgers and Fries, a restaurant designed to serve some elusive late-lunch and early-dinner market, prepared to close up for the day. Neither Ryan nor Ms. Roakes bothered to raise the outdoor umbrellas in the stormy winds, and no one spun the *FOOD* sign out by the road. Only a few lights in the windows told me that Ritz's might still be open. Cody parked the sedan at the front of the gravel lot.

"Let's go in," I insisted. "All of us." I opened my door, but Carson stayed put.

"Wait, why? Can't you just go talk to her? I think she's still pissed at me."

"Yeah, she is. She's pissed at all of us. Neither of us told her what she needed to know about AJ—at least, not until after the beach. It's my fault that Eliza's phone is gone. And Cody… I don't know; I guess maybe she didn't like your party on Saturday night. My point is, if Ryan's going to help us, she's gotta decide to help *all* of us. Team effort, right?"

"Yeah," Carson sighed, stepping out of the car and bracing himself. Cody followed too, but he seemed more confused than nervous.

"But I buried the phone, not Rain. Wait, what happened with AJ? And what the hell was wrong with my party? It rocked! Guys? How about 'thanks for the ride,' at least?"

Neither Carson nor I took the time to deal with him. I pushed my way through the door of Ritz's. Despite the lack of customers, Ryan stood dutifully behind the front counter in her fully red-and-white uniform.

"Lucianne!" She called back into the kitchen. Mrs. Roakes flung open the door behind the counter. She looked almost happy to see me… But not quite. An electronic cigarette dangled like a sixth finger on her hand.

"Good to see you again, Eldridge. Wasn't sure if you'd be coming back. If this is about asking for a raise, you're barking up the wrong tree. If this is about quitting, then… Well, I can't really blame ya. So, which one is it?"

"Neither." I said. Mrs. Roakes tuned in. "I'm sorry for disappearing like I did. I should've just told you what was going on; I'm guessing you know by now. You've always been honest with me—brutally, even—and I should return that favor. Jobs like this don't belong to one person: it's a team effort. So, if you're ready to let me back in, I'd be honored to work together again."

No one spoke. I wondered if maybe I just *thought* all those words; maybe I just stood silently for a minute, imagining myself talking. Finally, Ryan offered out her hand.

"Deal," she grinned.

"He was talking to me, hon." Mrs. Roakes crossed her arms.

"But I have some conditions. First of all, Cody: You're going to apologize to Bea because she deserves it, and not because you want to get back in her pants. Secondly, Carson: You gotta tone down the whole lady-killer vibe. Just live your life, and eventually you'll find someone who loves American military history as much as you. Now lastly, Rain: I have a great idea for this one. Lucianne, can you grab me a basket of poutine?"

Oh no.

Mrs. Roakes reached into the kitchen and handed over a steaming heap of fries, gravy, and cheese curds. Ryan accepted the basket and presented it to me. I wrinkled my nose at the smell. Ryan took far too much pleasure in my discomfort.

"Rain Eldridge, if you want to work with this team, you've gotta eat with this team."

I reached two fingers into the fries, trying not to touch the gravy. Ryan shifted the basket. I help up three fries, topped with slimy gravy and a marble-sized white cheese curd. A few feet away, Mrs. Roakes hummed the *O, Canada.* Carson and Cody joined in, and Ryan began to sing the lyrics.

"*O Canada, our home and native land...* C'mon, Rain, do it for the north!"

"Do it for the treasure," Carson suggested. Cody worked a more honest angle.

"Do it because we need Ryan's help!"

Do it for everyone, I told myself. I shut my eyes and dropped the fries into my mouth. The assault of so many flavors caught me off guard: Salt, cheese, potato, and Thanksgiving. Overall, it wasn't terrible. I swallowed and opened my eyes again.

"Yeah!" Mrs. Roakes cheered, and the others clapped. Ryan stopped clapping first, though; she heard what Cody said.

"My help? You need my help with what? Something new with Eliza?"

"Not Eliza," I sighed. "We've been trying too hard to solve the wrong puzzle."

Carson filled her in. "Rain slept alone in the pirate museum, so now he thinks he knows where to find Captain Heron's lost treasure. But we left our metal detectors in your house-truck-thing, so we need those back. Oh, and you can help us dig up the treasure if you want, I guess."

Ryan waited for someone to say "gotcha." When she came around to taking Carson seriously, she turned to Mrs. Roakes.

"Well, I'll be damned. Folk here've been looking for that maple chest a *long* time. If you think you've got it, well... You kids go have your fun. It's about time to close up shop anyway. Rain, Ryan, I expect you both here early on Monday. Grill training, both of you. Kapeesh?"

"Kapeesh!" We parroted. Ryan ditched her uniform's hat and rushed into the parking lot. The three of us struggled to keep up.

"C'mon, boys! Winnebago's around back." Ryan led us to the orange-striped beast, and we piled inside with our shovels from the back of Mrs. Welling's car. The engine roared to life, and a few fresh raindrops snaked down the windshield. "First condition, Cody.

Do you have Bea's address?" He shrugged. "Does anyone know where Bea is?" I raised my hand.

"Straight down Warley Avenue. I'll stop you when I see the house."

Ryan leaned onto the gas, and the house-on-wheels jolted forward.

"There!" I pointed. Ryan eased down on the brakes, then turned onto the driveway of Bea's friends' rental house. One of the Winnebago's wheels wobbled up and onto the curb.

"Damn driveway's too short. Am I in the street? Carson, Cody, can you tell?"

"Maybe a little bit! Should be okay."

"Fine." She cranked up the parking brake and killed the engine. "Go, let's go! We have apologies to make and gold to dig! Carson, if I catch you flirting with anyone in this house, I swear... Rain, what are you doing? Go with them. I'll be right up."

I wavered on the edge of the Winnebago's door. "Ryan, where's AJ?"

She looked away and took a deep breath. Maybe I shouldn't have asked.

"Okay. Alright, I guess honesty is a two-way street. I don't know where he is. He hasn't been answering his phone. Apparently, no one's seen him since you and Carson did. I don't know what to do."

"What I saw in Eliza's texts... I never got to tell you. I think AJ saw her after the party."

"I think so too."

"Oh. Well, do you know what that might mean?"

"I'm not assuming anything. I know there's a lot of evidence. I know what you're assuming about him, but don't. Not just yet. We can talk more later. Now go help those boneheads talk to Bea."

I jogged up the steps of the rental house as light raindrops seeped through my hair and curled around my ears. The front door opened for Carson and Cody right when I reached the porch. Bea stood at the threshold alongside the two girls from the beach. Behind them, three other girls peered in our direction from the living room. One of them pointed at me.

"That's the guy who ran through the house!"

"Yeah," another agreed, "and that's Bea's man who got arrested."

"Who's the chubby one, then?"

Bea closed the door a few inches to cut them off. I thought she might say something to Cody, but she waited for him to break the ice. Her two friends by the door stayed quiet too. After so many patient seconds, Cody could've planned out a careful explanation and apology, but to be honest, no one expected that from him.

"Bea, I… Okay, so, my mom bailed me out of jail. That's why I'm here. Not *why*, but like, you know? So, I'm here cause I gotta apologize about the washing machine. Not the washing machine… What I *said* with the washing machine, remember? I made a lame joke, and… Oh! And I didn't know your last name. That was bad. And what was the other thing?" Cody turned and whispered to me and Carson. "Guys, what else did I do?"

Lied to your family, trashed a house, gave alcohol to minors, stole a dead girl's phone and tried to destroy it, got drunk before a vigil, stole a car, hid from police, ran from police… I told him a few of these. He shook his head and bit his lip.

"That's too much, dude. You gotta write it down for me."

Bea closed her eyes and started to shut the door. Her friends covered their mouths and tried not to laugh.

"Get lost, losers," one of them sneered.

"Wait!" Carson jumped, placing his foot in the way of the door. His shoe squeaked on the hardwood inside. "*I'm* sorry, Bea. And I'm sorry for Cody. I don't want you to think he speaks for us. I know beach week is almost over, and I know you have people and parties to see before you go home, but you should really come with us instead. Let's just say... We have a better party planned. We'd really *treasure* your company."

Carson winked. Bea and her two friends raised their eyebrows, but not because they understood him. That wink was just too creepy. One of the girls stomped down on Carson's foot with a black platform shoe; I couldn't pull him away fast enough. He yelped in pain and jumped back from the door.

"These are Ralph Lauren!" He wheezed. "That's gonna leave a mark!"

I decided we'd wasted enough of Bea's time. Maybe I could've spoken my mind and defused the situation, but I wouldn't risk making things worse. I turned around to retreat toward the driveway, but Ryan pushed past me up the stairs. She marched straight to the door and planted her hands on her hips.

"Bea, I was awful to you when we met. I didn't understand you then, and I probably don't now, but I know how important you are to these idiots behind me. You're a natural leader. You know how to stand up for yourself. You can take a handful of chaos, throw it at the wall, and paint order. Ever since you handed Eliza's phone over to me, everything's gone to absolute shit. These two boneheads got arrested, and the other one interrogated my boyfriend! But that's not on you, Bea. We'll be okay. If you want to party with your friends all weekend, you do you. But if anything bad happens, if you need someone who's got your back, you know who to call."

I didn't expect it, but Bea smiled. Her friends didn't.

"Ghostbusters," Bea muttered.

"What?" One of her friends snorted. Bea cringed.

"Ghostbusters. You know? That's who I'm gonna call? That's… Never mind. Screw it. Carmen, you need to watch more sci-fi. Val? It's 2019; whether you like it or not, my identity is valid. Later, skaters. Let's go, team!"

Bea jumped over the threshold and slid down the railing of the house's steps. She stood in the center of the tiny front lawn and threw two middle fingers in the air. Her other friends rushed up to the door, and she began kicking the ground.

"Y'all are fake, just like this itty-bitty turf lawn! Grass doesn't grow this green near the Atlantic shoreline!"

Two of Bea's friends held up their phones to film her tirade. Meanwhile, Carson, Cody, and I ran down to the Winnebago and piled inside. Ryan came down after us and held the rear door open.

"You done, Bea?" Ryan waved to get her attention. "They're probably live-streaming you on Instagram."

"I know! I want the world to see this!" Bea ripped up a square of turf grass and tossed it like a frisbee onto the house's front steps. Clumps of sandy dirt scattered across the wood planks. For the first time, I spotted the house's name on a wood panel over the front door: "*Real Shore.*"

*
**

As the sky darkened into evening, the storm rains returned again. Buckets of water streamed across the windshield faster than the wipers could dance. The Winnebago rolled down Warley Avenue carrying more of us that ever before: Me, Ryan, Cody, Carson, and Bea. I can't say the reunion went smoothly, but it worked out okay considering the number of us in the confined space. Bea counted heads.

"What happened to AJ? I see everyone but him."

"Long story," I said. "I confronted him about something, and… Well, it's hard to explain."

"Who's got the phone?"

"AJ threw it into the ocean."

"Damn. Ryan, you weren't kidding about everything going to shit. What's the move now? Where are we going?"

"That's what those are for," Carson grinned and gestured to the pile of metal detectors and shovels. "Rain slept in the pirate museum last night during the storm. He thinks he found the secret location of Heron's treasure, so we're gonna go strike it rich."

"What the hell? Why didn't you tell me that first?!"

Ryan whistled to grab everyone's attention.

"Rain, are you sure about this? The storm's getting bad, and these headlights aren't great. I need evidence, not just your best assumptions."

"The drawing on Captain Heron's last letter matched the rock that Lars covered with that blue tarp. It's the *exact* same rock at the *exact* same place on the shoreline. It's been covered up for as long as anyone remembers. We already knew that Lars had been keeping secrets: Maybe not about Eliza, and maybe not even about a box full of pills. But he's been keeping that rock a secret, and the treasure is his only reason. It's there. I know it's there."

Carson nodded in agreement. Cody shrugged. Bea just soaked it all in.

"Alright!" Ryan exclaimed. "Let's go do some real digging!"

17: THE MURDER

E ven after the sun sunk away behind the clouds, forks of lightning lit the air like fireworks high above. Each time the white flashes snaked across the sky, the raindrops falling in front of us glowed like tumbling sparks from a fire. Not far ahead, a wooden windmill spun and clattered in the violent winds of the storm.

"Right up there," Carson pointed to remind Ryan.

"I know, I see it." She slowed the Winnebago and turned gently into the parking lot.

"I didn't realize the tower was so close to the museum," Bea added, gazing backwards across the street. The winds had ripped away most of the yellow police tape around the watchtower's dunes. It was like Eliza's story didn't matter anymore; the island forgot, and so did we. It was all about the treasure, in the end. It had all been about the treasure from the beginning.

Ryan parked the Winnebago and killed the engine. While Carson and I started gathering shovels and metal detectors, Cody cleared his throat. "Not the be *that guy* or whatever, but isn't this kinda illegal? Just trespassing on some dude's property and stealing his legendary pirate treasure?"

"Assuming it's there," Ryan shrugged. "Yeah, it's not quite legal. But if Lars goes to prison for drug possession, some bank will probably take his land and find the treasure instead. Lars is the only one who knows about it, right Rain? So, if we just take the treasure and make it look like nothing ever happened, no one will know the difference."

"Assuming the treasure's there," Bea repeated. "Didn't we have some policy about assumptions?"

Ryan laughed. "True, true."

One by one, we stepped out into the rain and carried our equipment over to the covered rock. The house and the museum stood like guards—like tombstones—on either side. In only a few seconds, water soaked us all from head to toe. I felt like nature turned against us, pushing us away and fighting to keep Heron's gold in the ground.

"Here's the power button!" Carson shouted over a thunderclap and held out his metal detector to Bea. She pushed the small button, and her detector's narrow screen lit up.

"Dammit!" Ryan shouted. She smacked one hand on her metal detector, over and over. "You guys got the nice ones from back at the house. This is AJ's metal detector. I think the battery's dead."

Bea began ripping wooden stakes out of the ground. Lar's blue boat tarp flapped loudly and peeled itself off the wide rock underneath. Drops of water quickly coated the dry gray surface, and it darkened like a mirror of the clouds above. "Rain, Cody, Carson, start checking around the rock!" Bea instructed while wrangling the half-freed tarp. We spread out and started panning our search coils over the muddy soil. "Ryan, if that detector's dead, do you want to wait in the car? I mean, truck? Whatever it is?"

"I'll stay close, just up on the porch of the house right there."

While Ryan wrung the rainwater out of her hair, the rest of us scanned the area around the rock. I began at the edge closest to the parking lot, then worked my way clockwise toward the intracoastal shore. *It can't be under the rock,* I told myself. *Captain*

Heron's crew couldn't have lifted this whole thing. It must just be close by. Maybe under one of the buildings? Is that too far away? I made a full circle around the rock, but the numbers on my detector's screen never even twitched. Cody, Bea, and Carson walked the same circle—maybe a bit wider—and still found nothing but mud and puddles.

"Rain, if you brought us out here for nothing, I might actually kill you." Bea slung her metal detector over her shoulder. Carson shook his head.

"I need to see Heron's letter again. The last one, with the drawing. Can we go in the museum? Do you still have Lars' keys, Rain?"

I checked my pocket and nodded. "I think I left it unlocked, too."

Sure enough, the museum door swung open. We dried our shoes on the carpet and used our sleeves to wipe water off the metal detectors. Carson took off his shirt and spread it flat across one of the glass cases. I rolled my eyes, but he kept trying to press water out of the fabric.

"C'mon, you know it'll wrinkle if I don't do this!"

Bea laughed. "I see you. Not the worst excuse for going shirtless, I admit." Without warning, Bea took off her shirt too, uncovering a blue sports bra that matched her hair. Rather than laying out her shirt neatly like Carson's, she flung it toward the door where it splattered and stuck on the pane of glass. Cody had to jump out of the way, and Bea frowned. "Shit, I missed that time. Oh well. We all good? Okay. Quit staring. We've all seen a bra before. Can someone point me toward the magical mystery pirate letter?"

Carson wrenched his eyes away from Bea's sports bra and directed everyone toward the glass case on the back wall. I already stood over it, checking every detail and hoping I hadn't missed something obvious. Four more heads craned over the drawing to inspect Heron's ink under the gleam of cell phone flashlights. Carson nodded.

"Looks like the right rock to me. I don't understand why we didn't pick up anything on the detectors. Maybe it's too deep. It would take us ages to search by digging. Do you think we could come back with—"

The museum door burst open again, and Bea's wet shirt flopped onto the floor. Streams of rain flew inside. Ryan marched through the entrance holding a soggy stack of envelopes. She reached the back of the museum in only a few long strides, then dumped the papers down on the glass case.

"Letters," she announced, "from the house's mailbox. Just… Just read what it says."

"You want us to open Lars' mail?" I picked up one of the white envelopes.

"No, Rain. Just read the address line."

I did.

Those words looked so obvious. Those words—just the first two words on the address line—felt so right. After almost a week spent puzzling over Eliza's death, I never considered that those two words could appear next to one another. I always thought of Lars as the fisherman, the curator, the unwanted guest, the criminal, and the treasure protector. At the party, when Carson added all those girls on Snapchat, he never learned their names. Cody made the mistake of never learning Bea's last name. If not for Fitz, Ryan might not have learned mine. Over and over, we all made the same mistake, and I was no different. For too long, I never learned the one name that mattered most of all:

Lars Murphy.

When Ryan and I saw him on the beach, Lars barely spoke. He shuffled up the sand with a caught fish in his cooler, eyes on the ground, until Ryan handed over his dropped knife. At her voice, his eyes widened in surprise—or was it surprise? It wasn't just the bloody fishing knife that scared us; it was Lars' frantic gaze. We always assumed he saw Eliza's body, but we never imagined he saw his *daughter's* body.

When Lars arrived at the vigil, I almost didn't recognize his bare face. He cleaned himself up to attend—out of respect for the dead, I thought. Fancy clothes and a clean shave should've done the trick, but his effort wasn't enough for Eliza's mom. But Georgia Murphy wasn't just a grieving mother; she was Lars' ex-wife. She kept his name and built her company on it, leaving him to waste away as a lonely museum curator. Whatever grudge Ms. Murphy held, it drove her to expel Lars from the vigil.

Wait a second. The bridge contract: Georgia Murphy brought her business to Warley knowing that her ex-husband worked on the island. Did she do it for him? If she felt such spite toward him, why bring her family closer? Lars tried to tell me something before Fitz arrested him. He said, *"I need someone to make sure she doesn't—"*

"The treasure," I spoke just seconds after picking up the envelope. "She knows about the treasure."

"What?" Carson blinked. "She who? What's going on?"

Everyone else stared at me. Even Ryan seemed a bit perplexed. For once, I fit a few puzzle pieces together before she could snatch them from my hands.

"I think I know what's going on. There's so much; I can't keep it straight. We need to get out of here. I think someone's—"

A bright beam of light swung across us from beyond the front windows. Tires crept down the parking lot toward us, and a large black car shut off its headlights.

"Get down!" Bea called out. All five of us ducked behind the glass cases of pirate artifacts. Ryan leaned around one corner to spy on the new arrivals. Cody breathed faster and started rambling in a hushed voice.

"Shit, shit! Whose car is that? Anyone know? Is it the cops? We can get out the back door. We'll just steal Lars' boat and make a beeline for Cuba. Warley cops won't even follow us to Georgia! What, no one's with me here? Carson, you and I are screwed if we get arrested again!"

"Shh!" Ryan hissed. "It's not the cops. It's Eliza's mom." Ryan pointed one finger at me, waving it up and down. "You're right. Geez, Rain, you're right! I don't mean to sound so surprised. No offense."

"None taken," I smiled. The rest of us craned our necks to watch Georgia Murphy step from her car into the rain. She wore a long black coat that nearly swept across the puddles in the parking lot. Her waves of golden hair quickly sunk down on her head.

Bea gasped. "I know her."

"Well yeah," Carson laughed. "You met her at the vigil with us, right?

Bea shook her head. "No, Cody and I were *plastered* at the vigil. I never met her there. I don't know where, but I've seen her before. It must've been here on the island, sometime in the past week. Ryan, Rain, any ideas? How do I know this old lady?"

The two of us shrugged.

"You probably saw her at the vigil," I guessed. "And is she really that old?"

"Wait!" Ryan exclaimed. "The party! Okay, Bea, do you remember… No, you definitely don't. You came up to me and Rain, and you started rambling. Something about stealing the party, something about Cody, your friends, Jell-O shots? Then you said some *old lady* tried to get into the party. You said those words, just like that. And a second ago, you called *her* an old lady. Bea, was Eliza's mom at the party?"

That makes no sense, I thought, recalling Bea's drunken monologue during the party. *Why would Georgia Murphy ever show up at some trashy party? Was it something with Eliza? What would Ms. Murphy want from people like us?*

"Oh shit," Carson muttered, but not at Ryan. His stare held on the car outside, and we followed it one by one. After Georgia, another long-haired figure stepped out from the car's passenger side. It wasn't another woman, though. He stood much taller. Carson took only an instant to recognize. "It's AJ."

As we hid in stunned silence behind the museum's display cases AJ and Ms. Murphy walked closer. I hoped that they would walk toward the rock, the boat, or the house. Unfortunately, after poking around the parked Winnebago for a minute, they aimed straight for us. Carson slid the metal detectors out of sight. Bea slid along the floor to grab her shirt and Carson's, which she brought back our hideout near the back wall. We could hide all of our stuff, but AJ knew the Winnebago. He knew Ryan would be nearby.

The door squealed open, and wet wind rushed inside. Footsteps thumped onto the carpet, accompanied by the *clunk* of the door shutting before quiet returned.

"Ryan? Are you in here?" AJ asked softly. Ryan never flinched.

"I told you, it's fine," Ms. Murphy reassured him. Her voice rose above his without a hint of fear. "We won't be here long. I'll search the back room while you wait here. If you want your money, you'll stay put. Try anything funny, and you won't see a single gold coin when were through."

"I don't care about the gold," he retorted. "I just want everything to be normal again."

Ms. Murphy paced up one side of the room and halted the side room door. When Carson and I visited the museum on Tuesday, Lars came out from that side room. Ms. Murphy pushed her way through the *Staff Only* door and disappeared into the next room. Before any of us could intervene, Ryan stood up and faced AJ.

"Ryan! What are you…?" He took a step back toward the entrance. His head spun from side to side, and he lowered his voice to a whisper. "You can't be here. She'll kill you; she has a gun. You have to get out before she comes—"

"What happened, AJ?" Ryan moved in front of the glass case, but the rest of us stayed put. "Last summer, you made a promise."

"Babe, listen. I want to talk, but not now. Not here. Not while she's right—"

"Just tell me. Be honest. Just tell me what you did. Nothing else."

AJ buried his face in his shaking hands. Ryan drifted closer. He lowered his arms and steeled himself. Meanwhile, hidden in the darkened museum, the rest of us listened.

"After last summer, I never saw Eliza. I *swear* to you, I never talked to her, and I never heard a word from her mom. Then last week, Georgia calls me at the shop to ask about a deal. I thought it was a trap, you know? Some sting operation with Fitz, or whatever, so I told her I don't deal anymore, and she hangs up. I thought it was nothing; I passed her test.

"Then this party last weekend, Georgia shows up and tells people she's looking for me. I go outside to meet her, ready to say, 'screw off,' but she says she'll pay for however much product I can deliver. I wanted to say no, but a blank check? That could mean a real house somewhere. You always said you wanted to settle down, and I saw a chance: One last deal, I'd ask you to forgive me, and we could go make a real home someplace.

"Now, I don't have much product in hand, but I know Ron does. So, I split from the party, and Georgia drives me up to the shop. I throw her stuff in a tackle box, lock it, and rip the *Ron's* sticker off the back. Georgia pays enough cash to keep Ron happy, then promises the rest for me later. She splits with the box and its key, so I leave the money for Ron and walk from the shop to the Winne. It was a done deal.

"Awhile later, I got the texts from Eliza. I'm guessing you know about those by now. You see, when I ripped the sticker off the tackle box, I didn't get all of it. One look at the sticker, and she knew I broke my promise to you. No doubt, she was ready to tell you about it unless I did what she asked. She wanted to meet me at the tower, just like last summer.

"I was freaked. I started sweating and crying and punching the walls of the Winne because I knew I messed up, and you'd be done with me for good. I had one last chance to make things right if I talked Eliza down, so I drove the Winnebago to the tower. She was there, but she wouldn't listen. She wanted me to be with her again, and she was ready to break us up for that. But all she had was that picture... That one stupid picture of a yellow sticker on her phone. All I had to do was get rid of that picture, so I took her phone. Pried it right from her hands. She hit me over and over, trying to get it back, so I climbed up the tower. She came after me. I couldn't get into her phone, couldn't smash it with that fancy case, but I saw that the tide was in, and I knew what to do. I took her phone in one hand and, and I just... I threw it as far as I could. Eliza was right there, and she reached... She jumped... She tried to catch the phone, but there was... She slipped, Ryan. Babe, she slipped, I swear. I never even touched her. It just happened, right in front of me. Ryan, I didn't..."

AJ choked. His chest heaved. I don't know how Ryan stayed so calm as she approached him. I thought she would scream, cry, or slap him in the face, but she opened her arms. She opened her arms and wrapped them around AJ in a silent hug.

"Ryan..." AJ croaked between sobs. "Did I kill her, Ryan? Did I kill Eliza?"

Ryan whispered into his ear, and I never heard what she said. In my pocket, my phone buzzed for an incoming call. My cheerful ringtone came with it, echoing like a siren through the tiny museum. *Shit!* I raced to silence my phone and decline the call. It was my mom, of course. She could wait; I could call back later. I pocketed my phone again, but the damage was done.

"Who else is here?" AJ reeled.

The side door swung open, and Georgia entered the room. At the sight of Ryan, her hand dove into her coat and pulled out a handgun. She pointed it at the two of them. The other four of us jumped to our feet and raised our hands.

"Don't shoot!" I shouted. Ms. Murphy whirled and aimed the gun toward me.

"What the hell are you all doing here?" She raised her other hand to cock the weapon, which she turned back to Ryan and AJ. "You, Ryan! Let him go. Or I'll have to shoot you both."

"What do you want?" Bea asked. "We have money."

"I don't want your money, young lady. Unless it's the chest of gold that my ex-husband hid away. I'm only here for what he owes me."

"We can help you find it!" Carson suggested, but I wished for him to stay quiet. "We have metal detectors, shovels, and two halves of a broken baseball bat. Right, Rain?" Carson widened his eyes at me suggestively.

Broken baseball bat? I strained to remember, but I couldn't focus with the gun several feet away. *You want me to hit her over the head with something? That's insane! And we threw away the baseball bat! What are you talking about?*

"Shut up!" Georgia yelled at Carson. The gun wavered toward him. "Shut up and put a shirt on!"

"It's okay," I said, deciding to play dumb. "Ms. Murphy, I'm sorry for what happened to your daughter."

She bit her lips together and pivoted to face me. "Don't you dare. Don't you talk about her."

Don't panic, I reminded myself, and continued.

"Listen, Ms. Murphy... I lost my dad. He died in a car accident on April fourth this year, early in the morning. I saw the crash right afterwards, before they pulled his body out, and I didn't cry. I didn't scream, faint, or vomit. I just stared at the burning car, and I thought to myself, 'This must be the worst day of my life.' I thought that, and I knew that, but I didn't feel it. You see, I never really knew my dad. He was very successful, and he traveled a lot. When he died, I didn't even care why it happened. I think that when you don't know how to love someone, you don't know how to mourn them either. I just wanted my life to keep going. I wanted to go to school the next day. I wanted to pretend the crash didn't happen. All I wanted was to move forward and away. So, I came to Warley Island.

"When Ryan and I found Eliza, I felt the pain immediately. You know, I barely flinched when I saw my dad's accident, but when I saw *her*—a stranger to me—I felt something powerful. Isn't it true that we're supposed to love people more when they die? I couldn't love my dad, but your daughter... Well, Eliza gave me a second chance to feel what I was supposed to feel. I wanted to know what happened to her. I wanted to find every piece of the puzzle she left behind. I wanted to mourn, to understand, and to really feel.

"I'm sorry, Ms. Murphy, about what happened to Eliza. But she taught me that good people can do bad things, and bad people can do good, but we all deserve some kind of love in the end. Now that I know what happened, not that I solved Eliza's puzzle, I know that your daughter didn't die in vain."

Georgia finally lowered her gun. Ryan let go of AJ. Cody, Carson, Bea, and I lowered our hands. Outside, the storm winds sang in sour notes. The calm inside the museum lasted for only seconds more. Beyond the parking lot, three pairs of lights flashed in red and blue. Ms. Murphy gasped and backed up to one of the glass cases.

Who called the cops? I wondered, but not for long. Bea snickered and tilted her phone screen toward me. Apparently, she'd been on the line with 9-1-1 for almost five minutes.

"Rain, remember? You can't call the cops when you're holding half a baseball bat? Throwback to like a week ago, when I met you two at the front door."

"I thought it was an easy hint," Carson shrugged. "At least someone got it."

"Carson, I think you're a bit of a genius." Bea nudged him, and he blushed.

"You!" Ms. Murphy screamed and pointed the gun back to me. "You said you know what happened to her. You found her. I saw you at the vigil. This has all been about you, you, you. Every time, you. I know it was you. You son of a bitch, you did it. You hurt her. You killed her. You took my daughter away from me!"

"No!" AJ bellowed, and Ms. Murphy jumped. The gun went off. Next to me, a glass case shattered. Captain Heron's final love letter swirled into the air, then settled back unevenly on its broken perch. A clean bullet hole carved out a circular space in the paper, right where Heron's signature drawing used to be.

"No," AJ repeated. "I killed Eliza."

Three police cars outside slid to a stop. Chief Fitz jumped out, weapon drawn, and ran for the museum's entrance. "Drop your weapon!" Fitz ordered, but instead Georgia turned. Carson pulled me away from the broken glass. Bea lunged for Georgia's gun. Ryan screamed. Cody covered his ears. Lightning flashed. The gun went off. I watched.

And AJ collapsed to the floor.

18: THE FUTURE

A few days later, the storm passed. Hundreds of wiped-out graduates left the island and returned to their homes across the country. For the first time, I saw the calmer side of Warley Island. Pelicans flew their patrols up and down the beach. Egrets and fiddler crabs wandered and scampered through the intracoastal grasses. The locals who hid away during beach week emerged from their homes to retake the public spaces of Warley. Everyone moved slower, and I think I needed that. About a week after Ms. Murphy shot AJ, Carson and I agreed to go fishing with an unexpected new friend.

"Water's calm today," Lars noted, but the boat still rocked like a seesaw on sunlit ocean swells. Carson groaned.

"Is it normal not to catch anything?"

"Oh, for sure," Lars laughed. "Sometimes I come out here for hours and never feel a bite. Doesn't stop me from coming back out, though."

Half a mile away, Warley Island lined the horizon with the pastel dots of beachfront homes. Up and down the coast, the old watchtowers rose at regular intervals like monuments to forgotten history. Forgotten to many, maybe, but not to us.

"You looking at the towers?" Lars pointed, and I snapped from my trance.

"Yeah. They look different from so far away."

"They sure do." Lars sat down on one of the boat's sun-bleached seat cushions. "You know, I barely remember that morning. It wasn't even two weeks ago, but it feels like a bad dream."

Carson reeled in his fishing lure, and I sat down with my rod across from Lars.

"You don't have to talk about it with us," I told him.

"I know, but who else am I gonna talk with? I've got no one left here or anywhere else. First it was my brother, Ned, eight years ago. He was a smoker, so he had it coming. I knew he'd leave the museum to me, so I was ready to move my family down to the island. That's when I lost Georgia, I guess. She didn't understand why the museum mattered so much to me, but I couldn't sell it. She was the one who got the divorce papers. Then started that company, you know. Millions of dollars pouring in. But then she brought her business here, and I was the fool to not know why."

Carson glared at me. During our first two hours on the boat, no one said a word about Heron or the treasure. After all, we never found it. Fitz sent us away from the museum before we could finish searching.

"You never guessed?" Lars grinned. I'd never seen him smile before. Carson seemed as confused as I felt.

"Guessed what?"

"The treasure," Lars said. "When Georgia had Eliza bring me that tackle box, I knew something was off. Eliza knew it too. I couldn't believe Georgia's story that the box came in the mail for me; she never gets my mail anymore. I never guessed that she figured out the treasure. I never guessed how far she'd go to take it from me. But I thought you two figured it out. And your friends, too. You were the ones who stopped her, so you must've found the treasure. Right?"

I shrugged. "We almost found it, I think. I saw Heron's drawing before Georgia shot the letter. I supposed you and your brother knew the treasure might be buried by the rock, so that's why you covered it up. We came with metal detectors and shovels that night, but we never found anything. I started thinking that all of us got it wrong—Georgia, too—unless you're saying we missed something."

Lars stood up and ran his hand over the edge of the boat's windshield. He reached into a compartment under the captain's seat and pulled out a brown pirate hat. Lars placed the hat on his head, straightened it, and smiled back at us. Carson nearly dropped his fishing rod.

"Museum owners are pirate fans too," Lars started. "Did you really think we'd leave the treasure in the ground?"

"*Saint Olga IV,*" Carson murmured. "So, there must've been two other *Saint Olga*'s after the original. Oh, wait… Heron kept the maple chest on his ship. You mean… If this boat is… Did you put the treasure on your boat?"

Lars moved back to the seat across from me, but he didn't sit down. Instead, he lifted the seat cushion and revealed a large wooden chest in the compartment underneath. This time, Carson's fishing rod clattered down to the deck. The maple chest pulled us closer like a magnet, and the whole boat listed to one side. Lars brushed one hand over the stained wood surface.

"My grandfather dug it up in the fifties. We've kept it aboard a boat ever since."

That's why he took the boat when the police came!

"All this time!" Carson exclaimed. "Every year, you told me and my dad where to go metal detecting! The treasure was on your boat!"

Lars sighed. "Yeah, well… I'm sorry about that. But I can't go telling everyone."

"That's why you never sold it," I thought aloud. "You never came forward with the treasure because it's better if it's hidden. People like Carson come to the museum—to Warley Island—because they think they can find Heron's treasure. It's brilliant. It's—"

"The ultimate tourist trap," Lars finished. He unlatched the warped iron clasp on both ends of the chest. With Carson's help, he lifted the lid off the chest and set it down on the boat's deck. Inside the maple wood box, stacks of gold and silver coins glinted in the sun.

"Take one," Lars told us. "Both of you, pick one."

During the rest of our fishing trip with Lars, no one caught anything. Even so, we loved every minute aboard the *Saint Olga IV.* In the afternoon, Lars dropped us off near the beach. Carson and I swam ashore, each with a gold coin in one pocket.

No matter how many times I called and texted, I couldn't convince my mom to stay in Ohio. After Carson's arrest, when I told her to come pick me up, there was no changing her mind. She arrived in Warley on the Saturday after Georgia's arrest, and she stayed at *All's Well* with me, Carson, Cody, and Mrs. Welling. Thanks to her, Carson and Cody were forced to share a room—not without significant protest. My mom didn't try to take me home immediately, but she didn't suggest any plans to leave without me.

The fishing trip with Lars happened one week after she arrived. By then, I think she started to like Warley. Maybe she needed the vacation even more than me. Later in the day, she joined me and Carson on the beach.

"Rain, do you want to take a walk?" She asked, but I knew her question was a demand in disguise. I had to go. Carson stayed back with our beach chairs while my mom and I started south down the sand. "You haven't said much this week. Have you been thinking more about coming home?"

I dragged one heel in the sand. "I don't know. I'm doing better now."

"You sounded really upset on the phone last week. I guess I just don't understand. Everything seemed so good before that one day. What happened?"

I bit my lip. I'd been dreading this conversation.

"I haven't been completely honest with you."

"Oh, I know. Carson's mom has told me some things that I have trouble believing."

"It's more than that. All those phone calls, I just told you what I thought you wanted to hear. The truth is, since I got to the island, everything's been a mess. First, we found Cody and Bea living in the house, which they had completely trashed. Then there was a party; everyone drank a lot. Not me, not Carson, but everyone else. Ryan and I found Eliza dead on the beach. The police interviewed us and searched the house. Cody stole Eliza's phone, which we realized during the vigil at her crazy mansion house. We tried to spy on Lars, but we almost got caught when the police raided his house. I snuck into a morgue. I punched AJ in the face!"

Mom massaged her temples. "And why didn't you tell me about this?"

"I don't know. I didn't want you to worry. I didn't want you to take me home. I guess even after all that stuff, I still wanted to stay here on the island. I still want to."

"You should," she smiled. "At least for the summer. Technically, you kept your promises. You got a job. You made new friends, spent time with the good people, and ate healthy—I think. You called me almost every day. You just... You did a lot of other things, too. But that's okay. You're doing well here. I don't want to drag you away from this place."

Warm sun streamed down from above. Kites flapped in the breeze, tethered to beachfront porches. Waves crashed onto wet sand in a soft, slow rhythm.

"Thank you," I said. "I'm sorry I lied to you."

"It's okay, Rain."

"Oh, and you know what else? I was talking to Cody last week. He thinks I might be aromantic. Or asexual."

She laughed. "Like a fern?"

"That's what I said! But no, apparently it's how some people are. I guess that explains why I didn't really date anyone in high school. Cody only said it because I told him I don't want to date Ryan. Like, I like her, but I just want to be friends. Is that weird?"

"No, of course you can be friends with Ryan without dating. However you are, you're still you. And I love you no matter what." She tried to hug me, but we were still walking, so she couldn't really hang on. "Have you written in the notebook at all?"

I shook my head.

"Well, it sounds like you have a lot more to write about now. Can you think of anything you might want to say?"

"I don't know," I told her, but an idea finally began to form in my head. It felt stupid, but maybe I could write it anyway. At the moment, it didn't matter. My mom and I kept walking down the beach, past countless sandcastles and seashells. Eventually, we headed back toward Carson and our chairs. We couldn't stay on the beach forever; we needed to get ready before dinner.

**

I never expected that Mrs. Welling would let Cody stay in Warley. Besides, once Bea and her friends left the island with the beach week crowd, I thought Cody would rush away to follow her. Instead, he hatched a surprising new idea. When he first told all of us, it sounded like a joke. Of all people, Mrs. Welling liked the idea most of all. If nothing else, it gave Cody a productive and legal way to occupy his evenings.

Carson and I met Ryan at Ritz's, where the familiar restaurant glowed with a brand-new energy. Thanks to Cody, Ms. Roakes found a reason to keep her business open after sunset. A modest crowd filled Ritz's tables inside and out. Ryan and Ms. Roakes opened up all the windows, letting coastal breezes and scents of cooking oil drift in and out of the small building. Outside, near the umbrella-covered tables, strands of outdoor lights illuminated the area. A barstool and microphone stood at one corner of the fenced outdoor space. Cody perched on that stool, tuning his acoustic guitar.

"I've never seen it like this," Carson marveled as we passed over the threshold. "It's a full house!"

"Whatever happened to predictability?" Ryan sang, but Carson never watched *Full House* as a kid, so he missed the joke. Ryan held a wide tray stacked with red baskets of steaming dinner food. "I gotta run these out to the tables; I'll be right back. Saved you some seats, right by the window."

Ryan pointed us in the right direction. From our seats by the window, we could see and hear Cody at the mic outside.

"How're y'all doing tonight?" Cody asked, and the crowd cheered slightly. "My name's Cody Welling. Thank y'all for being here. I'd like to dedicate this first song to a dear friend of mine, AJ Moss."

Cody strummed a familiar guitar riff. I recognized it from the Winnebago's horn. I don't think the Beach Boys classic worked as dinner music, but Cody carried on singing it anyway.

"If everybody had an ocean, across the U.S.A…"

"I wish he could hear this!" Ryan exclaimed, appearing behind us. There weren't enough chairs for her to sit with us, but she had to keep up with food orders anyway.

"How's he doing?" Carson asked. "Have the doctors said anything new?"

Ryan shook her head. "No updates. Critical but stable, they're saying. If we're lucky, he could be conscious next week." Ryan paused to listen to Cody. "Sorry if that's depressing. I mean, you did ask."

"It could be worse," I admitted.

"Right. I'll catch up more later, but I gotta keep moving. Enjoy the show!"

"Alright, talk later!" I called out, but she was already across the room.

"Admit it, Rain," Carson smirked. "You like her. Somewhere, deep down, you want to date Ryan."

I rolled my eyes. "I think you're projecting, as Freud would say."

"What does that mean? Is that a good thing?"

"If it makes you happy."

Another car pulled into the parking lot, taking one of the last spaces close to the road. I wouldn't have noticed, but the white car bore the familiar decals and lights of the Warley Island Police. Chief Fitz exited the car and approached the restaurant. Her signature orange sunglasses hung from the collar of her uniform.

"Oh, shit," Carson muttered. "What's she doing here?"

Fitz walked straight past Cody, hardly even noticing him. In fact, she almost smiled.

"Maybe she's here for dinner," I suggested. She passed the outdoor tables and entered the restaurant. Her eyes darted toward me and Carson but brought none of their usual sharpness or menace.

"Evening, boys," she greeted. "Either of you seen Lucy?"

"Lucy?" I puzzled, and Fitz quickly clarified.

"Lucianne. Ms. Roakes."

Oh.

"In the kitchen," Ryan pointed while darting between us.

"Thanks, Ryan," Fitz nodded and moved toward the kitchen. She knocked on the door, then leaned casually on the wall next to it.

"I think I just solved another puzzle," I announced.

"What now?" Carson groaned. "We already solved a murder and found legendary pirate treasure. We're done with puzzles! What else is left?"

"Remember when we hid under the dock and heard Fitz make that phone call?"

"Well, yeah, I guess. To her boyfriend, husband, fiancé or something. What about it?"

"I think I know who she was talking to."

Ms. Roakes pushed through the kitchen door, grinning. She dropped her e-cigarette into one pocket and embraced the police chief. Despite their notable height difference, Ms. Roakes had no trouble pointing her toes to reach up and kiss Fitz.

Ritz's Burgers and Fries, I realized. *It's all in the name. Roakes and Fitz: Ritz.*

"Wow," Carson said. "I didn't see that coming."

"They've been engaged for over a year," Ryan added, dashing past us with another tray of food. "I actually figured it out a week ago."

Carson scoffed. "We can't all be Sherlock Holmes!"

But Ryan was already outside.

After our dinner at Ritz's, Carson drove us back to *All's Well*. The trees of the driveway buzzed with their thousands of insects and frogs. We kept the pickup's windows down; the hot summer air clung to our faces, even at night. In the gravel driveway circle, Mrs. Welling's sedan and my mom's old car took up most of the space, so Carson parked further from the house near the cactus.

"Damn, I'm almost asleep," he groaned and slid out of the truck.

"Then why were you driving?"

"So, I could get home and go to sleep, duh."

We walked up the wooden steps to the front door, just like the first time two weeks earlier. Only this time, we arrived at no fanfare. No mess in the driveway, no raft on the roof, no clothes on the railings, and no dent in the garage door. Instead of wild parties and unexpected guests, the house hosted our moms in the living room, watching a recorded episode of the Bachelorette.

"I don't think your mom has talked to me all week," I whispered to Carson as we took off our shoes.

"Well, you *kinda* locked her out on the master bedroom porch during an overnight thunderstorm. Which was brilliant, by the way. Don't worry about it."

A phone buzzed in Carson's pocket, which surprised me.

"I thought your phone died after you jumped off the dock?"

"Right! I forgot to tell you; I got my first paycheck before the police arrested Ron. Turns out that I've actually *made money* from having a job. Who knew, right? But look, I bought a new phone with my same number, but I lost all my contacts. So, can you send me Bea's number?"

I narrowed my eyes. "You never had Bea's phone number before, did you?"

"Maybe I did. Maybe I didn't. I don't know; I lost all my contacts." Carson smirked.

"Fine," I gave in, and quickly texted her contact information to him. "Don't make me regret this."

"Bea and I will be just like you and Ryan: Two platonic friends who are extremely attracted to one another."

"Regretting it already!"

I tried to sleep, but a million thoughts nagged at my mind to keep me awake.

Two weeks ago, Eliza died. Chief Fitz and Ms. Roakes are getting married and moving to the mountains. AJ is clinging to life in a hospital somewhere. Lars is hiding a giant gold treasure on his boat. My dad is dead. I'll probably go to community college in the fall.

I sat up from my pullout bed and reached underneath it. My hand waved blindly across the carpet until I snagged the corner of my discarded notebook. I dragged it out from under the bed, slid into my flip-flops, and grabbed a pen from the kitchen counter. Carefully not to make much noise, I slid open the living room's glass door and followed the back steps down to the dock.

In Ohio, I could never see many stars because of the lights up in Cleveland. High above Warley Island, a million glittering lights filled the sky. The end of the dock felt like the center of a warm, sleeping universe. I took a seat at the very end of the dock, where the brackish waves tapped against wooden supports below. After a deep breath, I opened the notebook and began to write.

It wasn't easy. I don't know how my dad enjoyed his work. I crossed out words, lines, and whole sections of my writing before the final work took shape. Even then, my entry in the notebook covered only a few pages. It wasn't pretty, and it wasn't much, but I wrote it all anyway.

"You're writing," someone said, and I spun around. I nearly dropped the notebook into the water. Ryan stood at the back of the dock's platform, still wearing her *RBF* shirt. "Sorry. Didn't mean to scare you."

"It's okay," I breathed, sitting back down. My feet dangled inches above the water.

"Finally telling your story?" Ryan walked down toward me, then lowered herself to sit with her feet hanging like mine.

"Not exactly," I said, sandwiching the notebook between my hands. "It's personal."

"That's okay. I don't need to read it." She swung her feet, and the toes of her shoes cast ripples across the water. Reflected stars danced from side to side. "I wanted to tell you that you'll probably be busier at Ritz's soon. I'm going back to California."

"What?"

"Not tonight. Not tomorrow, either, but soon. AJ's family is coming to take care of him. Meanwhile, I need to take care of myself, and right now that means finding a real home."

I nodded slowly. "Will you take the Winnebago?"

"I don't think so, but I have some money saved. I can buy something used. I'll be okay, at least until I can get settled."

I couldn't believe my ears. I only just met Ryan; how could she leave so soon? Her reasons made sense, and I understood, but I wanted nothing more than for her to stay. I reached into my pocket and pulled out Heron's gold coin. Discreetly, I opened my dad's notebook and pressed the coin into the spine between its pages.

"Take this," I told Ryan, offering up the closed notebook. Even in the dark, I could see her smile.

"I can't take that. You know I can't."

"You need it more than me. It's what my dad would've wanted. Right there on the cover, it says *Tell Your Story.* I don't have anything left to tell. The rest of these pages belong to you. Maybe you can tell your stories even better than him."

Ryan accepted the notebook and ran her fingers over the engraved cover. We sat for awhile at the end of the dock, but Ryan never opened the notebook.

"It's a letter," I told her. "That's what I wrote. A letter to my dad."

"I won't read it, I promise."

⁂

Ryan left for California one week later. I don't know if she ever read my letter, but I imagined her opening the notebook on misty beach in California. I imagined the gold coin slipping from its pages and landing in the sands of that Western shore. I imagined Ryan picking up the coin and smiling. I imagine she'll slide the coin back into its space between inked pages. Maybe, without even trying, she'll read the letter I wrote.

Dad,

It hasn't been easy to hate you. It's been even harder to stop.

You always told a good story, and not just in your books. You told the world your stories, and everyone listened. In another way, I told a story too. I told myself the story of a father who ran from his son. I told myself the story of a helpless boy with nowhere to go. I told myself that I should never be like you, never travel far from home, and never take one sip of pride—because like you, I might drown.

I told myself a story where you were my en-emy. I thought that I could be a better person by never becoming you. I wrote your char-acter in harsher terms because I never un-derstood the gray areas between good and bad: The best of friends sometimes throw punches. The worst criminals can still show love. The strictest leaders can act with compassion, and the sweetest people often break the rules.

For years, I assumed that nothing could fix the hurt left by your absence. All that time, you tried to repay the debt: You ate dinners with Mom and me whenever you came home. You dedicated books to me. You never missed my birthdays. Meanwhile, I forced myself to hate you because I ignored any evidence that you loved me.

I told myself a story based on fiction and assumptions. You were a better father to me than I was a son to you. For that, I am forever sorry.

Thank you for the notebook, but I don't know how to fill it. You taught me that storytelling can bring great success. It can take us far from home and lead us in nine million directions. But at the end of every story, we come home to our lives. Maybe someday I will fill your notebook, but I plan to live a life beyond its many pages.

With Love from the Island,

Rain

ABOUT THE AUTHOR

S.C. Giedzinski is a Brooklyn-based engineer who designs solar farms throughout the United States. Giedzinski is also an audiobook narrator and designer of open-source 3D-printing projects. Giedzinski graduated from the University of Maryland in 2021 with a B.S. in mechanical engineering and a creative writing minor.

Giedzinski's short stories have been published by the Baltimore Science Fiction Society and *Stylus* Literary Journal. Giedzinski's short story collection, *Nine Million Marshmallows and More*, is available in paperback, e-book, and audiobook formats.